# OTHER BOOKS BY LONNIE BUSCH

*Cargo Hold 4*

*Project Übermensch*

*All Hope of Becoming Human*

*Turnback Creek; a Novella &/ Six Stories*

*The Baldwin Hotel*

*The Cabin on Souder Hill*

*Turnback Creek*

# PUSH ME

## FEISTY STORIES OF LOVE & LOSS

## LONNIE BUSCH

This is a work of fiction. All of the characters, organizations, and events portrayed in the novel are either products of the author's imagination or are used fictitiously. Any similarity to anyone living or dead is purely coincidental.

PUSH ME

Copyright © 2024 by Lonnie A. Busch

A UBiQ PRESS BOOK

North Carolina, USA

https://lonniebusch.com/

All rights reserved. No portion of this book may be reproduced in any form without permission from the publisher and/or author, except as permitted by U.S. copyright law. For permissions contact: author at airbusch1@yahoo.com

[No generative artificial intelligence (AI) was used in the creation of this book. The author expressly prohibits the use of this publication as training data for AI technologies or large language models (LLMs) for generative purposes. The author reserves all rights to license uses of this work for generative AI training and the development of LLMs.]

Cover Art by Lonnie Busch

ISBN: 978-1-964024-08-0 (hardcover)

ISBN: 978-1-964024-06-6 (paperback)

Library of Congress Control Number: 2024924038

First Paperback/Hardcover Editions, December 2024

# CONTENTS

*For my son and daughter,
the greatest miracles of my life.*

# PUSH ME

# THE FATE OF ECSTASY

*J*olene Dumont hadn't planned on destroying Ecstasy when she brought her report to our attention. After all, she was from Ecstasy. Almost everyone on the City Council remembered her—spelling champ three years straight at Ecstasy Middle School, head of the chess club and debating team at Ecstasy High. She left Ecstasy on a full scholarship, went to a prestigious university on the East Coast, then graduated and started working for a multinational tire company in the R & D department, where, doing research on tire failure and recycling, she discovered that Ecstasy accounted for more flat tires per capita than any other town or city in the U.S.

We acted surprised by her findings, even though we knew something had been wrong for quite some time. The gradual proliferation of retail tire outlets over the past decade had not gone unnoticed. It wasn't unusual to pass several cars a day pulled to the shoulder, trunk up, a hubcap full of lug nuts sitting on the ground.

We worried about the impact of Jolene's report on tourism.

The ancient beauty of the Appalachian Mountains was our big draw—rafting, hiking, fishing—bringing vacationers to Ecstasy each year, just like a dozen other towns in a hundred-mile radius. But if people had to choose between Ecstasy and all the other vacation destinations in the area, well... why risk a flat tire?

We voted to keep the report quiet, appointing a task force to investigate. That's when Aaron Tinkler told us about Glen Goode's Big People. He said Goode was an artist and a businessman, and collected enormous fiberglass figures—Muffler Man, Big John, the Uniroyal Gal. Aaron, his right leg pumping under the table like a jackhammer (the way it always did when he was excited about something), told us Goode's men stood over twenty-four feet high. Aaron often brought up topics tangential to the discussion, but we listened, ready to move on, when he threw his hands out as if trying to stop us all from jumping off a cliff. He waved his open palms at us, stating that Goode's collection attracted thousands of visitors to Gainesville, Texas every year.

"Don't you get it?" Aaron said. "We could be known for our *flat tires!*"

Our eyebrows rose, our curiosity igniting slowly. A giddy pride welled up inside us, a warm little volcano at the pit of our stomachs. No longer would our town's name be fodder for countless puns and jokes (and we'd heard them all). We could distinguish ourselves in a unique and remarkable way, even if it was just flat tires.

Over the next few weeks, we brainstormed every day, sometimes long into the evening. The secretary jotted ideas on a yellow legal pad: A gigantic fiberglass sculpture of a flat tire in the town square. New signs at the city limits, "Ecstasy—Flat Tire Capital of America." A Flat Tire Festival each year, with special discounted prices on a set of new rubber. An interactive tire museum. A tire-themed fun park. An enormous tire swing. Creativity was flowing.

Ida Landry, our resident author and copywriter, wrote press releases and articles for *The Voice of Ecstasy*. Brent Flanagan, our very own body-builder and fitness-guru, ran a series of ads for his gym: "Replace that old spare tire around your middle with a new "flat" one!"

Jolene's report had pumped new air into Ecstasy, and into the members of the City Council. We'd all served in leadership roles in our youth—head of the student council, prom committee chairperson, president of the glee club, master of ceremonies, protocol officer—but this was different; we were part of something important now, something rare, exciting! It was evident by the new pep in our step; even our spouses noticed. We didn't just go to lunch; we *did* lunch. An infectious spontaneity sprang up. We were exercising the *right* side of our brain, beginning to see ourselves no longer as city officials, but as innovators and promoters, and even... well, *artists!* The women started wearing sleeveless blouses, tank tops, designer coveralls with backless shoes, and changed their hairstyles—more *upflung* and frisky. They traded in their fake pearls for colorful, jangling bracelets and toe rings. Some of the men wore leather pants, grew beards and mustaches, had an ear pierced.

Change was sweeping Ecstasy. We were reinventing ourselves. At our meetings we made popcorn in an old-fashioned movie house popper, blew bubbles from those little bottles of soapy liquid, and listened to country music while discussing zoning issues and business permits. We took up hobbies—flying drones, stringing beads, posting on social media.

Over the past few years since Jolene's report, Ecstasy had become home to no less than thirty retail tire outlets, not counting the Super Walmart, AutoZone, and the many independent auto repair shops that also sold tires. We were hyped by Jimmy Fallon on *The Tonight Show,* made the cover of *GO,* Triple A's travel magazine, and were linked to countless vacation websites. We became a *destination!* Our status as the Flat Tire Capital attracted a staggering number of sightseers and vacationers, as well as a steady influx of curious risk-takers who believed they could beat the odds and drive home on all four originals. Stores offered ridiculous discounts on tires. Families purchased T-shirts and mugs and postcards. Visitors from all over the world lodged in our motels and hotels, and frequented our fine eateries and cafés. Many of us on the City Council became entrepreneurs, opening up B&Bs, souvenir shops, and operated street vending pushcarts selling hot dogs, pretzels, and kielbasa sausage. The multinational tire company Jolene worked for built a tire-testing facility in Ecstasy, creating over three hundred new jobs and numerous opportunities for local businesses. With funds donated by Jolene's employer, we built The Rubber Room, a city-block-sized entertainment warehouse with piped in music, strolling Michelin Man mimes, video driving games, a tire obstacle course, go-cart track, the Fire-Stone Pizza Oven restaurant, and a gift shop, "101 Things To Do With Old Tires," that sold, among other things, sandals with tread soles, and detailed blueprints for building your own self-heating shed from worn out steel-belted radials.

We held tire-sculpture competitions at our annual All-Weather Festival. We talked Glen Goode into selling us a replica of his Uniroyal Gal. And even with the economy off a bit over the past twelve months, it was still a good year, capped off by our Christmas Decorations Contest, the five-hundred-dollar prize going to Trojan Wheels for their darling Mr. and

Mrs. Snowman Family, complete with hats and scarves, and made entirely from huge inner tubes spray-painted white.

Even under the barrage of accusations and allegations of conspiracy and wrongdoing—neighboring townships blaming our governing members for the flat tires, claiming that we seeded nails and tacks along our streets—Ecstasy flourished!

Until last Wednesday, when Otto Fincke of the Ecstasy street crew discovered the source of our undeniable and mysterious good fortune. He had been carrying a tar sack, patching small cracks and holes in the streets near the town center, when he came upon a spike—not much more than an inch or so in height and an eighth-inch in diameter at its base—protruding from the pavement at the intersection of Boone and Redondo (the busiest streets in Ecstasy), directly under the suspended traffic light.

News of the spike got immediate traction. Rival towns, long jealous of our burgeoning success, flooded our little community with local reporters brandishing cameras and microphones, ready to expose the incriminating thorn to the world, set on destroying us. Ecstasy police set up roadblocks, diverting traffic away from Boone and Redondo. They put up yellow crime scene tape around the perimeter of the intersection, winding it around the crosswalk poles on each corner, ordering folks to stay back. Reporters shouted questions. Kids rode up on bicycles ringing those annoying, tinny little bells, and elderly couples, who'd lived in Ecstasy their entire lives, huddled close together as if they were witnessing a harbinger of the apocalypse, their ice cream cones dripping down the fronts of their shirts.

All of us on the City Council were vexed by the curious

spike, and well aware of its implications and the potential for embarrassment, but more than that, we were distracted by the noise and hubbub of the ensuing crowds. None of us could think. We voted on the spot to convene in private session at the courthouse.

We pushed our way through a throng of onlookers, repeating, "No comment, no comment," slinking serpent-like, hands clasped in solidarity, through the streets. At the courthouse steps, the police parted the sea of bustling, sign-toting rebels, holding them at bay until we were securely inside. We crowded into the elevator. The doors slid closed. A hand reached between us from the back and pushed the button for the second floor. We stood in silence, perspiring collectively, holding our breath.

Safely inside the meeting room, we locked the doors, pulled the blinds, ordered pizzas and five one-liter bottles of diet Coke, and a chocolate cream pie from The Cakery Bakery. We tried to remain pleasant and upbeat, calm and organized, logical and intelligent.

"Humiliating."

"Mortifying!"

"What will I do with all those T-shirts and mugs I just ordered?"

"An outrage!"

"Aliens."

*Aliens* was Cleo Soldier's answer to everything—when methane gas hung over the landfill one year; when thunder rumbled through the skies in the midst of a blizzard; when Ecstasy experienced a shortage at the gas pumps. *Aliens.* We all smiled and tried to remain focused.

"We have to remove it."

"We should wait, get more information."

"What if it's a *sign?*"

"What information?"

"We'll be laughed out of the state...or worse..."

"A sign of *what*? It's a prank!"

"Who would do such a thing?"

"We'll be torn apart by the media."

"High school kids."

"Aliens!"

Cleo sat arms folded, chin out, her eyes and hair the color of a thunderstorm. Just then, the pizzas arrived.

We hadn't even finished the first pepperoni when our cell phones went off, mothers and sisters and wives and uncles calling to ascertain our fate, to determine if the town's good fortune was in jeopardy, if we were doomed. They'd been sitting home watching their televisions, listening to radios, worried sick. One council member's grandmother said the little spike was the best thing to ever happen to Ecstasy. Someone's nephew claimed that if we removed it, we might as well board-up the damn town. Another said the scandal was like a broken nose that would *never heal*. The chocolate cream pie arrived.

Orville and Wilbur—twins named for the famous flight pioneers—were the longest standing members of the City Council. They said the spike was a prank, like the soap detergent in the town's water fountain years ago, and that it had to be removed. Orville and Wilbur agreed with each other on everything. But the rest of us, unwilling to listen to reason, argued back, pointing out that we would no longer be the "Flat Tire Capital of America," that people would stop coming, and that they'd probably start making fun of our name again; none of us could forget how unrelenting and cruel the jokes had been.

"Ecstasy will be a ghost town," someone added. Silence screwed down tight over the room. *Ghost town.* The words

7

hung over our meeting like a death sentence—which was exactly what removing the spike would be. "But the spike will be the bane of our town, now," Wilbur stated soberly. "Flat tires will no longer be a novelty. Just a nuisance and a plague. No matter what the consequences, we must remove it." Wilbur's twin brother, Orville, bobbed his head in solemn agreement.

We looked down at our clothes, then at each other, feeling like phonies. In years past, our town's *name* had been the joke; now *we* were. Our confidence was sliding. What had seemed perky and adventurous over the past few years—our new hairdos, our tattoos and facial hair, our Mick Jagger T-shirts—all seemed ridiculous and silly. Not only were we embarrassed for ourselves, but for each other. Even our children and siblings had started shaking their heads at us, smirking from the upturned corners of their mouths. We succumbed to self-pity and despair, then self-loathing for even considering something as evil and malicious as deliberately leaving the spike. We all looked to Wilbur, a faint knowingness and compassion coloring his eyes. After a somber and tearful recess, we came back to order and voted. Unanimous. The spike must go.

Our street crew hammered and tugged for several days trying to remove it, while cries of fraud and corruption echoed across newspapers, radio shows, and television broadcasts. We were a joke to the entire country, a farce, a hoax! The devil's machine! "Who could do something so underhanded?" people were heard to say. "Who would stoop so low?" We were called crooks, and scam artists, hucksters and soulless profiteers. Individual lawsuits were filed with the courthouse clerk. Class-action suits were rumored to be in the wings. Jolene Dumont lost her job at the tire-testing plant and was accused of collusion and left town in the middle of the night, alone, pulling a small U-Haul trailer. The multinational tire company laid off two hundred and ninety workers—retaining a skeleton crew in hopes that the controversy would blow over—and then took down their sign.

Police isolated the intersection of Boone and Redondo from traffic and passersby. The street crew labored on the small spike amid catcalls and booing. We came down to watch, all of us at first, our numbers dwindling under the constant pressure of questions and salvos of nasty remarks. We had brought shame to our town and ourselves. One person threw a hotdog with mustard at Aaron. Another yelled out that Ida's poetry collection was crap. One woman called Cleo a dike. Cleo shot her the finger.

The crew struggled on, utilizing trucks and chains, though it was hard to attach anything to the tiny spike, which was no bigger than a valve stem. They could not bend it, or break it, drill it or smash it. They tried cutting torches and titanium carbide tipped saws. They drove over it with a bulldozer, tried to yank it out with a backhoe. They suggested jackhammering the surrounding pavement, digging it out. "Extensive demolition," the crew foreman said. "It's the only way."

The City Council met again. We were haggard from unrest, demoralized by family ridicule and disapproval, ravaged by the press, frightened by threats of termination. We had received hate mail and countless threatening phone calls, tire stores and local business owners aghast that we would even consider removing the spike, then others, equally disturbed that we had pulled such a stunt in the first place, accusing us of installing nails in our city streets! We regarded each other with dismay and suspicion; animosity grew between us like kudzu. Our home lives were splintering and so was our group. Orville and Wilbur sat at opposite ends of the conference room, worn and bald, their faces pale as whitewalls.

Then someone placed an enormous bottle of Jack Daniels

on the table. We all looked at it, then at each other. Cleo removed the cap and brought it to her lips. We passed it around. At first, we were polite, taking sips, wiping the rim with our shirttail or sleeve before passing it on. Within thirty minutes, no one would have cared if an eyeball had been floating in the bronze liquid. When the bottle was empty, we tiptoed down the back steps of the courthouse building, giggling and shushing each other, then piled into Orville's Suburban, laughing and howling as soon as we were outside the city limits. We drove thirty miles to Weaver, where no one knew us, and purchased whiskey and vodka and gin at the ABC liquor store, and bags of snacks—potato chips and dip, pretzels, corn curls, M&Ms—from the BiLo.

Back at the courthouse, we poked fun at each other—our armadillo skin cowboy boots, our spiked hairdos, our nose and tongue posts—laughing with the unbridled fervor of second graders on a trip to Disney World. One member removed her expensive hair extension and tossed it out the window, another showed us the lightning bolt tattoo on her left hip. Aaron exposed his pierced nipple. It wasn't long before we were telling off-color jokes and reciting limericks and yodeling like lunatics.

We were bonding through adversity, the criticism and chastising we'd had to endure over the past weeks fusing us together like victims of a near death experience, like rubber-raft survivors of a sinking ship.

It was dawn when Cleo woke us and said we should vote on the excavation. Hungover, exhausted, and too humiliated to face each other eye-to-eye, we voted quickly, and discreetly, to excavate, then slinked home to our loved ones.

Later that afternoon, before we could enact the order to dig, a team of scientists and metallurgists from a major university arrived in a big blue van pulling an even larger blue trailer to study the spike. Wilbur had forgotten to tell us about the call. He apologized and left the room sobbing. We all thought he was being a little dramatic for his oversight, but Orville explained that Wilbur was embarrassed by the previous evening's shenanigans, and not to worry, that he'd be back.

When Orville stepped to the window, we crowded around him and watched from the second story as scientists unloaded micrometers, electron microscopes, spectrometers, and a tuning fork. They used particle detectors to check for radiation. They set up computers and generators and banks of work lights, laboring through the night in shifts, measuring, testing, documenting, creating 3D models, using crystallography to identify the properties of the spike, taking sonar readings of the ground. Several days later, their findings were released to us behind closed doors.

The papers rattled in our hands, the report nearly incomprehensible to everyone except Aaron, who had worked in the aerospace industry for several years. The report stated that the spike was only the tip of a much larger object beneath the street, and that it had most likely crashed into our planet over eight thousand years ago where it has remained buried beneath the soil, pushing up slowly for centuries due to hydrostatic pressure, or maybe geothermal forces, possibly even a seismic anomaly. The impact of the object may have thinned the earth's crust sufficiently enough to initiate a convection process, allowing for a small mantle plume. The report concluded by stating that extensive research was required to answer all those questions adequately, but one thing was certain—the object, whatever it was, was *not of this earth!*

We watched from the windows as the blue van and trailer drove away. After a few moments, we took our seats, cleared our throats, adjusted our chairs. We were stunned. We looked at Aaron quizzically. He nodded, confirming what was in each of our heads: *An object from outer space!* Everyone looked over at Cleo. She gave us a gentle shrug and her *I told you so* grin. We discussed contacting Homeland Security, the president, NASA, then decided unanimously that we needed to keep this quiet.

It leaked. That was all the reporters needed. "Bizarre object, NOT OF THIS EARTH, discovered in Ecstasy!" Magazines and newspapers called night and day requesting interviews. "Is this another hoax?" "Have you no conscience?" "Will you folks do anything for a buck?" "Is this space debris scheme just a fabrication to cover up your toxic waste dump?" A few reporters evidently recalled the methane gas issue we'd had a few years back.

At home we disconnected our phones, and kept our cells off in our pockets. Some of us had our car windows tinted. Our spouses and lovers and families complained of being scared, humiliated, annoyed, disappointed, incensed, suspicious, confused...

Visitors came in droves, not the usual sightseers we would normally throw open the doors for, but ufologists and psychics and alien abductees, motorcycle gangs and fortune tellers, weirdos and kooks of every ilk. Indigents with aluminum foil wrapped around their heads camped under shopping carts and deserted cars on the Food Lion parking lot. Religious fanatics in black tennis shoes and blue robes recited incoherent prayers and carried lit votive candles through the streets. Bygone hippies in tie-dyed shirts smoked pot and ran naked through the car wash. The multinational tire company finally shut its doors forever, skulking away one evening while the town slept, rumbling over the hillside in enormous eighteen-wheelers. Motels switched on their "No Vacancy" signs so they wouldn't have to rent rooms to self-proclaimed "saviors," "angels," and "Martians." CNN, NBC, and Fox helicopters flew over the town, reporting the carnage to the world, their denouncements hidden from us by the thump and thrum of their rotors. We were ripped apart on all the late-night monologues— Colbert, Fallon, Corden, Kimmel, and Maher—the Ecstasy jokes delivered with renewed vigor and devastating punch lines.

We convened at midnight, chauffeured to the courthouse in unmarked police cars, while reporters slept unbeknownst on the courthouse steps. Urgency hung in the air like smog from a nuclear winter. Some of the council members believed this could be a bigger boon to Ecstasy than the flat tire shtick, but most of us weren't convinced of that, citing the new demographic populating our streets and stores and eating establishments.

"But those nutcases won't stay," they tried to assure us. The rest of us were skeptical, certain the "nutcases" would never leave.

For the first time, we were divided. A sad gulf was opening. A hush fell over the meeting as we contemplated our fate. That's when Connie Learst announced that her husband filed for divorce. We all looked at her, sympathetic to her plight. Humiliation left a puncture hole in all our chests. Nevertheless, Connie wasn't alone. Most of us were experiencing the same upheaval in our own homes. Spouses had gone to live with loved ones. Some of us were told to leave and never come back. A few of us were living at the Budget Inn out on 141.

Tina LaFleur—an outsider from Idaho, and the youngest and newest member of our committee, but a stolid supporter of the council's commitment to tradition and values—brought pot to our meeting. She rolled a fatty. Wilbur said smoking wasn't allowed in government buildings, and his twin brother,

Orville, said, "Oh, horseshit, Wilbur!" and proceeded to climb on the table and disable the smoke detectors. We had several joints circulating while we discussed our options. Most of the conversation eventually turned to our childhoods and high school sweethearts, Wilbur trying desperately to get us back on track. Orville took out his harmonica and started playing Willie Nelson tunes, while some of us attempted to learn the two-step from Amy Woolfitt. Bill Stylie produced a handful of darts and an 8x10 glossy of Jolene Dumont. We taped Jolene to the door and took turns. Her mouth was twenty points, her eyes thirty each, her nose, fifty. She had a cute, but hard to hit, little bud of a nose.

The National Guard arrived that evening, along with the FBI and NSA. We stood at the windows of the meeting room, bleary-eyed, stoned and sniggering like idiots, watching Ecstasy become a spectacle. Wilbur went out for food and never returned. Ida Landry sat in the corner penning a play on a stack of napkins, entitled, "The Thorn that Destroyed Ecstasy," to be performed at the Ecstasy playhouse if it ever reopened.

Needing the strength of numbers, none of us left the courthouse building—sleeping on the floor, napping in chairs, bathing in the restroom sinks, ordering in Chinese—until a few days later when the mayor appeared with a police escort, informing us the City Council was being disbanded. He instructed us all to go home—those of us who still had homes —that the town was no longer under local government control, that our power and authority had been expropriated due to the rare nature of the cosmic debris, using terms like, "martial law," and "eminent domain." He urged us to vacate the premises immediately, then departed with his entourage.

Most of us had no idea where to go, and were staring out the window when an advisor from Homeland Security arrived with a convoy of military vehicles—Humvees, trucks, jeeps—along with a passel of scientists and astrophysicists armed with X-ray fluorescence micro computed tomographers, Si(Li) fluorescence detectors, PIN diodes, infrared CO2 laser lights, and even a Scanning Kelvin Probe, a very rare piece of equipment, indeed, Aaron said. They circled RVs and tractor-trailers around the intersection of Boone and Redondo, erecting massive poles adorned with halogen floodlights. They fired up riotous, clattering generators, and threaded thick black cables across our sidewalks and lawns. A carnival of bulldozers and cranes arrived on flatbed trucks. They posted Keep Out signs, four feet high, eight feet wide. In less than fifteen hours, Ecstasy had been transformed into a military compound, complete with Uzi toting sentries, revetment walls, and razor wire.

We piled into Orville's Suburban, eating Taco Bell take-out and singing, *One Hundred Bottles of Beer on the Wall,* and met in a barn twenty miles outside of town on Cleo's farm.

In her barn, we sat on hay bales (something many us had never done before) and grew glum over the demise of Ecstasy. Orville jumped up and announced that Bill Stylie was an excellent caller, and suggested a square dance. We all stood. Orville played his harmonica and Bill shouted for us to allemande left our corners, then allemande right, and do-si-do our partners, then heads promenade. Sixty-six calls later we were laughing and singing, joyous once again, straw stuck in our hair, armpits soaked with delight. We had pushed all the ugly images from our thoughts, had managed to forget how miserable we'd all be. Some of Tina's new friends—hippies from upstate New York—clapped and whistled and slapped their knees as we danced with our partners, until we all collapsed in a heap in the middle of the dirt floor. We got up laughing and giggling, our gaiety dwindling slowly to a few guffaws, dying further to faint titters and nervous coughs, until nothing but silence and despair engulfed us. We sank deeper and deeper knowing our town was gone. Our lovely Ecstasy was gone forever. Most of us were still wearing the same clothes from a week earlier. We smelled. We were homeless. We were stoned and sweaty and morose. That's when Cleo told us to follow her.

We walked single file down a steep slope to a pond where she had built a sweat lodge. Cleo started an enormous bonfire and heated a dozen cantaloupe-sized stones, which Aaron and Orville helped carry inside. We stripped down to our underwear and crawled into the blistering tomb made of willow branches and blankets, the searing rocks steaming in the center of the black space like a portal to hell. We sat cross-legged, trying to breathe the dry, sweltering air. We grew hot and dizzy and disoriented. We hallucinated and cleansed and bared our souls. Cleo went first, telling us that several years ago she'd been abducted by extraterrestrials. Orville admitted he'd never once paid his income taxes. Confessions poured forth like perspiration.

"I have only four toes on each foot."

"I had sex with several men at the same time."

"I poisoned my neighbor's yapping dog."

"I'm still a virgin."

The purging continued until dawn. When the rocks finally cooled, we staggered from the sweat lodge and leaped into Cleo's pond, washing and splashing, drying ourselves in the sunlight, engulfed by lush, green grass. Vibrant and purified, we hiked back to Orville's Suburban and drove to Weaver, pooled our pocket change and went to Shoney's out on the Interstate for the breakfast buffet. We were ecstatic!

$\sim$

16

But it didn't last. We fell silent, the miracles of the previous twenty-four hours fading under the scrutiny of a harsh new day and the burden of a full belly. We picked our teeth and wondered out loud if we would be alone the rest of our lives, if we'd ever find jobs again, where we would sleep that night. Hippies in a nearby booth tried to lift our spirits, telling us life on the street wasn't so bad. Some of us broke into tears, others of us shook until our dessert pancakes fell off our forks. Tina put breakfast on her Visa, explaining that she didn't plan to pay it off; she was going to live in a commune. None of us knew those still existed, and for a moment we felt optimistic. We crowded into Orville's Suburban, quiet as cadavers. Cleo told him to drive us back to her farm.

That evening, Cleo cooked a huge pot of bison stew. After supper, Aaron informed us that he was moving back to Saint Louis with his wife to work for McDonnell Douglas.

Aaron not only had a *job*, but still had a *spouse?*

We wished him well, but none of us meant it.

After Aaron left, we moped around, ignoring one another, perusing Cleo's books and cassettes—self-improvement, calming meditations, affirmations, *Qigong.* Tina started to read aloud a quote from a Deepak Chopra book and we told her to *stuff it!* Cleo calmed us down, then said she wanted to show us something special. She was rapidly becoming the council cheerleader and our high priestess of hope.

We followed Cleo up a knoll, to the top of a barren ridge, nothing but sky and undulating fields. She told us to open our minds as the heavens changed from deep blue to black. Stars magically appeared, a smattering at first, then more and more as the sky blackened to reveal a pageantry of glittering lights. The answers we sought were not in Ecstasy, she told us, nor in the space junk beneath the intersection of Boone and Redondo, or in the security of big homes and nice jobs. Her body cut a bold silhouette against thousands of constellations as she pointed her finger, crinkled slightly with arthritis, at the Milky Way.

Merge your thoughts into one solitary, energetic declaration, allow it to emanate out into the universe, Cleo urged. Summon your distant brothers and sisters from other galaxies, invite them to join us, *reclaim* us. We were a little scared.

"Connect with your celestial ancestors," she proclaimed. "Embrace the power of the galaxy, the light of the universe."

We sat under the weight of a strange new stillness, our hands clammy, clasped together with our neighbors, our collective thoughts burrowing deeper into the cosmos. For a moment we were buoyant, nearly euphoric, until our inner voices—recalling what the hippies had told us—tried to convince our brains that life on the street wouldn't be so bad.

# ALLEY FIGHTER

(Appeared originally in *Portland Review*)

Phyllis got me good this time. All ten of my white Van Heusen dress shirts are knotted at the sleeves, strung together like cutout paper dolls, or a chorus line. There's no time to undo the knots, and even if there were, the sleeves would look like flexible straws.

My wife did this. Phyllis calls them practical jokes, but I can't find anything practical about them. We've been married two months and I'm seeing a side to her I've not seen before.

On my way to the office I wonder if Phyllis noticed that I had changed the tire on her new 280z. Last night, while she was jogging, I slipped out to the garage and removed her passenger side rear wheel, replacing it with her spare, one of those dreadful little donuts short on tread and character. I put her original tire in the trunk of my car. I doubt she will find my joke inventive or intriguing, because I am not even sure what the joke is about, but it was all I could think of. I'm new to this. She tells me I better "get up to speed" if I'm going to be a contender. She and her brother played these games on each other since they were kids, continuing well into adulthood, until her brother died in a skiing accident three years ago. It happened before I met her. She told me about Michael on our honeymoon in Maui.

"He probably died thinking I planned his accident somehow," she said. Michael had a stroke while riding the ski lift and fell to his death. Doctors said he was probably dead before he hit the snow. The man sitting next to him on the chair lift said he slumped over and slipped beneath the bar. The man grabbed Michael's coat, but couldn't hold on.

"Michael would have been comforted knowing his death was the result of one of my pranks, even though it wasn't. How could it be?" Phyllis was smiling, staring past the palm trees outside our bungalow window, when she told me. When I noticed her eyes pooling, she got up and went to the bathroom. A few minutes later she said she was starving and suggested going to dinner at the Blue Crab Café. She hasn't talked about her brother's death since.

When I get to the office, Byron is the first to notice the burgundy polo shirt under my suit jacket. "Casual today, huh?"

My desk is stacked high with policies but I can't concentrate, my mind on Phyllis's new 280z, the donut tire I put on her car. What if it blows out on the highway, causing her to crash? Or what if it goes flat in a bad part of the city? Suddenly my neck is itchy and my armpits are swimming pools. When I asked Phyllis about the rules of engagement, she said, "Fun stuff. You know. You don't want anyone to get hurt." One night when she'd just returned from the store, I thought it would be a good trick to tell her she'd had a phone call from the office, even though she hadn't. When she got off the phone, she was shaking her head. "You don't understand," she told me. "This isn't like April Fool's stuff. Don't you know what a practical joke is?"

I thought I did.

"You have to be creative," she said. "But you don't want to hurt anyone." That word *hurt* was the troubling detail. Did she mean physically? Or emotionally? The guidelines were vague. For instance, the night she put cayenne pepper in the Dixie cup of mouthwash I gargled, and it burned like hell, I questioned her about it. When she stopped laughing, she told me I was a baby, then rolled over to go to sleep.

I call her at the office because I need to know she arrived safely, that the donut didn't explode, sending her careening off a wall, or into oncoming traffic. Her receptionist answers and says she isn't in yet.

"Did she call?" I ask Mimi. "It's after ten-thirty."

"No, Mr. Markinson. Not yet. Should I have her call when she comes in?"

Visions of mangled and fiery metal glow inside my skull.

"Early lunch today, Kevin?" Byron asks, as I hurry past his office toward the elevator.

Driving down Highway 40, I can't believe I pulled such a stupid stunt. Even if it doesn't turn out badly, Phyllis will not be pleased. She will claim it was a bad prank, that the potential for physical harm was too great, practically inevitable. Of course she would not use those words, even though she's a lawyer. She would say something like, "What the hell were you thinking about? I could've been killed, Kevin."

Not finding her car on the highway, I drive past the Crazy Beans coffee shop, then Sammi's Delicatessen in the Central West End. She could be in court today, but Mimi would've told me that and I have no idea where Phyllis might be, so I go back home thinking she might be there, that maybe she forgot her depositions or something. The house is quiet, the garage empty. I get back in my Audi and retrace her route from house to office. Nothing, and now I'm panicked. My cell phone battery is low and I can't hold a signal, so I find a parking spot near her office building and head up to the twenty-first floor.

The polished brass plate—Law Offices of Giarnese, Siler, and Frick—greets me when I step from the elevator. Phyllis is the Giarnese third of the title. Mimi is on the phone when I hurry to the reception desk. "Is she in yet?" I ask.

Mimi nods and smiles, holding her palm over the receiver. "Yes, Mr. Markinson. Go on in."

Relieved by the absence of shock and horror on Mimi's face when I asked about my wife, I hurry down the hallway toward Phyllis's office secure in the belief that everything is okay.

"Nice shirt!" Phyllis says, smiling up from behind her desk.

When she stands to welcome me, I seize her in a bear hug, afraid to let go. I don't like this game. I'm not good at it. Growing up for me was a T. S. Elliot kind of thing, a childhood of quiet desperation. The most jarring incident I can remember as a kid was my dad's flannel shirt catching fire during Christmas dinner when he reached across a candle for the ham platter. I had no idea flannel was so flammable. My dad quickly patted out the fire with his other hand, then wrestled a huge slab of pork onto his plate.

"You're kind of frisky today," Phyllis says, caught in my embrace, unable to read me. Mistakenly she interprets my trepidation as a sexual overture. "Should I lock the door?" she asks.

When I don't respond, she apparently senses something wrong. I feel her hand slide up my back, a soothing touch, caressing my shoulder blades, my head, my scalp.

"Baby, are you all right?" she whispers in my ear, leaning back enough to study my eyes. At first, I can't meet her gaze, too embarrassed by what I must tell her next. After I explain about the spare tire, she just stares, her lips slightly parted, her eyes expressionless. She steps to the door and eases it shut, then sits in one of the chairs next to her fichus.

"That's kind of dangerous, don't you think?" she finally says. "I mean, what was the point of the gag? Was I supposed to be killed in a car accident on the way to work today?"

I sit in the chair next to her, limp with shame, unsure myself what effect my prank was intended to produce. "Let's don't do this anymore, okay?" I say, reaching out to take her hand.

"Okay, if that's how you want it," she says, the disappointment in her voice almost as crushing as the guilt. "It can be a lot of fun, though, Kevin. You just have to think a little, you know. I mean, it wasn't a bad prank really, kind of creative. But those goofy spares aren't very safe on the highway. I don't think you're supposed to go over forty with one. And you know how I drive."

I feel dejected, my head slumped in disgrace, my eyes fixed on the weave of Phyllis's carpet. She lifts my hand from the chair, cradling it in hers. I am running scenarios of devastation through my head, her 280z tumbling end over end down the highway like an Olympic gymnast. I wonder how Phyllis will handle being married to someone who doesn't really enjoy practical jokes, how she will feel living a hoax-free life. Will she lose interest, become bored, seek thrills elsewhere? Even though this is her first marriage, it is not mine, but I hoped it would be my last. Phyllis pulls my face up by my chin and her short black hair is a wonderful, chaotic experiment, her eyes, shimmering, exotic seaports. She leans in and kisses me on the lips, her tongue mingling with mine, a couple of baby penguins. I am immediately aroused.

"Can you take off early?" I ask.

"No...but I won't be late tonight. We can order pizza, get

naked under the comforter on the couch and watch a movie. How does that sound?" For some reason, being naked on the couch is more exciting for her than being naked in bed. I, on the other hand, don't really care where we get naked.

I nod, pulling her close again, smelling her hair, her neck. I get up to leave. "Where's your car parked?" I ask. "I'll change your tire." I don't tell her that I have her tire in my trunk, that I had left her without a spare. So far she has taken this pretty well. I don't want to send her into apoplexy. She tells me her car is in the parking garage, section C, space 67, and thanks me for taking care of it, assuring me that it was a good prank, even though we both know it wasn't.

After getting my car from the street, I drive to the parking garage and take the ticket from the attendant, then drive to section C, easing my Audi along the parked cars until I find her burgundy Z. I am horrified when I pop open my trunk. Her tire is gone. Did I leave it in the garage at home? I am almost certain I put it in my trunk, thinking I might have to bring it to her. Then it hits me. I walk around to the passenger side of Phyllis's car, spy the sleek, cast aluminum alloy wheel, the shiny black tire, and can almost hear laughter twenty-one floors above me. I recall how long she was in the garage this morning before I heard the garage door open and close. It's unsettling that she could turn my prank back on me. How did her brother endure this? How could anyone? Nothing to this point in my life has prepared me for such a relationship and I am afraid the pranks will spin out of control, cause irreparable damage somehow. I deal with actuary tables every day, probabilities, it's how I make my living. This is risky business and someone will get hurt. It's inevitable. And the casualty will probably be me.

However, I don't want to be a bore, a dud. I give her tire a little kick with the toe of my Florsheim and walk back to my car, knowing I will now have to pay five dollars to get out of the parking lot. Perplexed, and caught in a vortex of spiraling dread, I find some solace in the fact that at least Phyllis discovered my trick before she was hurt.

"High jinks," as my mom would have called them, were not part of Phyllis's and my courtship. We met at a fundraiser for the Literacy Council and started dating a week later, then married shortly after, no more than five months. That's when the games started. I wanted to be flexible, embrace the spirit of mischief, but I was terrible at it. I sought the Internet for answers. I did the Saran-Wrap-over-the-doorway-of-a-dimly-lit-room thing, then tried the plastic-bag-duct-taped-over-the-showerhead thing. I had no idea what effect these gags were supposed to create, but after a week or so of my inept attempts, Phyllis, obviously disheartened by my inability to grasp the finer points of pranking, said, "Kevin, honey, don't go online for practical jokes. Most of them are lame, especially the duct tape ones. Be creative."

She was right. They were lame, like pinning a glass of water to a wall. You were supposed to tell someone you could pin an actual glass to the wall, and when they challenged you, you held the glass filled with water up against the wall, then fumbled with the pin, surreptitiously dropping the pin to the floor. When they bent down to pick it up for you, you were supposed to pour the water on their head. I didn't get it.

Cuddled naked on the couch beneath the comforter, Phyllis and I have just finished making love and are trying to decide who will order pizza, and who will pick the DVD. I offer to order, she will pick. When I come back with the phone, she has just started *Nothing to Lose* with Martin Lawrence and Tim Robbins, one of her favorites. Thirty-five minutes later the doorbell rings. On the television, Lawrence and Robbins encounter the two killers for the first time. "Ooh, pause it,

Kevin, I love this part!" She grabs the remote and pauses it herself, then pulls the comforter up over her shoulders, letting me know with her naked youthful smile that I need to attend the pizza guy, as well as pay for the pie.

When I return with the box, Phyllis is laughing, kneeling on the cushions. The movie is playing and I can hear the actors arguing, then gunshots, then, "Here it comes, Kevin!" Phyllis says, leaping from the couch, standing naked in the middle of the living room. "God, this is so funny!"

"Shut the fuck up!" Lawrence says, pointing a gun at the killers, the killers countering with, "No, you shut the fuck up!" Then Robbins, "No, you shut the fuck up!" then Lawrence, "No, you shut the fuck up!" Then Phyllis joins in, "No, you shut the fuck up!" waving her finger at me like a gun. She waits a moment, then, "Come on, Kevin. You say it now."

I shake my head. I have never liked this movie all that much. She implores me again, coming closer. "Come on, Kevin."

When I finally say it, it isn't good enough. She chides me, the Lawrence film playing on without us, the sound muted. I try again. She starts directing me now, deepening her voice, scowling. "No, you shut the fuck up! Come on, Kevin, it's fun. No, you shut the fuck up!" When she starts poking her finger-gun in my chest, I know she is not going to let go of this so I jump to my feet and give it my best. She howls and says, "Yes. That's it! No, you shut the fuck up!" Then I shout back and we continue like this for a minute or so, her stamina for this shtick seemingly inexhaustible.

"Can we eat pizza now?" I finally say.

"Wouldn't that be fun to pull at Trevor's next weekend?" she says. "That would blow them away!"

Phyllis has more close friends than I have policyholders. She is a raging extrovert and I was somewhat unprepared for the entourage that attended our wedding. I had forgotten about Trevor's dinner party on Sunday afternoon. She begs me to run the joke on them. I have to admit, it would be fun to work together for a change, someone besides me receiving the punch in the nose, the kick to the groin. She tells me that all we have to do is find the right "opening." "It'll be easy, Kevin. I'll start talking about your driving, or something, then you can say, 'Shut the fuck up!' Then I'll say, 'No, you shut the fuck up!' then we'll just go off back and forth. 'No, you shut the fuck up!' It'll be great. But you can't laugh. It'll ruin it."

I watch the movie, eat pizza, and sip my beer, wondering what's wrong with my driving.

Phyllis does not try for a gag every day, which I am glad about, and the week for me has been pretty successful, my pranks beginning to gain approval. She is still way out ahead. On Tuesday it rained. That's when I found out she'd drilled tiny holes in the soles of my Florsheims. I worked in soggy socks that day. On Thursday she changed the password on my home computer, making it inaccessible to me, threatening to withhold the new password until I came up with a "really killer gag." She thought it was clever when I Super-glued her leather briefcase shut, but it didn't buy me passage back into my laptop. It wasn't until she was getting ready for work Friday morning that I scored enough points to gain entry. She'd been dressed and ready to go, searching for her wristwatch, and asked if I'd seen it.

I told her it was in the kitchen. When she still couldn't find it, she called to me. I went to the kitchen, opened the freezer and took out a 2-quart Tupperware bowl. I turned it upside down under the faucet, running water over the bottom until the chunk of ice fell out and banged around in the stainless-steel sink. Encased in a thick chunk of ice was her expensive Timex. I couldn't tell if it was still running.

27

"That watch wasn't waterproof, you know," she said. I reminded her my Florsheims were no longer waterproof either. The pranks were getting expensive and I was beginning to feel like an alley fighter, always looking over my shoulder, always on guard, never sure where the next attack would come from.

On the way to Trevor's, she goes over the plan again, reminding me to be forceful when I say shut the fuck up. I tell her I can handle it, not to worry.

"Look how well I've done this past week?" I remind her.

"Yeah, just great," she says, looking at her empty wrist. "Just don't miss your cue. And don't get cold feet. This will be hilarious."

"What's wrong with my driving?" I finally have to ask. It's been bugging me all week. Phyllis, under the spell of some special reverie, ignores me.

When dinner ends, people drift toward Trevor's living room. The resolve I'd experienced in the Audi is growing thin. These people are mostly strangers to me, some of them Phyllis's chums from the fifth grade. Not only that, each one of them appears to have known her brother, Michael, and suddenly I'm an interloper, an outsider, no longer certain how this bit will go. It feels risky. A few times during the evening, Phyllis winked at me, gave me her little grin. It made my stomach lurch. Not because it was romantic, but because it meant we were going through with her plan.

Trevor asks Phyllis how she likes her new Z. "It's fabulous," she says, "but I won't let Kevin drive it. He's a terrible driver." She glances over at me and smiles. I know that's my cue, but I can't move.

"What's wrong with his driving?" Trevor asks.

"He changes lanes without checking his mirror. And

doesn't use his signals. He practically ran a guy off the road a few weeks ago."

I want to object, tell everyone that her statement is only partly true. The guy had been driving in my blind spot. And he hardly *ran off the road*. He caught a little gravel on the shoulder, then laid on his horn and gave me the finger when he passed, but that's standard road etiquette anymore.

"He does it all the time," Phyllis adds, buying time for me to ratchet up my courage. "I don't think he knows it's against the law."

"Shut the fuck up!" I yell. It's forceful, it's angry, it's aggressive, and for a flash of a second it doesn't feel like acting. All eyes are on me, a hush falling over Trevor's apartment. Just then, Phyllis flushes red, rushing from the room in tears. I protest immediately, telling everyone it's a joke, explaining about the Martin Lawrence movie, how Phyllis and I are running the gag on *them*. A couple of her friends clear their throats, look away. Trevor grins weakly (the kind of charitable expression you give the checker who doesn't know how to ring up the leafy green vegetable you placed on the belt), then pads slowly to the bathroom to console Phyllis. I am devastated by the betrayal. I never expected our gags to go public. Not like this.

About then, Trevor and Phyllis stroll out of the bathroom, laughing, everyone joining in a second later. Obviously, the whole gang is in on it. The game has turned vicious.

On the drive home I tell Phyllis how I feel, bringing up the "hurt" rule, asking her to elaborate. She leans across the seat and fondles my earlobe. "I'm sorry. Everyone thinks you're adorable. A real sport. Trevor thought you took it better than anyone could. And I love you for it. Michael would have been proud."

Proud of "whom?" I wonder—me for being such a dolt, or

29

Phyllis for her cunning. Maybe as some kind of recompense for my public humiliation, Phyllis tries to initiate car sex. When this fails (I am still far too mortified to muster an erection), she pulls a small plastic bag from her purse and starts rolling a joint. This is yet another new facet of her personality.

"Where'd you get that?" I ask.

"Turn off the air conditioner, will you?" she says, rolling down her window. "It's really nice out tonight."

She draws deep, sucking her cheeks in, releasing the smoke only after it has marinated her lungs for nearly five seconds. Without a word she offers the joint to me. I haven't smoked pot in over twenty years. I don't even like the smell.

"Where did you get that?" I ask again.

"Trevor," she says, pulling the joint to her lips and sucking. "I rarely smoke anymore. Sure you don't want a hit?"

A *hit*. From this point, the trek home grinds on without conversation. When I pull into the garage, Phyllis hurries from the car and rushes in the house before I can shut the engine off. I tap the garage remote and wait for the door to rattle shut.

When I walk in the bedroom I can hear Phyllis sobbing on the bed, her back to me. She's still dressed, except for her shoes. They're lying on the floor next to her purse. The back of her dress is undone, the white strap of her bra like a bandage across her ribs.

"I miss him, Kevin," she says without turning to face me. She folds her legs tight to her bottom and there's a hole in the toe of her nylon, her painted nail poking out.

"Trevor?" I ask.

"My brother Michael. I miss him so much."

For the next several days my concern for Phyllis grows. She has lost her spunk, moping around the house, sitting in front of the television watching one inane cable channel after another. Not one prank all week. The absence of foolishness comes as a relief—our lives seeming almost normal—but it worries me just the same. I have never seen her so listless. However, we've only known each other a short time. I was married to my first wife for nine years and she was still a stranger.

On Monday morning, Phyllis is seated at the kitchen table in dorm pants and a purple bra. "I'm sorry, Kevin," she says, using a fork to probe the macaroni and cheese she just microwaved.

I ask what she's sorry for and she tells me that she thinks she hasn't grieved fully for her brother, that maybe the pranks have been a way of keeping him alive. "It's not fair to you, Kevin. I've been using you."

I don't really want to broach this subject as I'm walking out the door. Monday is my worst day. "Can we talk about it when I get home from work?" I ask.

She nods, then reaches her arms out to me like a small child begging to be lifted. I bend down and hug her, kiss her on the forehead, then the lips, tasting the salty trail running down her cheek. She didn't go to work on Thursday or Friday and isn't going today. I am a little scared to leave her. I tell her I'll call her later and hurry out to the garage.

I'm already late for the morning meeting and the highway is jammed. The day is humid and when I switch on the air conditioner, downy white feathers gush from the vents until the interior of my Audi resembles a snow dome. Feathers land on the dash, the seats, the headrests, only to be stirred once again by the blowing vents. I open the window, hoping the feathers will be sucked out. The fresh air only seems to agitate them more. Apparently, at some point during the weekend, Phyllis must have been feeling her old self again.

There is no time to pull over and clear the car. The highway is slogging along, so I find a lane that is moving, then find another when it stalls. I pop into the next lane that opens and suddenly I have flashing blue and red lights in my rear window.

After bullying my way through three lanes of traffic, I veer onto the shoulder and stop. When I roll the window down, feathers drift past my eyes, sticking to the steering wheel and the hair on my wrists and knuckles. The officer is at my window, asking for registration and license. I oblige, trying to ignore the feathers, hoping he will too.

"Mr. Markinson, is everything okay?" the officer asks, waving his hand through the feathers floating out the window. One sticks to his blue shirt.

"Yes, just a little joke my wife played on me this morning."

The officer glances toward the back seat, allowing his eyes to rove every square inch of leather, then back to me. He holds my license up, comparing the picture with my face.

"Would you mind stepping out of the car?" he says. "Please be careful. Lot of traffic this morning."

I open the door, cars lumbering by, little heads craning to see what I've done wrong. Another officer walks past me and starts to search the car.

"Is there a problem?" I ask.

"Probably not," he says. "You were switching lanes sort of dangerously back there. You probably didn't know you cut right in front of us, did you?"

It seems I would have remembered a police car, but I don't.

"That's kind of a dangerous joke, don't you think?" he says, snatching a feather from the air. Before I can answer, the other officer walks over holding a small plastic bag.

"Is this yours?" he asks, holding it by the corner between his thumb and forefinger like a dead robin. I recognize it immediately—Trevor's marijuana. How could Phyllis leave it in my car? In the midst of my astonishment and shock, I suddenly realize, this wasn't an accident. She planted it, hoping I'd get pulled over, knowing the police would find it. Maybe that's why she put the feathers in my air vents, to attract the police, to distract me. She's gone too far this time.

"That's my wife's idea of a prank," I say. "Like the feathers."

"The drugs belong to your wife?"

"No, they're not my wife's... they belong to..." I can't finish the sentence without further implicating Phyllis, and dragging Trevor into it as well. I guess the police wait as long as they can without an answer, then handcuff me and stick me in the back of the cruiser. One of the officers locks my Audi and we speed away.

Phyllis picks up on the fifth ring. "Hello?"

I tell her it's me, that I'm at the police station. My fingertips are black and I've just been photographed from the front and side, like on television. I hear bawling on the other end of the receiver.

"Phyllis, I need you now," I say. "Please pull yourself together."

She sniffles, and takes a deep breath. "There's not much pot there, less than an ounce. Recreational," she says. "It's obvious you're not dealing."

The sudden cavalier tone of her lawyer voice is enervating and I want her to explain to the police about her prank.

"I'll get dressed and come down," she tells me. "Don't say anything."

I pull the phone close to my mouth and ask her how she could do such a thing, plant that crap in my car like that. "This is serious shit, Phyllis!"

"I didn't plant it. I completely forgot it was there, Kevin. I'm done with the tricks. I promise."

"Really! What about the goddamn feathers, then? How did those get in my car?"

33

There is silence on the other end, that numbing void usually reserved for churches and conch shells.

"I forgot about those," she finally says. "I rigged that Sunday when Roger picked you up to play tennis. I thought it might make me feel better. It didn't. I'm sorry."

Phyllis is down at the police station within the hour. She comes to the holding cell first to speak with me, still wearing the plaid dorm pants, only now she has put on the mauve-splattered sweatshirt she'd painted our bedroom in. Her hair is a shrub, leafing out in all directions. She asks what I've told them.

"Not much." I squirm a little because I told the police it was her fault.

"They don't have much," she says.

"They have the pot!"

"Yeah, but there's not much there. And besides, you don't have any priors."

*Priors!* I can't stand being the recipient of her legalese. It feels detached and institutional, and dangerous, like the words: incarceration. And felony.

"I'll post bail and we'll get out of here," she says.

"How much is it?"

"The bail? What does that matter?" she says.

"I just want to know."

Phyllis stares at the floor a moment, then looks up at me. "I have to leave my new Z."

"Your car?"

"Yeah, And my new Rolex." She rotates her new watch at me and while I'm trying to parse this information, a half-moon of a smile opens across her face. Within seconds, she's howling, trying to apologize through tears of amusement. The arresting officers come in holding the bag of pot, chuckling. They hug Phyllis, handing me the bag through the bars, telling me they no longer need the *oregano* as evidence. She introduces them as close friends of Michael's, then explains how they waited near the freeway for me to drive by.

The tall one, Brad, opens the holding cell and tells me he hopes it wasn't too harrowing, then counsels me on how I really should be more careful with my lane changes, that I was a bit careless out there "on the track" this morning.

The sun is burrowing down when I push through the front doors of the police station. Phyllis is trying to catch up to me, clopping down the steps behind me in her yellow Crocs. Just as she grabs the sleeve of my suit jacket, I spin on her, push her hand away.

"Please, Kevin," she says. I can see her fighting back a laugh. "Look, I'm sorry. Really," she continues. "I truly was depressed. Trevor thought a good gag might get me out of it. And it worked. But from now on, no more foolishness. Not at your expense, anyway."

I turn from her and walk to the curb.

"My car is over here, Kevin," she says, coming up behind me.

I shoot my hand out toward an approaching cab, grabbing the door handle as soon as the driver slows enough for me to jerk it open. She begs me to come with her.

"He didn't fall," I say to Phyllis, throwing myself in the back seat.

"What? Who didn't fall?" Phyllis says, somewhat confused.

"Your brother. Michael," I say with all the self-righteous smugness I can muster. "He didn't fall... he killed himself because he couldn't take it anymore!"

Through the glass I watch Phyllis slump away from the curb, her fingers cupping her mouth, her eyes blank as stones, and I feel something rupture between us, the air rush out. The driver twists toward me. "Where to?" I glance at the meter, at his nameplate and photo, at the chain of colored beads dangling from his rearview mirror. The world has stopped and I know I'm waiting for something, I'm waiting, but am not sure for what. In the darkly impatient eyes of the driver, I finally see what I'm waiting for and picture Phyllis running up to the cab, laughing, turning my insensitive blunder into an Olympic gold prank, announcing that Michael isn't dead after all, that in fact, he never existed. And it's her knock at the taxi window, her bright face at the glass, her laughter, her ability to make this lethal schism between us disappear; that's what I'm waiting for...

# SHE CALLS

She's always drowning. Her words are booby traps. Her head's a busy, dangerous intersection. Before we were kids we spent time in the same uterus, but that's where the similarities end. And because I'm older she thinks I have answers. I'm forty-four and still trying to figure out high school—Caroline Munger and her mysterious orgasms, all three semesters of chemistry, Sister Mary Baxter's rants about fish falls, alien abductions, spontaneous human combustion; clear signs of the rapidly approaching apocalypse. She was forced to retire the following year but I still wake up in a sweat, my elbows on fire.

Talking to my sister is penance. My mind is losing traction, but I listen. I pick my toes to stay focused. I tell her to leave him. Wrong. "But I love him," she says, "you never liked him," she says, "you're jealous," she says. At some point I pray the phone will explode and save us both from this evening. "Jealous?" I say. "Of what? The 90k he makes a year thinking up clever ways to market beer to alcoholics? Or the sable Beemer he drives? Or his girlfriend with the amazing silicone rack?" That last one sticks pretty deep. "Bastard!" she says, "you rotten bastard!" I apologize, grab my parachute and jump.

I know my ears are bleeding but I can't get off the phone. She needs me, she says. Emotional safari, I call it. Big game hunting for truth and fidelity in the new millennium. She's too young to remember Nixon and that's too bad. But what about Clinton? Would it break her arms to pick up a newspaper?

Stone Sales. Why didn't I think of that? They sell stones. Fireplace stones, walkway stones, patio stones, columns of stones three feet high stacked on wooden skids. Driving the forklift is a dark-haired, athletic looking woman I'm itching to meet. But I have no use for a large column of stones wrapped in chicken wire so I continue down the road. "Are you listening?" she says. "Yeah, Bernadette, but I'm trying to drive here!" I'm hurrying home to an empty apartment to make stir-fry. "He hasn't been home in two days," she says. I say, "Maybe he's on a business trip he forgot to tell you about." What does she expect? She collects ceramic gnomes and embroiders farm scenes on white pillowcases. Roger, straying husband in question, creates killer ad campaigns and does Jell-O shooters and blow off the hipbones of high-voltage models.

"Please come over," she says. An army of cracked and shattered gnomes lie scattered across Bernadette's living room floor. She hasn't dressed or bathed in two weeks. Her hair is going dread. I shower and dress her and break a brush in her hair. I find her a hat and take her to the Sizzlin' for dinner. She stares at the ribeye on her plate, then jabs it hard with her fork. Before I can stop her, the ribeye goes sailing across the restaurant. "Roger, you bastard!" she screams at the ceiling. In the parking lot some idiot in a black Jag rolls down his window and whistles. Bad timing. It's a few minutes before the pepper spray wears off and he's able to see. By then, Bernadette has left a deep crease down the passenger side of his car with the fork she stole from the Sizzlin'. Misdirected rage, maybe, but at least she's fighting back.

"I'm filing for divorce!" she says. "I don't deserve this!" "You're too good for him, Sis," I say. "You deserve better." West Wing is coming on. A six of Heineken is chilled on the coffee table. I mute the Viagra commercial. "Do you think I'm doing the right thing?" she says. "He's a dog, Bernadette," I say, "he's slime, he's excrement!" I tap the mute button off so I can hear what Bartlet is saying to Zoey. "You don't know him!" Bernadette says. "His loving, caring side. No one knows him like I do. No one understands him!" Now everything has stalled. The gyro between my ears is wobbling. "You never liked Roger," she says. "No one in this stupid family has ever liked him!" she says.

With a little ingenuity I know I can find a use for a pile of rocks. Today I stop. Up close she's more delicious than I thought. "Do you work out?" I ask. She looks down from the forklift, points at her ear and mouths the words: "I can't hear you." The forklift is loud and I love the way her lips work. She's wearing short-shorts and clearly has thighs bigger than mine. She tells me her name—Kitsi. Pulling from the parking lot, I hear the rear bumper of my Saturn drag a little on the pavement, an expensive scraping metallic sound. In the mirror I see sparks.

"Roger called me today," Bernadette says. "He wants to talk. What should I do?" It's no wonder my folks took off and left their house to her. "No, really, dear," my Mom had told her. "Your father and I want to live in the RV for a while, try life on the road. You stay here in our house until you figure things out with Roger." Kitsi's coming over in about forty-five minutes to watch the *Godfather* trilogy on DVD. She loves Marlon Brando. "Remember *Last Tango in Paris*," she said, loading stones into the trunk of my Saturn. Oh, yes. Who can forget! "Well? What should I do?" Bernadette says. "Are you listening to me, Herbert? I have a big dilemma, here." "I don't know exactly how to advise you, Sis," I say, unwrapping a brand-new stick of Land-O-Lakes for the butter dish.

"Roger was here!" she says, her words dizzy with provisional joy. When worlds collide. Roger and Bernadette married just out of high school, their futures hijacked by stupefied hormones and intoxicated corpuscles. Who knew then how they'd turn out? "Herbert, we had sex this afternoon," she says. "For eight months he doesn't touch me and *Wham!* we're on the floor of mom and dad's living room as soon as he walks in." I hear the doorbell. Kitsi's standing there, gray tights and a white pullover. What she's doing to that sweater is illegal in 48 states. "I miss him," Bernadette says. "He makes me laugh, Herbert. Do you know how rare that is?" I take Kitsi's purse, walk her to the couch and hand her the remote. "You're extremely fortunate, Sis. Can I call you tomorrow?"

Jack finds the horse head under the blankets. Where's the star on the horse's head? "See, it's not the same horse!" I whisper to Kitsi. The evening is unspooling nicely. "He just called and begged me to come home," Bernadette says. On the couch Kitsi's toes are flirting with mine. Hers are the painted ones. "You should go home to him, Bernadette," I say. "I'll talk to you tomorrow, okay?" On the DVD, the severed horse head is paused, the grizzly image etching into my long-term memory. "He brought me a new gnome this afternoon when he came by," she says. "I forgot to tell you about it. It's so beautiful. Roger wants us to fill our entire house with gnomes, our own little gnomes, Herbert. Children! I think I still love him." Kitsi seems bored now, walking around the apartment, inspecting the baseball trophies I won as a kid. She picks up the postcard from Arizona and the photo of my folks standing in front of a vortex in Sedona. "I've always wanted children," she says. "What should I do, Herbert?" The vortex is not visible in the photo. "I think you should pack up and go back home. Roger is a wonderful guy, a great catch! I'll talk to you tomorrow, okay?" Kitsi is picking up her purse and writing a note. "Now you're defending him?" Bernadette says. "You don't even like Roger. You've never liked Roger and now you're…"

~

I think one of the rear springs under my Saturn is broken. My folks' house seems abandoned with the RV missing from the backyard. My sister's Element is parked in their driveway. "Thanks for coming, Herbert," she says. "You're the best brother in the world." I pop the trunk and lift out a stone. "Can you grab one of those, Sis?" We stack them around the garden. "You're so thoughtful, Herbert, bringing these for mom's garden." My new DVD, *Last Tango in Paris,* is sitting on my front seat. I reach in and put it on the floor so it doesn't turn into a taco in the sun. "I think I'm going to move back with Roger," she says. "He's started rehab and he's giving up his girl-friends." I notice that the right rear of my car is still lower than the left. I check the trunk for stones. It's empty. "Do you think I'm making a mistake?" she asks. I'm anxious to get home. Kitsi is giving me a second chance tonight. She thinks it's cute that I'm such a nurturer. "No, Kitsi. I think you're making the right move. Marriage is an institution, a vow, a promise, a pact, a pledge, a covenant, a sacred… thing." "You called me Kitsi, Herbert. Who is Kitsi?"

~

"The bastard!" Bernadette says. "The no-good bastard! I went home and caught him in our bed with two women! They were naked! All of them!" Out in the kitchen, Kitsi is humming the *Battle Hymn of the Republic* and making popcorn. I can hear it percolating in the microwave. "They had their whore hair all over my embroidered pillows and Roger was holding some kind of...I don't know...disgusting sexual device...ugh!" I feel my ear going numb. "Where are you now, Sis?" I ask. "I'm back at mom and dad's. They'll be home in a few days. Jesus, Herbert! My life is shit! My whole life is shit!" Kitsi sets the bowl of popcorn on the coffee table, puts her blouse back on and heads for the bathroom. I say, "You're at mom and dad's, you're safe, you seem reasonably together. I'll call you tomorrow, okay?" "Tomorrow!" (Crying, sobbing, wailing, whimpering.) "Bernadette? Are you okay? Bernadette?" Kitsi waves and throws me a kiss as she walks out the front door. "Kitsi! Wait!" "Herbert! Who is Kitsi? Are you listening to me at all? Don't you care anything about me? My life is crumbling and..."

"Bernadette is going with us," my mother tells me. Kitsi must have changed her phone number. I've tried it ten times this morning. "Your father and I have decided to sell the house. We're going down to South America to pick up a load of Copado cactus for your father's rainsticks, then travelling up the West Coast into Alaska. We're going to live in the RV and Bernadette has decided to go with. We wanted to know if you're interested in going along, Herbert. We're starting our lives over." I pick up the remote, click scene selection trying to find the butter shot. "I'm 44 years old, Mom. What would I do in an RV? What would I do for work?" I can't get the remote to function. The batteries must be shot. "Like I told you in my letter," my mother says, "your father is painting rainsticks. I'm making jewelry and Bernadette can sell her embroideries. You could paint. You've always wanted to paint." I don't recall anything about dad making rainsticks, whatever the hell those are. But then I never really read the letters. "We'll get a camper to pull behind the RV," she says. "You can stay in that." The batteries look fine when I open the back of the remote, but batteries always look fine unless they have that brown foam oozing out the seams. "Herbert? Are you there?" The batteries fall on the floor. They're dead. "Yeah, Mom, I'm here. When did you say you were leaving?"

# WHITE BULL

(Appeared originally in *Southwest Review*)

When Sheila walked in the house from work, Walter was seated at the kitchen table studying a blank piece of inkjet paper, holding it up to the light like a surgeon with an x-ray. He was wearing the same blue and yellow boxers he'd had on when she'd left that morning. Walter turned to look at her, his wire-rimmed glasses slunk down on his nose, his thumb and finger holding the sheet out by the corner. The paper made a crinkling sound when he waved it. Sheila noticed he hadn't even bothered combing his hair.

"I got fired today," Walter said.

Driving home from the bank she'd pictured herself languishing all weekend on the back patio, absorbing juicy rays in her yellow bikini, losing herself in her new Berg novel. In the evenings she planned to lock herself in her studio, order anchovy and pineapple pizza, finish the stained-glass window she started over three years ago. Now, watching Walter toggle the sheet of paper, she felt defeated.

"Kline read my column and told me it was no good," Walter said, placing the sheet of paper on the table, picking up another. "Actually, Sheila, he said it stunk! Then he fired me."

The truth was, Walter had been fired over two years ago. He and Sheila had been living in Chicago, and when the *Tribune* released him, they moved to Indiana where Walter took a job on a small newspaper, writing obits and local puff. After a few months, he just stopped going to work. He'd spend most of his day around the house, cleaning and dusting, scrubbing the bathroom, beating the upholstery with a Wiffle ball bat, chasing the airborne dust with the Dirt Devil. He washed the dishes by hand even though they owned a new Maytag dishwasher, then carried them out on the deck to dry; plates, saucers, bowls, and glasses lined up along the railing like a booth at a flea market. When he finished with the inside of the house, he'd take the sweeper outside on a long extension cord, climb a stepladder and vacuum the gutters.

Walter didn't seem to miss writing, apparently finding greater solace in housework. With Sheila's income as bank manager at Fidelity Savings, and a few cuts here and there, he didn't really need to work anyway. And other than a small assortment of compulsions, he seemed as normal as anyone— going out to dinner with friends, going to the movies—except when he became the "other." That was the only way Sheila could think to describe it to friends, as if she were talking about Jekyll and Hyde. When he became the "other," he'd do nothing all day, just sit at the table thinking, wondering about things like: Did corn and tomatoes once grow wild in the forest? And how was concrete first invented?

"I don't know how they make paper," Walter said. "I mean, do they slice it like cheese to get it so thin, or do they compact it on a huge press? Sometimes I think maybe they just pour liquid pulp into a centrifugal cast of some kind. Don't you wonder about that, Sheila?" Walter made a raspy noise when he scratched his fingernails across his unshaven jaw.

During Walter's inquisitive moments, Sheila had thought he would have enjoyed spending his day Googling, or typing questions into howstuffworks.com, but Walter wouldn't go near the computer anymore, said the glow from the screen was etching white lines along the anterior lobe of his brain. She never bothered to ask how he knew that.

"Where's Mark?" she asked.

Walter picked up a scrap of paper from the table. "He left you a note."

Mark's note said he was going to a party with Trevor, and that Trevor's mom was driving them. Sheila squeezed the note into her palm.

"See what he bought me." Walter held up a book of statistics. "It looks interesting, but I'm not sure why he thought I would enjoy it."

Sheila wasn't as surprised. Mark knew that Walter never read anything anymore, wouldn't even watch television, yet Mark persisted in trying to mastermind a breakthrough for his stepfather where doctors had failed. He wanted to believe that if his stepdad would just take an interest in real things, it might snap him out of his malady.

"Are you too warm, Walter?" she asked, draping her jacket over the chair.

"Yeah, it's real stuffy in here, don't you think?"

She checked the thermostat. Sixty-eight degrees. "I'll turn it down a little," she told him, even though she didn't.

"Hey, what about the museum?" Walter said, his expression growing brighter, as if wired to a rheostat. "I think they're open till eight on Fridays." Walter had told her he felt the most peace when he was at the art museum, said he could breathe easier, felt lighter. He attributed it to the art.

Caught in a crawl of traffic on Skinker Avenue, Sheila eyed the other motorists who looked to be dressed for the symphony, or the theatre, men in suits and ties, ladies in evening gowns with pearls and diamonds sparkling on slender necks. There were also women in baggy sweatshirts with clipped up hair—maybe meeting for margaritas, discussing boyfriends, lovers, affairs—and couples kissing at stoplights, strolling hand in hand into stores, restaurants. Walter brought the blank sheet of paper with him—a touchstone? —she had no idea. He flipped the paper in his lap, the crinkling noise driving her mad. She mashed the brakes, honked at the jackass in front of her who stopped at the green light.

"White bull," said Walter.

Her attention shifted momentarily from the couple crossing the street as she waited to make a left turn. "What?"

"The white bull. That's what Hemingway called the blank page," Walter said. "The white bull."

About to ask why, she decided she didn't have patience for the answer. "I have to stop at Walmart for pads," she said. "It'll only take a minute."

"Sure." Walter opened the glove compartment. Oil change schedules, the automobile manual, cassette tapes, a box of tissues, and condoms crammed the small space, the condoms spilling over the edge, falling to the floor. Foil squares glistened like candy on the car mat. Walter picked them up one at a time, placing each back in the compartment, using his palm to staunch the flow, while others slid past his hand, collecting around his shoes, glimmering. A Saturn attempting a left turn blocked oncoming traffic. Sheila checked to the right for an opening, ready to abandon the turning lane. Traffic approaching from the rear cut a scorching white light across her mirror. Walter was losing the battle with the condoms.

"What are you doing, Walter?" she asked, distracted, frustrated with his clumsiness.

"Looking for a pen."

"Here. In my purse, Walter." She tossed her bag across the seat, smacking his thigh.

"Did you ever think about where the first grocery store got its stock from?" he said, peering into her purse. "I mean, no one would process food and print up expensive boxes and packaging if there was no place to sell it, right?"

Doctors told Sheila that Walter was not really insane, but couldn't say what he was. She'd asked if he was bi-polar, if his condition was the onset of Alzheimer's, and if he was dangerous to himself or others. They prescribed medication and said it was a mild psychosis, occasional breaks with reality. With low doses of Clozapine, he should function just fine most of the time.

"It's like the first automobile owners," Walter said, his hand swimming in her purse. "Where did they buy tires and gas? And the tires, rubber tires! Did you ever think about those, Sheila? I mean, some inventor had to think up the idea for rubber tires, then figure out how to make rubber, develop an elaborate metal mold, devise a way to inject the rubber; then he had to have some kind of factory for all the equipment before he even made the first tire to know if it would work! It's pretty amazing, don't you think?"

Sheila nodded, waiting for the boy on his skateboard to scoot past the entrance of Walmart. She drove Walter to the front doors and asked if he'd run in and grab them real quick.

"What kind?" he asked.

"Freedom. With the wings."

Cars pulled in behind her, waiting, headlights glaring in the rear glass.

Shoppers with white plastic bags swinging from their arms crossed between the yellow lines. Walter disappeared into the store. Sheila eased forward as people cleared the crosswalk. She gave the side mirror a glance, then fixed her eyes on the exit ahead; she could make a quick right onto Lindell. She imagined the glowing block letters of Walmart shrinking in her rearview mirror, her car blending back into traffic, her taillights joining a long line of anonymous taillights. How hard would it be to leave Walter behind? What would he do when he came out of the store? It would be so easy, just drive away. Eventually someone would find him, bring him home, if Walter could remember where he lived. Even if he couldn't, someone would check his wallet, his address, call a cab. But it was unthinkable, Walter standing on the curb with her Freedom pads, waiting calmly for her to drive up in the Toyota, take him to the art museum. She pictured him standing at the curb when the Walmart lights went out, waiting in the dark while burrito wrappers from the nearby Taco Bell blew across the deserted parking lot. He might stand there till seven the next morning when they opened. She pulled past the line of shiny green riding lawnmowers and made a left down the last parking lane. She paused a moment by the *KFC,* smelling the crispy-sweet odor of chicken fried grease before returning to the entrance of the store to wait in the fire lane.

The art museum was a fifteen-minute drive from the Walmart. Walter placed the *Freedom* pads in the backseat, buckled his seatbelt. He stared out the front window for most of the trip. Sheila didn't bother checking what Walter had bought; he always bought exactly what she told him. But his silence was beginning to worry her, even though she was thankful for the Walter-free time. Did he know who *she* was? Or where *he* was? She could never be sure. His unchanged expression reminded her of "Tituba the Witch" in the Salem Wax Museum. Walter had enjoyed that trip.

"You still want to go, don't you, Walter?" She hoped he'd forgotten about the art museum and was ready to go home.

"The museum? Sure." Walter never took his eyes off the road. Sheila wondered if he missed driving, if he ever thought about it.

"How do you think the idea of UFOs got started?" Walter asked. "I've never seen one and no one I know has ever seen one, yet they show up in everything from television to novels. There was a picture of one in Walmart, a display for some kind of candy or something."

Walter's eyes flickered wildly with oncoming traffic and Sheila had to look away.

"Did you ever have an eight-track stereo player?" he asked. "My dad had one when he was a kid. I think it might have been the last one ever made. The tapes had only one spool inside and I could never figure out how the tape could wind on and off the same spool without breaking, or getting tangled."

She'd heard of eight-tracks, but had never really seen one. Walter was eleven years older and often recalled things she'd never heard of, like Lik-m-aid and Estes model rockets.

Children were jumping from a van at the entrance to the art museum when Sheila pulled to the curb. A woman climbed out the passenger side and gathered the children around her, then waved the van away. Sheila stopped the car and told Walter to go inside and she would park. He looked over at her and smiled, an unexpected, knowing smile that at times made her feel that he was faking his condition, that at any moment he would touch her cheek and say, "I'm still crazy for you, Sheila," the way he had done each morning before he left for work. She looked at him and couldn't believe he was the same man who had rolled off her the first time they'd spent the night together and said, "You make a man want to spend his entire heart and not ask for change." When she'd smirked, he'd said, "What, too corny?" It had seemed mawkish at the time, but now she longed for sentimentality, anything that sparked of normal.

She was about to reach across the seat and touch his hand when he shut the door and strode up the museum steps, never once looking back. Maybe he belonged in some kind of care facility, but she couldn't consider the idea, and her boys would never stand for it, not now. When she and Walter first married, her boys wanted little to do with him, calling him by his name instead of "Dad." Walter never seemed to mind, assuring her they just needed time to adjust. She knew it was much more than that. Todd and Mark still held onto the *ideal* of their biological father, still worshipped him even though they saw him only once a year, those visits lasting less than a week, some only a few days. To Sheila's surprise, those infrequent trips were enough to keep the myth alive. It was only after their father failed to call or write for three years that they finally started calling Walter "Dad." Walter had smiled and said, "See, Sheila, they just needed time."

Sheila drove to the parking lot on the side of the building. The fresh scent of rain rode the air and the evening suddenly seemed too unspoiled to waste in an art museum. Walter would be studying the Early European collection, rocking back and forth to some motet playing in his head, enthralled with the Old Masters—Bartolomeo Manfredi, Artemisia Gentileschi, Titian. Though he'd never seen the actual painting, he'd once told her that Jacques-Louis David's *Oath of the*

*Horatii* marked the end of a great era in painting and the beginning of modernism. He'd explained why but she couldn't remember the reason. He rarely talked about art anymore, seemingly content to just linger in the Early European room— he said the paintings left him feeling light, alive. Sheila could never understand it; to her the Old Masters were dismal and gloomy.

She paused on the front steps and lit a cigarette. After smoking it to the filter, she squashed it under the toe of her pump and lit another. She realized she hadn't even changed clothes from work. She thought about Steve, the motel at lunch, his anxiety over the possibility of his wife finding about their affair. "This has to be the last time, Sheila," he'd said. Naturally he'd waited till after sex to reform. She was glad it was over. Steve's apprehension had become so tedious she hadn't had an orgasm in two months. As soon as sex was over, he'd ask a thousand questions while they dressed— "Can you still get AIDS using a condom? How long do you think we've been here? Do you think anyone can see the car from the highway? Is Walter suspicious?" That was her favorite. "Is Walter suspicious?" Walter didn't know what day it was.

Reaching for another cigarette, Sheila looked up at the entrance to the museum and knew she couldn't go in. She dashed back to the car, unlocked the door and threw herself into the front seat. She coaxed the key forward. The engine lit smoothly. Before she could change her mind, she jerked the shifter into drive, made a left on Museum Drive, and headed toward the city.

～

Kelly Kat was the name of the bar. Sheila had no idea what the name meant, but she'd never be recognized or remembered here. She checked her watch. An hour till the museum closed. She slid onto one of the stools and ordered a Vodka Collins from the girl behind the bar. When the girl pushed the drink across the polyurethaned wood, Sheila reached in her purse for her wallet.

"I'll collect when you're finished," the girl said.

Sheila smiled, curious about the raven tattoo across the girl's shaven brow. It gave her the look of Frida Kahlo. A moment later, the girl put a different drink on the bar that looked more adventurous than her Vodka Collins.

"What do you call that?" Sheila asked, but the girl obviously hadn't heard and turned away.

"White Bull," a man said. Sheila spun on her stool. She hadn't seen him walk up.

"It's kind of a sissy drink. My girlfriend's favorite." He nodded toward two young women in the far booth, a blonde and a brunette. "Mine's the blonde."

His girlfriend's dress was sliding off one shoulder, but she didn't seem to care. Both girls laughed at some whispered secret, their eyes flitting toward Sheila, then back at each other. They couldn't have been much more than twenty-one. The man seemed to be in his early thirties. Sheila shook her head and turned back toward the wall of bottles behind the bar.

"Tequila, Kahlua, and lightly whipped fresh cream."

"What?" Sheila said, turning to face him.

"Tequila, Kahlua, and lightly whipped fresh cream. That's how you make a White Bull. I could make you one some time."

Sheila smirked, then glanced at the two women in the booth before downing her Vodka Collins. She signaled the Kahlo girl for another. The man went back to his girlfriend and Sheila slowly nursed her second drink, studying the girl behind the bar. The girl seemed to be about the same age as her oldest son, Todd. She wondered if Todd was dating girls in college that looked like her—black fingernails, maroon hair, nose rings. The girl was pretty, but the seemingly permanent scowl on her face had all the allure of peeling paint. Sheila figured it for some kind of defense system. Apparently it worked; no one lingered at the bar attempting conversation.

Sheila finished her second drink and was about to order another when she checked her watch. The museum would close in seven minutes. She threw a ten and five on the bar and walked to the parking lot.

"Want that White Bull now?" It was the man with the whispering blonde, but the girl wasn't with him. Surprisingly, Sheila wasn't afraid. For whatever reason, he seemed harmless, or maybe she just didn't care anymore. She knew it was wrong to think only of herself, take dangerous chances, not considering Todd and Mark. If something happened to her, they would have no family, would have no one, and probably would feel compelled to take care of Walter. That wasn't fair, not for two boys whose entire lives were yet unmapped.

"Not tonight, cowboy. Besides, it looks like your dance card is full."

"Dance card?"

Sheila hated that she'd used one of Walter's adages She wasn't even sure what a dance card was.

"What happened to your blonde?"

"She went home with her friend."

"You should have gone with her."

"You know there are only three kinds of people in the world," the man said. "Those who read stories about people who live interesting lives, those who write stories about people who live interesting lives, and people who actually live interesting lives. Which are you?"

Sheila looked at the pavement and shook her head. "You're a writer. Christ! Who else would come up with such crap?"

The man laughed and walked closer. He pulled a martini glass from the hood of a parked Mazda. The liquid in the glass was a frothy white on top, black on the bottom. "One White Bull for the lady."

"No more for me tonight. You drink it. I've got to go." Sheila unlocked the door and pulled it open. The dome light failed to come on. The parking lot was dark and the absence of light unsettled her.

The man stepped closer, set the drink on the roof of Sheila's car, then leaned in past her. Her breath caught for a second. She was about to protest when the dome light came on.

"The switch was in the wrong spot. I hate when my dome light doesn't come on," he said. "Makes me feel like the whole car is broken." He smiled again and stepped back. Sheila reached up and took the drink from the roof.

"One sip," she said. "What's your name?"

"Cole. What's yours?"

"Sheila." She checked her watch again, then invited him to sit in the car for five minutes while she finished the drink. Their conversation led quickly to Walter, the gold band on her left hand.

"He's at the art museum," she said, the truth sounding more stupid than a lie.

"You don't like art?"

"No, it's not that. It's just that he loves it more than I do." She didn't want to talk about Walter, didn't want to talk at all. She and Steve never talked, not about anything important. "Walter says it makes him feel lighter," she finally said, her statement feeling like a betrayal. "He says it makes him breathe easier. It makes no sense."

"Actually, it does," Cole said, his lips forming the words gently, like a priest or minister. "The museum has a controlled environment. Perfect temperature. Perfect humidity. For the paintings."

Uneasy with the simplistic explanation, Sheila shifted in her seat about to rebut Cole's theory when she spilled her drink down her jacket. "Shit. Grab that box of Kleenex from the glove compartment, will you?"

Cole popped open the lid, condoms cascading to the floor. He looked over at her, then fished out the small daisy-covered tissue box. He said nothing, quietly picking up the foil packets, pressing them down into the glove compartment with his fingertips.

When Todd had started driving, Sheila filled the glove compartment with condoms, explaining to both her sons there was no excuse for unprotected sex. She showed both boys, even though Mark was only twelve at the time, how to put one on, demonstrating with a carrot. Both boys had chortled and smirked, obviously embarrassed, but she didn't care. No one else would show them, certainly not their biological father. And to ask Walter felt unreasonable, even though he would have done it without hesitation. But she never would have asked, and in many ways she knew she kept Walter on the periphery of her relationship with her boys. The five years she had spent raising them by herself had formed them into a unit, The Three Amigos, making it difficult to let anyone else in, even Walter. Men in her life might come and go, but Todd and Mark would always be there for her and she for them. Still, Walter was a wonderful father, driving them to hockey practice, helping with homework, showing them how to use a computer.

"I've got to go," she said to Cole, humiliated by the condoms. She noticed Cole had forced Walter's sheet of inkjet paper down into the cup holder beneath her drink to soak up the mess.

"Wait," Cole said, laying his fingertips on her wrist. "Not just yet."

She couldn't tell the color of Cole's eyes as he leaned over to kiss her, the Kleenex box exhaling a whoosh as he accidentally crushed it beneath his hand.

"I know this sounds like a line, but my apartment isn't far from here," he said.

"No. Thanks."

Headlights drifted across the headliner from a car pulling into the parking lot. She drew away from Cole and for a moment he reminded her of Steve—same charming smile, same stale cigarette breath. She wondered if her breath reeked of nicotine. He massaged her shoulder, his gaze unflinching, like a television poker player. She glanced between the headrests. She hadn't had sex in a car since she was a teenager, five months pregnant with Todd, her soon-to-be husband Roger deciding it would be fun to christen the rental car on their trip to meet his folks in Oklahoma. It had been ninety-five degrees that day, dust rolling through the opened windows, Roger's sweat soaking her dress while she lay squished into the upholstery gulping for air. Sheila didn't know it at the time, but that gritty romp in the back of the Plymouth would serve as their only honeymoon.

Her cell phone rang. "I have to get this." She fully expected it to be Walter, even though he often forgot the number. It was Mark.

"Can you pick us up?" Mark said. "Trevor's mom had to work late. We need a ride to the party."

"Where are you?" Sheila felt Cole's hand on her knee and pushed it away. Mark was giving her directions to some girl's house but Sheila had never heard of the streets. "Just wait,

Mark. Let me call you back in fifteen minutes and get directions. I'm in heavy traffic right now."

"Where's Dad?"

"Right here. Where else would he be?"

She shoved the phone in her purse, glancing briefly toward the back seat, the Walmart bag still sitting where Walter had left it. When Cole leaned in for another kiss, Sheila pecked him on the cheek. "You've got to go...and I've got to go," she said, checking her makeup in the mirror, even though the interior was too dark to see anything.

"Are you sure?"

"Yes. Very."

"Can I see you again?"

"We'll see." The same two words she'd spoken to Todd and Mark the entire time they were growing up. Her own mother's words. Every mother's words for anything that was not likely to happen. The lines that defined her were blurring. She took Cole's number and promised to call him. As he left to take the empty martini glass back to the bar, Sheila started the engine. She didn't want to be there when he came out.

Pulling from the parking lot, she glanced at the dash clock. The museum had closed forty-five minutes ago. She pictured Walter standing on the steps of the museum, staring up at the stars, except there were no stars. Raindrops began to flower on the windshield. Would Walter find cover, or just stand in the rain? She thought about Cole, finding his theory about the museum and Walter both amusing and sad. She was sorry she had divulged so much about Walter, suddenly upset that Cole had reduced Walter's panacea down to something as mundane as air quality.

She dialed Mark.

"Jeez, Mom, I thought you'd never call back!"

"Don't smart-mouth me, Mark. Just give me the directions."

She told him it would be an hour, that she and Walter had a few more errands to run before they could pick him up. Mark protested the delay. Sheila told him he could find another ride if that wasn't satisfactory. Mark said they could wait.

Rain battled the wipers.

The museum was dark, the front entrance empty. She parked at the front and ran up the steps, thinking she'd find him tucked under the overhang trying to stay dry. She walked around the building, called his name. "Walter. Walter!" She went to the sculpture garden and called his name again. She walked through the parking lot, down the road, then across the street into the park. "Walter!" Removing her pumps, she stepped across mud puddles and walked toward the Henry Moore sculpture opposite the entrance to the museum. Walter loved touching the Moore sculpture, running his fingers along the slick bronze skin. Even though he'd never cared for modern art, Walter had told her once that Moore was a genius, yet never explained why.

She looked down the hill. "Walter!" Water trailed down the hair stuck to her forehead, dripped off her nose, her chin.

Hurrying back to the car, she thought she spied someone near the fence. She ran toward the figure, calling Walter's name. The man looked up, his beard white and bushy, his spine bent like a fishhook. Sheila turned back toward the car, jumped inside, and locked the doors. Her clothes were soaked. She brushed her hair to one side and started the car. Thirty minutes later, after scouring a ten-block radius around the museum, she called Mark and told him he'd have to find his own ride.

60

"Jesus, Mom! You said you'd take us. Now what are we supposed to do?"

"Call your father in Italy. Have him take you to the goddamn party."

Sheila had never hung up on either of her sons before. She couldn't even remember the last time she'd yelled at Mark. She tossed her cell phone on the front seat.

Crawling the car past every McDonald's, Burger King, and Starbucks within two miles of the museum, Sheila hoped to see Walter's hunched frame sitting at some window booth, sipping a Coke, plucking fries from a cardboard pocket and dipping them in mayonnaise. He loved his fries with mayonnaise. She tried it once. Even though it wasn't as disgusting as it sounded, she preferred ketchup.

After searching another twenty-five minutes, she thought about calling the police, but was too afraid of what they'd say, too afraid she'd feel horrified, then relieved, then ashamed, if they said his body was in the morgue. She often wondered what it would be like if he just died. Some simple death. Uncomplicated. No pain or fear.

Maybe the police had called the house trying to contact her. Maybe they found him. Maybe he was in a hospital. She dialed the house and checked messages. Only one; Mark calling to see if she could take them to the party, saying he'd try to reach her on the cell. She tried to figure out where to look next. She drove to the hospital. She called the police station. "No ma'am. No one by that name." She drove past deserted store windows, all-night convenience stores, grocery stores, restaurants, pizza parlors. Rounding the corner, she spotted someone wearing a dark red jacket, tottering like Walter. She pulled to the side of the street, put the car in park, and jumped out. "Walter!" The man turned, his jacket open in front, the silver black hairs on his chest bleeding through the drenched white shirt. "Oh,

Walter!" She ran up to him and he smiled that knowing, disturbing smile.

"You won't believe what happened," he said, scratching his head. "Kline read my column today and said it stunk. Then he fired me. I'm sorry, Sheila."

She cradled her arm around his shoulders and led him to the car, helping him with the passenger side door.

"You won't believe what else happened," he said, when she settled in behind the steering wheel. "I completely forgot where I parked my car. I've been walking around all day trying to find it. Can you believe that? You must think I'm a mess." She looked over at him. He was smiling. His glasses were fogged, hiding his eyes. Water dripped from his hair.

They sat in silence, the street lamps illuminating the interior of the car. Walter's wet clothes appeared brittle under the glassy light.

Sheila was about to put the car in gear when she noticed Walter reach down between the seat and console. He twisted forward holding the wrinkled sheet of inkjet paper. The stain from her White Bull stood out like a target, Cole's phone number written in the center of the ring. She'd meant to throw it away.

"You know what's strange, Sheila?"

She shook her head, embarrassed that Walter had found the paper, was touching it, staring at the bull's-eye. She moved her gaze to the window where a girl was locking the front doors of a Dairy Queen.

"A man's nose and ears keep growing until he dies," Walter said. "What purpose could that possibly serve? Isn't that peculiar, Sheila?"

She wanted to discard Cole's phone number, but when she looked back at Walter's hand the sheet was gone. She had no idea what he'd done with it.

"If I live long enough, I'll probably end up looking like an elephant," he said.

She started the engine, checked the side mirror. Walter was leaning forward, palms on the dash, gazing out the windshield. Water dripped from the cuffs of his jacket. She studied him a moment, then leaned over and eased his glasses from his face. She wiped the lenses with a Kleenex, then carefully replaced the glasses, weaving the thin wire arms behind his ears.

# PRINCESS OF HUB CAP CITY

(Appeared originally in *The Iconoclast*)

"There's a child dancing on those old junker automobiles out there!" the woman screeched, horrified, standing in the doorway of my office with an eye on me and an eye on the junker automobiles. She was referring to my auto salvage just beyond the chain link. The woman had come inside to pay for the shifter knob in her hand. While she craned around the door jam, I slid the sawbuck from her fingers, smiled, and slipped her back a little less change than I should have. That old shifter knob she found on the table wasn't worth more than fifty cents, if that, but it appeared to have a story and that's all anyone cares about anyway, a story.

"Yeah, mister, a young girl, jumping around from hood to roof," the husband chimed in, eager to be a part of something important—all the while their own little yard-apes were running wild through the parking lot, knocking over my columns of stacked caps. Cooped up in the car too long, I suppose. I don't much care; nothing but junk anyway, as long as they don't hurt themselves.

"What was she wearing?" I asked, but I already knew the answer.

"A blue dress with little yellow flowers," the woman said, her face pinched with disapproval and looking like a weasel. "And she's bare-footed!"

I could tell the woman was perturbed with Anna Beth's appearance, her unkempt hair and filthy dress. I've had complaints before, worse than this.

"That's my daughter, Anna Beth," I said. "She's out there dancing on those junkers every day about this time. I don't know how she does it, frankly. The child must have soles made of asbestos. That metal out there is hotter than a griddle-iron in a 24-hour diner.

The woman's eyes grew bigger than baby moon hubcaps. She glared at me for a second, then shot an "aren't you going to say something?" look at her old man who couldn't recall how to shift his brain out of park, so conditioned he was to rephrasing the little woman's thoughts. Probably couldn't remember the last original idea he had. He just stood there slack-jawed, slumped over like he might have hit his head on the windshield a time or two.

"Oh, no need for concern, ma'am," I tried to assure her by standing up and walking toward the door. "Anna Beth is a little ballerina. Never so much as a bruised toe!" I tugged on my trousers to lend authenticity to my statement, even though I was wearing suspenders.

By now her two little boys were into some sort of mischief out by the Studebaker front ends that my granddaddy had welded together. He thought it was funny, and I must say it is humorous to see a car with two identical front ends facing in opposite directions. Anyway, the taller boy was poking on the little one's head or something, making him cry. The wife huffed out of my office and the husband slinked out behind, dragged along in her wake. Pretty soon those folks were in the parking lot hollering at their little renegades, shooting glances over in Anna Beth's direction and shaking their heads. They hustled the boys into the Explorer, spit a little gravel as they left the lot, and continued on their vacation. I always get a lot of folks on vacation this time of year. My place is a novelty, I guess, though it's nothing special, really, just home to Anna Beth and me.

The big sign next to the highway is what brings them in. Made it myself. Twenty feet high and sixty feet long. HUB CAP CITY. All capital letters made out of hubcaps. All *caps!*

Listening to cars rush by up on the highway, I felt the sun hot on my head where my scalp's gone to seed. The sun can get hot here, even in June, especially when the sky gets wide and blue like a million miles of ocean. Today's one of those days, without a breeze, and I usually wear a cap if I'm gonna be out very long. But I try to stay inside if I can, where it's cool. I glanced over toward the sea of wreckage wedged in beyond the chain link, looking for Anna Beth, even though I knew I wouldn't see her.

I wasn't much more than a kid when Charlene got pregnant with Anna Beth, maybe nineteen, twenty at most. We weren't married, but we pretended to be in the backseat of my Chevy. The day she told me she was pregnant, I said, "Charlene, if I don't love this child, I can't stick around!" Charlene just smiled, but I was dead serious. It may sound like a cruel thing to say, like I should've been more responsible-minded and all, but I had plans. Big plans. And they didn't figure to include a wife and child.

I was headed for Nova Scotia to work on the fishing boats. Met a fella once who told me about the job, said it was hard work, fourteen hours a day, four or five months during season, but after they rolled up the nets and docked the boats your time was your own, and you had enough cash to last you the rest of the year. I loved tilling the sea. Back when I was in high school, I worked a few summers in Charleston on the fishing boats and took to it like a gull on a mullet. No seasickness for me. Some of the new boys spent the afternoon bent over the rail studying the food they had for breakfast. And not all of them were boys either; some were men shouting their grits into the brine. But I just hauled nets and laughed. I guess God blessed me with the constitution of a humpback whale.

One day, a cold snap whipped the ocean into a fury, waves spitting and spewing, had been since three that morning. Several of the men were on the rail, but one boy in particular had done run out of menu. The boy looked terrible, green as seaweed, and dry heaving nothing but foul air. The captain walked over to him, turned him around, and said he saw something peculiar inside the boy's mouth. "Boy, I'm not sure what that red ring is in there," Captain said, with a grave tone, "but you better swallow hard, I think it's your asshole!" Captain and I laughed until we about fell off the deck. That was the life for me and I knew it.

But it didn't work out that way, of course. Life happens while you're making other plans and I married Charlene and ended up hanging drywall with my old man. Not bad work, but hard work, and dirty, and I imagine my lungs look like broken sacks of flour from all the plaster dust. Probably wouldn't have worked out anyway, the Nova Scotia thing. I would've spent the off season stewing my liver in Jack Daniel's and losing all my cash playing stud in the back room of Ruby's.

I ended up with this place. My granddaddy owned it, called it "Bill's Auto Salvage." Name wasn't a real bell ringer and when he died my daddy got it and quickly passed it off to me like a sack of copperheads. It was ten acres of has-been vehicles when it landed in my lap, an automobile graveyard all the way back to the sycamores. A few years after I got it, I decided to sell hubcaps, so I pried them off every wheel of every car beyond the chain link and stacked them out front. Stacks of hubcaps everywhere, like columns in a palace; hell, it was a palace, still is.

Eventually I put out some folding tables, made a little flea market, and filled the tables mostly with useless junk: little glass bottles, farm tools, shifter knobs and what not, but that's what people want, long as it has a story. From time-to-time folks will buy a hubcap or two, but mostly caps are a curiosity. Folks like to look at them because they're shiny and odd, and they see their reflection in the chrome. They hold them like a steering wheel in their hands, rotate them slowly, watching their reflections slip around the swells and valleys like fleshy pools of quicksilver. But they can't figure what to do with caps other than what they're doing, so they smile and put them back on the stack.

Now Charlene would never have moved here to live in a junkyard, but then neither would I if she was still with me. It was sad when I committed her to Harris Gloams Hospital, leaving her with folks that were screaming at walls and eating checkers. It broke my heart, what was left of it. But she had to go before she hurt herself again and I couldn't stay home from work every day to make sure she didn't. I only visit a few times a year now, not near as much as when hope was still an option.

Now it's just Anna Beth and me, most times it's just me. I remember when Children's Services came out here to check on Anna Beth a couple years back. Had it fixed in their mind to take her away from me. Seems that one of my customers had called them after seeing Anna Beth dancing barefoot across the junkers, thought it was irresponsible of me, that I was unfit to have such a beautiful child. Hell, they might be right.

The woman from Children's Services showed up wearing a tan skirt and jacket with a blouse the color of a canary and matching high heels. She had white hair as straight as a waterfall that ended at her narrow shoulders and little blue eyes that were so close set that it looked like the thin bridge of her nose was the only thing keeping them from a collision. She was friendly, in an institutional sort of way, but her smile was kind of sad, like the grill of a '53 Buick Skylark.

"I'm Trudence Galloway, from Children's Services," she said. "Are you Mr. Wiley Tiller?"

I nodded. She held out her hand and I took it, even though I had just finished jerking a carburetor off a '68 Mustang for a fella. She grimaced when she saw the grease on her manicured fingers. I handed her my rag, but it was dirtier than my hands. She pulled one of those wet wipes from her purse and cleaned her fingers. I figured she must have had plenty of run-ins with junk dealers to be that prepared.

"Mr. Wiley...I mean, Mr. Tiller, we've had a complaint about your little girl running around barefoot in your junkyard, playing unattended on the wreckage? Is that true?"

I didn't know what to say to this poor woman, so I shrugged. I think she took it as a sign of moral ineptitude and demanded to see Anna Beth at once.

"I don't know where she is right now," I said, scratching my head and leaving a big greasy spot on my scalp.

"Where is Mrs. Tiller?" she asked.

"She's indisposed indefinitely," I told her, and she didn't appreciate that answer either, putting her hands to her hips, obviously vexed.

Her features seemed to be shrinking, sucking in tighter toward the center of her face.

"I must see that child at once, Mr. Tiller!" she said, rigid as a fence post.

"Why don't we walk outside," I said. She followed me into the sunlight.

"*There* she is," Trudy shouted, pointing, and looked appalled. "Mr. Tiller, that child hasn't been bathed in weeks, and her hair, does it ever get brushed? She's filthy and she...she is not wearing *shoes!*" That just made her madder than a moth in a street lamp. She stomped off stammering about tetanus and infection and germs and said she'd return with the law. She held to her word, I'll give her that.

Pretty soon, here come two patrol cars and her green Impala screeching into the parking lot kicking up dirt like a stampede of wild horses. Doors are slamming and people are muttering but mostly I hear Trudy's shrill voice like a train whistle coming through the door. She's all fired up, high strutting ahead of this pack of lawmen like Wyatt Earp with a lynch mob. Trudy plants her feet in front of my desk and shoots a bony finger straight out at me, then looks over at the officer.

"Mr. Tiller, I'm Officer Duncan. Sir, we need to see your daughter, now!"

"Well, I can't help you. Like I told Trudy, I mean Ms. Galloway, I don't know where Anna Beth is right now. But if you'll follow me out to the parking lot...."

Officer Duncan took my comment as proof that I was lacking parental fortitude and moral fiber, and that I mustn't have a booger's worth of humanity anywhere in my old wreck of a body. He promptly escorted me into the backseat of his patrol car and commenced to making calls and running checks while the other officers searched the premises. Poor Officer Duncan spun like a dervish in the front seat of the patrol car when the news came over the radio. He glared at me around

71

the headrest. All I could offer in the way of explanation was a shrug.

Still waiting in the backseat of the patrol car, I could see the color drain from Trudy's face when Officer Duncan explained that Anna Beth had been nine years old when she disappeared, and that had been over twenty years ago. Never heard from since. Trudy shook her head, pointed out beyond the chain link, moved her lips in defense of her eyes, and rattled her head some more. She was starting to remind me of Charlene— just before I took her to Harris Gloams. Officer Duncan escorted Trudy to her car and she drove off slowly, but not before sending her eyes over the chain link several more times.

Officer Duncan warned me that even though he didn't know what was going on, he would 'upend the dirt' until he found out. Well, Officer Duncan never returned and neither did Children's Services.

For years folks had been stopping here and seeing Anna Beth dancing out on the wreckage, and for the first four or five years I'd run out to see, too. But I never saw her, even when folks said they were looking right at her. I wished I could, though, before Charlene got so bad. Maybe she could've forgiven herself, not that there was anything to forgive. Charlene just got caught in traffic on her way to pick up Anna Beth from dance class, got there ten minutes late. Ten minutes— that's not much time, but enough to change the bearing of someone's life forever. Anna Beth had been wearing the blue dress Charlene made her, the one with the little yellow flowers, and was waiting on the street. When Charlene got there Anna Beth was gone.

Charlene took it hard and I wasn't much help. We grieved like opposite ends of a candle. She grieved fiercely, her hope and heart burning away steadily while I was the cold end, hiding at the bottom, beneath the residue of her sorrow. She grieved for both of us, I suppose, until the flame went out behind her eyes.

"Charlene, if I don't love this child, I can't stick around!" What a dumb thing I had said to Charlene that day in the Chevy when she told me she was pregnant. Hell, I didn't even know what *love* was until Anna Beth was born. When I came to the hospital and looked at her through the glass, my heart melted like warm sap in a maple tree. I couldn't stop looking at her, like the part of Wiley Tiller that was lost at sea had finally come home to port.

Anyway, for years I wished I could see Anna Beth the way strangers did, and I didn't understand it. One night, long after Charlene was gone and I had moved here, I couldn't hold a composed vigil anymore. I ran out in that parking lot in the middle of the night and started screaming at the stars, hurling hubcaps at God until it looked like Hub Cap City was under siege by UFO's. The hubcaps seemed to hang there in the night air, flying and circling overhead, but not coming down. Finally, one by one, they landed in a crooked path between the chain link and me, the last cap falling at my feet. I closed my eyes a second, to let my soup settle, but when I opened them, Anna Beth was dancing across the caps like they were stones in a creek. I sat down on the gravel, waiting for her to come near so I could hold her, clean her face, brush her hair, but she didn't. After an hour or so the sun came up and she was gone.

Sometimes Anna Beth is sitting at my kitchen table, 29 years old now I guess, that's how old she'd be—is—I don't know. I picture her at the sink, her two children at the kitchen table eating their cereal, rushing off to school. Sometimes I see Anna Beth reading under a tree; a fine young woman with blond hair wearing a summer dress, bare-footed, looking so much like Charlene it squeezes at my chest. But it's the only way I see Anna Beth now, through a quirk of the brain cells, a trick of the heart.

I still can't and haven't to this day been able to see Anna Beth the way strangers do, during the day, dancing across the hoods and roofs. But on the nights I can't sleep, after I've coaxed the last bit of Novocain from the television, I take my lawn chair out on the parking lot, cozy up near a stack of hubcaps, and toss them one after the other toward the chain link, toward the sea of wreckage, and they sail away, shiny and bright like moons.

# STARGAZER AND THE BELLY DANCERS OF SHARM EL-SHEIKH

(Appeared originally in *Potomac Review*)

This is me standing in front of the Red Sea. This is me wading out into the waves with my pants rolled to my knees. That's Rebecca. Those are her naked breasts. She said she wasn't going to spend all this money to come to Egypt and return home with tan lines, as if tan lines were the Mark of the Beast. If it bothers you so much, she said, stop taking pictures of me with your phone. This is Rebecca walking away, her yellow thong battling the snug cleft of her butt cheeks.

The next morning I thought we were taking the camel safari to Ras Abu Galoum. Rebecca changed her mind, slipped her thong on and headed for the beach. Are you going topless again? I said. And what about the camel safari? She used her Betty Boop towel like a sarong. I followed down the hall in my chinos and polo shirt. I don't want to ride a stinky camel, today, Rebecca said in the elevator. It's too beautiful out. You're forty-one with two daughters, fanatical Christian parents, and a successful marketing firm, I told her. What's that supposed to mean? she said. It's the bio of someone who wears a top with her swimsuit.

She stopped down the beach ahead of me and straightened her towel on the sand. I stayed back, not wanting to be seen with her. Topless bathing was supposed to be illegal on Egyptian beaches, I'd thought, but Rebecca wasn't the only one doing it. This is the girl I saw at breakfast yesterday, the one with the tattoo of a bluebird on her shoulder. This is the elderly woman from the bus tour who probably shouldn't be on the beach at all, much less topless...her skin's already like luggage. This is the woman with hair the color of sunset. She looked straight at me and smiled when I clicked the shot. and didn't seem to mind me looking at her chest.

I glanced back at Rebecca, then out at the Red Sea. Salt water eventually makes my skin itch. Not when I'm in the water, but later, when I'm eating dinner or sipping a martini at the bar. Itching aside, I waded into the surf, my pants rolled to my knees. I went out fifty yards, maybe more—it was very shallow—stiff-arming my phone away from my body to get a picture of myself to show my daughters how adventurous I was. That's when I felt it, a sharp prick in the bottom of my foot. Ouch! at first, but the pain went from ouch! to fuck! so fast I thought I was going to faint. I tried to get Rebecca's attention, waving my phone hand, but she was lying prostrate, face away, hands in supplication on the sand. A true worshipper. The thudding in my leg matched the one in my neck. My chest felt tighter than an army sheet. I tried to yell but the only thing that came out was a desperate ball of air.

I finally managed a screech as I slogged toward shore. I knew I was going to die. My body was on full alert, all the alarms going off. Any minute now I would probably keel over, foaming at the mouth, hungry with madness. The first person to notice me was the woman with sunset hair. She smiled at me until she realized I couldn't smile back. That's when she splashed into the water, hopping through the waves, arms bobbing, breasts flopping, and grabbed me, trying to keep me from going under. Several times her breasts grazed the top of my head. One time they mashed into my face as she tried to help me up, a nipple dragging across my lips, along the edge of my nose, over my eye. The sensation broke through the barrier of pain, etching an irrevocable link in my long-term memory. Suddenly everything tasted salty. Maybe it was the lingering tang of her breast, or the seawater rushing into my open mouth. She squealed and struggled to lift me. She asked if I could breathe. Oh my god! Help! she shouted.

From fifty yards away, Rebecca acknowledged my dilemma in stages, first with mild disinterest, followed by curious concern, then concentrated panic. She shot up from her towel and dashed toward me, sand splashing from her feet. I handed my phone to the woman with sunset hair. Who should I call? she cried. Quick, take my picture, I said.

Together, Rebecca and the sunset woman dragged me onto the beach. My leg was redder than a three-day sunburn, and my foot had swelled to the size of a Reebok. The beach patrol lifted me onto the back of a four-wheeler and sped me to the entrance of the Hilton where they loaded me into the rear of an ambulance and rushed me to the hospital. In the ambulance, Betty Boop stared down at me from my wife's towel with those big black spiky eyes of hers. The EMT held up a syringe. Wait! I said. It's just lidocaine, she said. For the pain and inflammation.

I thrust my phone at Rebecca and told her to shoot me, my leg and foot. Get my face in there, I said. Back in Pittsburgh I had a classroom full of sixth graders who would never believe me without photographic evidence, unless of course, doctors had to amputate. Give him the shot, Rebecca said, folding her arms and refusing to take my phone or my picture.

I thought the EMT would jab the syringe directly into my heart like a doctor I'd seen on television. Instead, she gently pricked my foot in several places around the wound. Is the barb still in there? I asked, figuring I'd been attacked by a stingray. No, she said. Looks pretty clean.

The drug worked fast. The pain dispersed as swiftly as it had come, leaving me weightless, floating, woozy. Rebecca touched my forehead and for a second I thought she *was* Betty Boop. At the hospital, I asked the doctor if I could die from a stingray attack. He chuckled and said it wasn't a stingray. He poked his fingertip into my ankle, then my calf, and told me when people step on stingrays they usually get stung in the leg. Probably a stargazer, he said, explaining about their forward dorsal ray fin equipped with venomous spines. Stargazers are quite aggressive during spawning, he added. I told him I thought I was having a heart attack. He grinned and said I must have gotten a good dose of poison. He cleaned the wound and stuck a Band-aid on it. I expected a more trophy-sized dressing for my affliction, some sort of gauze and plaster badge of courage to drag around the lobby of the Hilton. The woman with sunset hair was suddenly in my mind, on my tongue, the salty taste of seawater. The doctor handed me a prescription for *Piriton* and *Darvon,* explaining that the antihistamine would help alleviate allergic reactions to the poison and the *Darvon* was for pain when the lidocaine wore off. Here's a couple *Darvon* until you get the prescription filled. You should be fine, he said. Resume your normal activities, walking, jogging, whatever.

On the cab ride back to the hotel I was a little loopy from the *Darvon.* When we got back to the room, Rebecca pushed me down on the bed and started jerking my clothes off. She

tossed away her towel, wrenched her thong down and strad-
dled me. For whatever reason, Rebecca always became more
aggressive sexually when I was impaired. Drunk after a party.
A little stoned on pot once after a concert. The time I took
codeine for three days after breaking my ankle; that was
more sex than we had on our honeymoon. I always wondered
if I was more appealing to her when I was less of my normal
self.

When Rebecca finished, she rolled off me and went to the
bathroom and took a shower. I fell asleep and when I woke
Rebecca was seated in the chair by the reading lamp looking at
my phone. You have a lot of pictures of Ginger Campbell's
breasts, she said. Who is Ginger Campbell? I asked. The
woman who saved your life, she told me. Ginger, Ginger
Campbell, the woman with sunset hair, I thought, mortified
Rebecca had seen the photos, even though I only remembered
taking two. Rebecca asked if I ever thought about anything
other than breasts.

I couldn't really answer that.

She brought the phone over and sat next to me on the bed. I
was shocked to see so many crazy angle close-ups of Ginger's
breasts. Apparently, in my frantic state during the rescue, I
inadvertently kept pressing the button. This is Ginger's breast
mashed against my cheek. This is her breast covering my left
eye. This is her breast glancing off my chin. Was that your
tongue? Rebecca said, telling me to go back one shot. No, of
course not, I assured her. Go back, she said.

It *was* my tongue, the tip, captured in my moment of terrified capitulation, inebriated with visions of death, reaching out
to that tiny eraser-shaped port of safety, that primordial icon
of salvation. Perched on the tenuous string between life and
death, I had no control over the most primitive instincts of
survival, the archetype of deliverance directing my tongue

forward. Michelangelo's David reaching out to God on the ceiling of the Sistine Chapel.

Did you lick her nipple? Rebecca said, incredulous. Jesus, you're fucking drowning and you still managed to lick her nipple? A perfect stranger?

It was true, Ginger was a stranger, but her breasts weren't. I felt I had known them for all ages, a cosmic familiarity all men share with breasts.

That evening we called our girls in Pittsburgh. My mother answered the phone and asked if we were having fun. I told her about my run in with a stargazer, then I told my girls. My youngest daughter, Melissa, asked what a stargazer was and I told her it was some kind of fish. Carmie, my oldest, thirteen, told me to email her pictures of my swollen foot. I just emailed you a photo of a stargazer, she said, then told me she couldn't believe anything that goofy looking was dangerous. I opened my laptop and brought up her email. The fish was half buried in sand and gravel with hideous teeth and huge, bulging eyes like a Chinese fu dog. It was ugly and vicious looking. Melissa thought he looked like Bert on Sesame Street. When Rebecca got on the phone she told my daughters I was saved by a damsel with "sunset hair." I was stunned.

That evening at dinner I asked her what she meant by "damsel with sunset hair?" She said that was all I kept muttering on the ride back from the hospital. A second later, as if responding to some divine cue, Ginger was standing beside our table telling us how relieved she was that I was okay, dwarfed by a big man she introduced as Gobel. Just Gobel? I thought. Rebecca invited them to join us. Gobel sat opposite me, his black drug-lord hair swept back from his forehead ending in a long fat ponytail down the back of his shirt. I understand Ginger saved your life, Gobel said.

Yeah, and he's got the photos to prove it, Rebecca added.

We ate lobster and sea bass and drank martinis and the Campbell's invited us up to their room for a nightcap.

Rebecca accepted the invitation without even looking at me.

The elevator took us to the top floor. The penthouse suite?

As soon as we walked in their room, I knew the Campbell's had herpes-wealth, the kind of money you can never get rid of no matter what you do. Rebecca and I had erection-wealth; all we had to do was get fucked once and it would be gone. Gobel mixed drinks at the bar while Ginger talked about her *Swift-Signs* business back in New Jersey. She purchased the franchise for sixty thousand, with another thirty thousand startup costs, and was making over two hundred and fifty thousand a year. I quit high school when I was seventeen and here I am making a quarter of a million dollars a year, she said. That was a lot of money, but not the kind to afford a room that probably went for two thousand a night in this hotel; it had more square footage than our home back in PA. Gobel brought the drinks over.

My daddy didn't think I would be successful, Ginger added, and, well...here I am. She threw her arms up in the air, her breasts jostling under her silky sparkly top. Ginger said her father expected her to go into the hotel business. He's CEO of *United Hotels Worldwide,* Ginger said. Have you heard of it? They own resorts all over the world.

We stay for free, Gobel said. Wherever we go. Sweet deal.

Gobel stated their good fortune with the enthusiasm of a man awaiting his own execution.

What do you do? I asked Gobel.

Not much, he said. Ginger quickly corrected him, coming over to hug and kiss him, plopping down on his lap, telling us what a wonderful poet he was. Rebecca asked him to recite one of his poems. Gobel seemed distressed. Go on, Gobi, Ginger said. Tell them *Abalene's Escorts*. This is such a great poem! Ginger looked like a little windup toy on Gobel's massive Sphinx lap.

After much cajoling, cooing, and kissing on Ginger's part, Gobel recited *Abalene's Escorts*. From what I could tell it was about a pest control guy named Paul who starts dating a hooker only to discover that the reason he kills bugs is because he's jealous of them. It felt longer than *Ancient Mariner* and weirder than *Metamorphosis*. In high school, Mr. Babich had us read Kafka's bizarre story. After that, Billy Stemmes would fall down on his back in the halls between classes, kicking his legs and arms in the air begging for someone to please turn him over. Stemmes was usually stoned.

Recite another, Rebecca said. Gobel said he needed a fresh drink. From the bar he asked what Rebecca and I were doing the next day. You should come with us tomorrow night, Gobel said. We're going to a nightclub in Sharm El-Sheikh to watch the belly dancers.

Rebecca said we were going on our camel safari to Ras Abu Galoum, but should be back before dark. You should go to Gabr El Bint. It means "dead girl" or something in Arabic, Ginger said. "Grave of girl," Gobel corrected, pulling a small pouch from his pocket. He rolled a joint, lit it and passed it around. We smoked and had another martini and Rebecca said she was wasted and needed sleep. This is Rebecca back in our room five minutes later, wiggling out of her dress, tossing her panties at my phone. This is her attacking me on the bed. This is me sucking on her middle finger. I have no idea why that turns her on.

I was relieved the next morning when Rebecca wore a bra and blouse to breakfast. We talked about the Campbell's and their wealth and Rebecca started telling me about when she was seven and how she loved when her mother's Sears catalog arrived in the mail, the lacquer smell of the ink, the way the shiny pages crinkled. She said she'd go straight to the toy pages and circle everything she wanted for Christmas.

It was cute. In twenty years of marriage she had never shared that story. Did you get everything you circled? I asked.

No. A few things, I suppose, she said, I don't remember. But I loved circling them.

After breakfast, we headed down to the camel tour office. A young woman named Panya with a seashell necklace and gold rings on her fingers told us we would take a Jeep eight kilometers to Blue Hole, where we would pick up our snorkels and dive equipment, then travel ninety minutes by camel to the small fishing village of Ras Abu Galoum. I pulled Rebecca aside and told her I didn't feel comfortable going in the water. What are we going to do the rest of our vacation, she asked—clearly disappointed with my cowardice—if you're not going back in the water?

This is the back of Rebecca's head in the front seat of the Jeep, hair flying, on the dusty road to Blue Hole. I sat in the back. This is Rebecca riding her camel to Ras Abu Galoum, her skin coconut brown even under the blaring sun. These are my legs, white as bone, like I vacationed in Antarctica.

At Ras Abu Galoum, Rebecca went with a guide, Musa, snorkeling the reefs, returning around lunch. This is Rebecca in her back-up bikini, the turquoise one that covered her breasts and most of her behind. This is Musa, the gray-haired man with sinewy arms and hairy legs and a smile big as a waterslide. We ate lunch together and he assured me nothing would attack me. I make peace with sea for you, Musa said. I dove that afternoon with Rebecca and Musa and we saw coral gardens and gigantic sea fans. At one point Musa swam to the bottom and rousted a funny fish from the sand, pointing and making crazy eyes at me through his mask. I shrugged. He swam over to me and yelled through the water, his voice garbled with bubbles. Stargazer! Stargazer! Stargazer! he said, pointing at the peculiar little fish swimming away, its black dorsal array of venomous spines erect. The fish wiggled wildly along the bottom, stirring up a cloud of silt, trying to bury itself again. A minute later it was gone, all except for its big golf ball eyes sticking from the bottom, staring up at the sky.

The sun floated above the mountains when we started back on the camels. Rebecca fell asleep in the Jeep on the drive to the hotel.

We met the Campbell's that evening. Gobel drove us in his rented Mercedes and Ginger told us they wanted to buy us dinner at this great little restaurant called *The Funky Flounder.* After dinner and several martinis, we walked to *Goddess of the Nile.* This is Olufemi, the belly dancer who gave me her red silk scarf. This is Rebecca wrapping the scarf around her head and over her mouth and nose like a veil, leaving only her eyes exposed. Rebecca batted her eyelashes concubine-like and I ordered another round of drinks, insuring my impairment for when we got back to the hotel.

Walking past the shops and restaurants on King of Bahrain Street, Rebecca told Gobel and Ginger about the stargazer Musa flushed from the sand earlier that afternoon. It was this big, Rebecca told them, laughing, holding her fingers eight inches apart as if to say how could anything that insignificant have caused such a big scene. Rebecca and Ginger snickered and made big stargazer bug-eyes at me, obviously forgetting how dangerous dainty can be, so I reminded them of the black widow spider. Gobel remained neutral rolling another fatty— that's what Billy Stemmes always called them—then lit it and handed it to me. Before I could exhale, he pulled a flask from inside his jacket and pressed it into my palm. Ginger and

Rebecca took the joint and passed it between them, taking turns dancing and whirling with my new scarf.

Tourists dressed in pastels and whites, some kind of vacation dress code like my pink shirt and cream shorts, bumped in and out of shops. Gobel, whose life was obviously much simpler, always wore black. When we walked by *The Sheik's Harem,* Ginger grabbed Rebecca's arm and pulled her toward the door. Come on, everybody! Ginger said. They tried on hip scarves, dresses, jewelry and tiaras, finally settling on harem pants, silk scarves and bustiers. When the woman at the register told them about amateur night at Nekhbet's, Rebecca and Ginger decided to wear their new outfits to the nightclub, both of them giggling as they bounded from the shop.

This is the neon sign over the entrance to Nekhbet's. This is Ginger and Rebecca cheek to cheek, their faces flushed red from the frizzle of neon gas. Those are Ginger's fingers holding the joint. This is Gobel paying the doorman the cover. We drank more martinis and watched more belly dancers. After the professionals left, they opened the stage to amateurs. This is Ginger and Rebecca goading each other. I'll do it if you will. I'll do it if you will. I'll do it if you will. This is the woman who actually did it, twirling around the open floor surrounded by tables of flickering candles. She also must have known about amateur night at Nehkbet's by the clothes she wore, the sheer chiffon dress, the bejeweled bustier. Rebecca and Ginger sniggered, whispering to each other that they could do better.

Afterwards, in the parking lot, they gave it a try. Gobel opened the doors of the Mercedes and cranked up the stereo, some Middle Eastern mix of sitar, flute, and tambourine. This is Rebecca and Ginger barefoot on the pavement, wheeling around each other, dragging their scarves over one another's shoulders, wrapping them over their faces, their breasts, their eyes locked on each other's. This is the crowd that started gathering. This is Ginger and Rebecca howling, making a mad dash for the car.

Gobel and I jumped in behind them and Gobel drove off. Ginger rolled a joint and passed it over the headrests, giggling, bouncing. Between drags, Rebecca burst into laughter, then crawled up on my lap and started kissing my ear. I think that's when Gobel suggested the game of Harem Share 'em. When Rebecca asked how to play, Gobel pulled the Mercedes to the shoulder. Ginger got out and jumped in the back seat with Rebecca and me. This is Rebecca and Ginger licking my ears, my neck. This is Gobel's fat ponytail as he chauffeured us back to the hotel.

We staggered through the lobby chortling and hooting like Americans and when the elevator stopped on Rebecca's and my floor, Ginger stepped out with us. I thought the game was supposed to end at the hotel, but the elevator doors closed on Gobel's blank face and he was whisked away to his penthouse. Alone. I looked over at Rebecca and wondered how far she was going to take this as she fumbled for the key card. As soon we were inside the room, Rebecca hurried to the bathroom and Ginger found the stereo in the nightstand and put in the CD she'd taken from Gobel's Mercedes, then started dancing on the bed. Rebecca joined her when she came out and a funny thing happened when they started undressing each other; my mind snagged on our life back in Pittsburgh, our two daughters Carmie and Melissa, our home in Hampton Acres, my sixth graders, Rebecca and I sharing popcorn at the movies, sitting on our deck sipping martinis, reading in our bedroom.

Ginger and Rebecca danced around me naked, trailing their scarves, orange and golden flames, then started undressing me since I hadn't done it myself, pulling me toward the bed. When Rebecca switched off the lamp, the three of us kissing, touching, arms and legs entwined, Ginger and Rebecca apparently experiencing no discomfort with the situation, all of us still very stoned but me sobering quickly, I found myself unable to keep up my end of Harem Share 'em. Rebecca tried to caress me back into the game but I couldn't follow. When Ginger tried to help I was more embarrassed than ever. After several minutes Ginger stood, dressed, and smiled as she fastened her bustier. Rebecca, sitting next to me on the bed, looked miserable. When Rebecca got up and started to put *her* costume back on I asked where she was going. Didn't you listen to the rules of the game? Rebecca said. It's Gobel's turn now.

Gobel's turn?

Ginger used the bathroom while Rebecca brushed her hair in the mirror over the desk. I watched the hard bone of Rebecca's elbow, her arm levering the brush, her features concentrated in the glass. I wanted to tell her not to go. Ginger came out of the bathroom and walked straight to the bed and kissed me on the lips. Goodbye little stargazer, she said. She smiled and told Rebecca Gobel didn't need a turn. Rebecca smiled glumly and said a deal was a deal. A second later they were both gone, the solid click of the door latch like a gunshot in a cave.

This is me waiting on the bed, sober. This is me thirty minutes later, still wondering what happened, still waiting on the bed. I got up, dressed, almost pushed the elevator button for the penthouse but went to the lobby instead.

I walked along the beach, the surf a convocation of ghosts rushing toward me on the dark water, breaking into a million pieces on the sand. I pictured Rebecca—her pale appendix scar and belly button ring—on top of the giant Gobel, the enormous man undoubtedly possessing a boundless reserve of stamina and a huge everything, and Ginger, her sunset hair, and all their hands roving each other's flesh like starfish on the ocean floor. What would happen to our life in Pittsburgh?

Would anything ever be the same? Would Rebecca and I be able to chalk it up to inebriation, a dope-induced adult time-out, and move on? And Carmie, Melissa, what would they think if they ever found out? The reverie had all but paralyzed me when someone walked up and called my name.

I turned to see Gobel strolling along the beach.

Didn't expect to see you here, he said.

The feeling was mutual. He raised his joint to me and I declined. Why aren't you...you know, upstairs with...you know? I asked. I was going to ask you the same, he said. After a few minutes he explained that there was something wrong with his hydraulics and he hadn't had an erection in over two years. Probably in my head, he said, turning to face the surf. After the pills, doctors, and therapy, he just gave up. Then he said it didn't bother him, Ginger sleeping with other men...and women; he was just glad she hadn't left him. We've done it before, he said. Harem Share 'em. It was my idea. It satisfies her I think.

Gobel seemed distraught telling me, unable to look my way. Sometimes I feel like a pimp, though, you know? he said.

This is Gobel walking down the beach, away from our hotel. On the way back to the Hilton I was giddy with relief Rebecca had not slept with Gobel. For whatever crazy reason, it didn't seem as critical if she just had sex with Ginger. When I thought she was with Gobel it felt like we'd crossed some line in our marriage that we couldn't return from—the way I always imagined having an affair might feel.

When I got back to the room, Rebecca was in bed, the room dark, the blankets bundled up over her shoulders. Was I supposed to know she hadn't had sex with Gobel? And how did she feel about me touching Ginger, about her touching Ginger, Ginger touching us? I had no concept of the emotional playing field I was stepping onto. I couldn't even sort out my own feelings about the evening. And even though I was relieved about Gobel, something still felt broken.

I undressed and stood at the window. This is me staring out over the Red Sea, a hundred billion stars spinning above me, hundreds of thousands of stargazers buried in the sand at the bottom of the ocean, their eyes aimed at the sky. Was it their fate to gaze constantly at the heavens? Could they read those tiny points of light, ascertain destinies written there?

I heard the mattress squeak as Rebecca turned over. Are you coming to bed soon? she asked. Her eyes glinted in the darkness like stones on the ocean floor. I slid under the blankets and wedged in behind her. I don't want to talk tonight, she said. Maybe tomorrow, okay?

This is Rebecca sleeping, her lips parted, her eyelids flickering under the spell of a dream. This is me sitting in the dark with my back against the headboard, watching the stars sneak across the sky, waiting for the sun to come up over the Red Sea.

# ANOTHER MAN'S GOLD

(Appeared originally in *Willow Review* & *The Worcester Review*)

Zoe loved running naked across Lake Chiloahoa when it froze to a blanket of snow, knew all the words to every song Woody Guthrie ever wrote, could skin the bark off a birch tree with a draw knife (lost her index finger to the knuckle as a kid in Ottawa), could unload fifty-five-gallon drums of diesel from an Otter seaplane all by herself, and wasn't afraid to pick up a drowned beaver, so I married her. The fact that she was mute didn't bother me none; I wasn't much of a talker anyway.

But it wasn't a real marriage, with a church and a preacher. Don't even think it was official. Huey Dent, a sheriff from Idaho Falls, married us one evening after we'd been sitting around the campfire passing a bottle of Canadian Mist and singing Guthrie's *Hard Travelin'*. Huey had come up to our lodge in northern Ontario to fish with his two boys. The boys were in the cabin playing video games or something, and Huey was sitting under the northern lights with Zoe and me, showing us his pistol, talking about his divorce and how he missed his wife. Campfires were powerful serum. Canadian Mist helped a little, too.

When he learned Zoe and me weren't hitched, he jumped up, snapped his suspenders, and said no time like the present, then rounded up his boys for witnesses, took off his own wedding ring and handed it to me. "Best institution in the world," he said with tears in his eyes, and Zoe's eyes sparkled too, in a way I'd never seen before, like stars on the surface of a moonless lake. Through all the seasons Zoe and me'd been together, the subject of marriage never came up. It was kind of understood that neither of us could see ourselves anywhere but with each other, so there'd been no reason for a ceremony. But I have to admit, when Huey pressed that ring into my palm, and I slid it on Zoe's finger, and he spoke some words that sounded real and binding, I felt my stomach lurch, like my canoe'd just pitched off a high waterfall. It was exhilarating. Zoe wrapped the bottom of Huey's wedding band with first aid tape until it hugged her finger as if it had been fashioned for it from the start. How easy it was, it seemed, to make things fit. We made love all night, the linoleum-covered plywood floor of our cabin creaking and sighing under the rattle of our old four-poster. The next morning we ignored our chores. Noah and our summer camp staff took over, filling gas tanks for folks, filleting their fish, making shore lunch, cleaning cabins. Zoe and me packed up our canoe and headed for the Jaspunlaska River, something we'd thought about doing for years but never did on account of all the work.

The next morning when Huey came out of his cabin in his jeans and suspenders, all sobered up from the night before, he smiled the biggest saddest smile I'd ever seen on a man and I figured he was going to ask for that ring back. I was prepared to trade him the entire lodge for it—boats, motors, cabins and generator—knowing how it'd break Zoe's heart to have to give it up. And I would've done it, too; I was no stranger to leaving everything behind—I'd done it before. But Huey did no such thing. He strolled over and kissed Zoe on the cheek, then wrapped my leathery hand in his own thick paw and gave it a vice-grip squeeze. Not the kind some men use to dominate others, but the kind that lets one man tell another he loves him without hugging and gushing lots of silly words. Huey bent over and gave the point of our canoe a shove, waving from the bank as Zoe dipped her paddle in the lake, guiding us toward the Jaspunlaska.

It would take a day and a half of paddling to get there, down the Chiloahoa River, across thirty miles of Lake Tipookoalal, past hundreds of beaver dams, islands and a few trapper shacks. With every stroke of Zoe's paddle, I watched that new gold ring shine on her finger, surprised by the warmth it brought me. Even though it wasn't really my ring below her knuckle, it bound me to her in a way I'd never thought possible, like we were tethered by some invisible, unbreakable cord. I couldn't be sure if Zoe felt the same way, but every so often she'd look back at me over her shoulder, glance at the ring and smile. We pulled over just before dark, made camp, built a fire, ate, then took off our clothes and splashed naked in the moonlight. When we got to shivering, Zoe went to the fire while I split a few more logs into firewood, chuckling at my own squirrel and acorns flapping around in the dark. I'd never chopped naked before.

When I finished, I carried the wood over, threw a few pieces in the fire, then sat on the log next to Zoe, our bare hips pressed against each other. She handed me a cup of coffee, the metal handle hot, the smell delicious. She shared her blanket with me, draping it over my shoulders. We stared at the fire, loons yodeling out on the lake and I was grateful for my new life. My old one ended over thirty years earlier, in 1969 like so many other young men, only their lives ended courageously in rice fields and jungles of Vietnam, while mine dissolved slowly, disgracefully and unnoticed north of the Canadian border.

My first few months in Ontario were spent in an abandoned camping trailer out in the middle of nowhere, surviving on berries and leaves, getting sick a lot, catching a fish when I could coax one from the stream, and checking the highway when I heard a car drive by. Didn't matter if it was day or night, I'd rush out to the road buck-naked to see if a tourist had killed me a possum, coon or marten. Martens were the best because they were small, about the size of a ferret, and easy to clean. By then, taste didn't matter anymore. When winter came things got tougher—less tourists, and the stream iced over so the animals stopped coming. That's when I hiked the eight miles back down the highway to Icy and Lew's convenience-store-gas-station. On my trip up that summer, I'd stopped there to buy groceries—beans, chips, bread and peanut butter—then spent the last of my cash on a cheeseburger and a six-pack of Coke. They were nice folks, and I think they knew I was running, so they threw in some chips and candy bars at no charge. I knew I'd never rob them, no matter how hungry I got. But I'd never really known hunger before. It put a worse hole in my stomach than I'd ever imagined.

The place was dark when I got there and I almost turned around, picturing the delicate wrinkles on Icy's cheeks when she smiled, her eyes green as mint leaves, and Lew, a stovepipe of a man with legs to his chest and hands big as work gloves. The sound of the glass breaking almost brought me to my knees, and I could hardly believe what I was doing. Lew and Icy had no burglar alarm and I reached my hand through the opening and unlatched the door. I stuffed myself with Spam and chips in the dark, washing it down with Coke until I thought I would throw up. I jammed my pockets full of candy bars, my coat with cans of beans, corn and chili. I took a couple of magazines off the rack, and stole a flashlight from the pegboard hook. Then I figured I'd better get some fishing gear before I left, hooks and weights and line. Before I knew it, I had gotten so drowsy from all the food and pop, I sat down on the floor to rest a minute and fell asleep.

Next morning Icy was standing over me with a plate of waffles, potatoes and a ham steak she'd cooked up. "Come to the back and eat," she'd said, holding her hand out. I sat up next to the fishing equipment, my ribs sore from sleeping on the cans of beans and chili, noticing the plaid blanket she'd covered me with. "I'm really sorry," I told her, folding the blanket into to a lumpy misshapen mess. She sat me at a table in the back where they kept extra stock and I figured Lew would show up any minute with a chain saw and hack off my legs, then stick me on a post out by the highway with a sign that said, "We prosecute shoplifters." I wouldn't have blamed him if he had. When Lew finally did come in, it was with a fresh pane of glass in his hands, a knife for cutting and a toolbox. He showed me how to replace the pane, but made me do the work. For a while I think he questioned his choice of punishment, because I broke every piece of glass I tried to cut. After several more tries I finally got it.

That afternoon, Lew and Icy introduced me to a friend of theirs, Frisk Mcinnes. Frisk took me out to his lodge on Lake Chiloahoa, taught me how to build a cabin, strip logs, play the fiddle. He showed me how to spot a beaver's runaway channel, how to place a trap so when the beaver got caught, the weight of the trap would pull it under water, drown the beaver, keep the pelt safe from predators and freezing temperatures. My first winter on Lake Chiloahoa, Frisk taught me how to harvest an ice field. That was the most fun and the hardest work I'd ever done. The ice field had to be laid out as soon as the lake froze solid, then shoveled clean every time it snowed. Most of our ice fields were about twenty-five meters square. We shoveled a much larger area than we planned to cut, because he explained that if we didn't, the weight of the snow would force water onto the ice during cutting and ruin the harvest. Frisk had built his own cutting machine from a thirty-six-inch sawmill blade and old Clinton snowmobile engine. It was a dangerous looking contraption. He pushed it from behind like a lawnmower. It sliced a perfect even grid in the ice easy as a straight razor through coffeecake. The blocks then had to be lifted from the water, each one weighing anywhere from 100 to 150 pounds. We loaded them onto a sled with tongs, then pushed the sled up a rail made of metal pipes into the icehouse, and layered the blocks with sawdust to keep it through summer.

I learned so much from Frisk and he never asked me why I was in Canada, yet he knew I was from the states. Then one winter, while we were putting runners on the front of his Ford truck to winch it out of a snowdrift, he said he knew why I had come to Canada and there was no shame in it, no shame at all. "Hell, boy," he'd said. "You didn't invent fear." Maybe I hadn't, but I felt like I'd put a fresh coat of paint on cowardice. And I know I shamed my family with my crime. My daddy, a vet himself, quit everything on account of me—quit going to the VFW Hall out of embarrassment, quit his job at the Chrysler plant for the same reason and started working at a garage two counties over where no one knew him, and he quit taking my phone calls. Eventually my momma quit taking them too. I think she was afraid he'd quit on her if she continued talking to me. By the time President Carter initiated his amnesty program, my old life had been bleached clean out of me.

Frisk never said anymore about it after that day, and we spent our evenings playing fiddle and drinking liquor, and it didn't matter what kind. One night he told me he didn't have family and was leaving the lodge to me if I wanted it, but I told him he'd outlive me and we both laughed—me, because I knew Frisk never went into town to make a will, and Frisk, hell, I guess I'll never know why he was laughing.

In the spring, Frisk showed me how to grow vegetables at the lodge. The ground around the lake was inhospitable, mostly a thin padding of loam over granite, so over the years Frisk had collected quite an assortment of Styrofoam coolers fisherman left behind. He filled them with rich soil he'd mined from the silted-in bays. He grew enormous tomatoes, squash, and peppers in those coolers. One spring, while he was tending his garden, he fell over dead. When we flew his body out, doctor said a blood vessel burst in his head. Doctor said Frisk was probably gone before he hit the ground. Hell of a thing for a man who loved life as much as Frisk. By then, Frisk and me had spent almost every hour of our lives together for the past ten years. And to my surprise, he left me the lodge in his will. I still have no idea when he'd found time to meet with a lawyer.

Frisk was the kind of guy you wanted beside you in a place like life. The loss devastated me, so much so, I could hardly keep up with the chores around the lodge, much less the fishermen arriving in floatplanes expecting to have boats and motors and leeches and worms. That was the summer Weber Kilbride came out to give me a hand, helped me fix the cabins, made shore lunch for the guests and I owed everything to him. He'd been a good friend to Frisk, helped us harvest ice a few times, drove over a hundred miles out to the lodge in a snowmobile over frozen lakes battling sub-zero temperatures. But it wasn't until that following winter, just as I was getting ready for ice harvest, that he brought his daughter Zoe out with him.

For the three weeks she was there, she never spoke a word, just smiled and chopped wood for the fire and threw hundred-pound ice blocks onto the sled with metal tongs so cold they'd take the hide down to bone. It wasn't till late one evening after a bout with Canadian Mist and some fat Cuban cigars that Weber told me she was dumb. I was shocked at first, hearing the word roll off his lips, but he'd used it for its true meaning, that she was mute. But I still thought it was a mean word for such an unfair condition.

Late that night, long after the fire had gone out in the cabin, I woke up and decided I needed a smoke. I rolled a cigarette and went outside in my bare feet, freezing the wrinkles off my soles. There in the middle of the moonlight was Zoe running naked across the frozen snow of Lake Chiloahoa, silent as a dream. I puffed my cigarette, watching her skin flash like a rainbow trout in a clear pool. When I finished the first cigarette, I rolled another. She started toward the cabin then and I thought she'd be embarrassed or angry when she saw me gawking, but she just smiled and took my hand. I was never sure if Weber knew we'd made love that night or not, or if he figured he'd never get Zoe married off in town, but he left her out there with me after ice harvest. Zoe seemed not to mind and I'd never been happier in my life.

It's hard to say how Huey, being a proud and patriotic man, would have felt giving his wedding ring to a draft dodger, and I guess I should have been straight with him from the start, but last night when he married Zoe and me, I experienced something I thought I'd never feel again, a sense of home, as if he'd not only wed me to Zoe, but to everyone who'd shown me kindness since I'd fled to Ontario over three decades ago, as if he'd wed me to this land and culture, to a place I'd never felt I deserved or belonged. And even though it was another man's gold on Zoe's finger, I wanted to hold onto that feeling, fearing it might be as false as our marriage and fade at first light. In the morning, this place, this feeling, might be like that oversized ring, something I hadn't paid for, something that was never mine in the first place, something I had no right to share with anyone.

Zoe tapped on my knee. I looked up, surprised by her face, relieved she was next to me. I'd forgotten we were both naked. The loons were quiet and the fire spit sparks toward the black lake. Zoe touched her opened mouth, tapped her ear, then pulled blank sheets of notebook paper from her backpack. "Sure, I said. How about, *Budded Rose?*" She grabbed her pen and wrote out the lyrics. I don't know how she remembered all the words to them songs. I unpacked my fiddle and sang with my best Guthrie voice, while Zoe mouthed the words, thumbing the wedding band, a tiny fire flickering in the gold.

# OVER THE TOP

(Appeared originally in *ELM _Eureka Literary Magazine*)

*H*eath Jarrell's third quarter estimated tax payment was somewhere in the San Francisco Bay. The IRS letter stated that on Sunday, September 11, 2005, an accident occurred on the San Mateo Bridge near San Francisco involving a courier transporting payments to an IRS Payment Processing Site. The letter went on to say that the truck carrying the tax payments overturned, causing approximately 30,000 Form 1040ES quarterly estimated tax payments to be ejected into the San Francisco Bay. Heath couldn't understand how his payment, mailed from Chicago to the tax office in St. Louis, Missouri, could possibly have been on that truck, even though it was obvious by the letter his check hadn't reached the proper agency.

With the Internal Revenue Service, Heath wanted to remain as unremarkable as a blade of grass. He didn't like anything IRS, not since his audit in 1998. It wasn't that he was doing anything illegal, or had anything to hide; the process just filled him with dread. Wearing only boxer shorts, his bare thighs were already sucking to the vinyl seat of the kitchen chair. He sipped his coffee and glanced across the table at Carol. She was reading the newspaper. He wanted to tell her what was happening without sounding distressed, dramatic. "Everything's a crisis with you, Heath," she'd told him on numerous occasions. And since they weren't married, the IRS notice was his problem and his alone.

He glanced down at the letter again, remembering his audit, how he'd asked Carol if she thought he should purchase an expensive brief case to carry his documentation to the IRS office. One of those intimidating leather ones lawyers use. She'd smirked and handed him her backpack. "Use this." The green and gray pack seemed too trail mix and *Nike* for the IRS, but he'd used it anyway and felt like a fool, his receipts and bank statements crammed into it like the stuffing in a badly upholstered couch.

Did the IRS expect him to send another check, Heath wondered, skimming the letter again? What if he didn't send them a new check? After all, it was their fault the money was lost. But that argument seemed weak and potentially risky recalling Ms. Owens, Heath's caseworker in 1998. Her dark eyes were like freshly waxed floors, not to be walked upon, and her skin smooth and blemish-free as a manila envelope. The absolute correctness of Ms. Owens' short, stout body wrapped in her no-frills white blouse and navy skirt made Heath feel fraudulent for being tall and bony, and ridiculous wearing a backpack over his sport coat. But it was Ms. Owens' smile that unhinged him the most—both kind and alarming in the same instant.

Heath turned the crisp paper between his fingers until it made a crinkling sound, hoping Carol would notice and inquire into the letter. The mail had been sitting on the kitchen table since the previous afternoon, neither of them bothering to go through it, both of them too drunk and tired after Carol's opening the previous evening. Heath looked over at her again, this time noticing how angry she seemed, her lips tightened to a dry, pink line, her attention fixed on her newspaper. Still in panties and bra, she had folded her right leg up against her breast.

"Bastard!" She flattened the newspaper on the kitchen table, poking the small black and white photo. Each time she jabbed the man's face with her fingertip, the fork and plate beneath the newspaper made a tinkling, scraping sound as if the man's face were made of tin. Heath pictured the underside of the newspaper sticky with pancake syrup and gooey yellow egg.

"Bastard!" Carol wrenched the pack of Marlboros from under the newspaper, shook one out and lit it, drawing deeply, as if she were out of breath, the smoke pure oxygen. She took another drag, then shot away from the table, wrestling plates and cups into the dishwasher. Heath leaned across and surveyed the article upside down. Kenneth Korman. Art critic for the Chicago Times. Heath was afraid to swing the paper around to read the review, certain the newsprint was stuck to the remains of Carol's breakfast.

"That bastard must have a degree in accounting!" she said, shoving forks and spoons into the plastic cubbyholes. "It's obvious he doesn't no jack-shit about art!"

Heath got up, went around the table and settled into Carol's chair. He gave a little poke at his glasses, fixing them on the bridge of his nose, then leaned over the review.

**Carol Henley's, "Mother. Daughter. Stumble. Stab," which opened last night at The Charon Gallery, is yet another disappointing evocation of sentimentality and melodrama shoveled onto the ever growing heap of egocentric, ego-**

**driven indulgences attempting to pass themselves off as art. Letters, photos, diary pages ripped from a childhood (that was, yes, painful! yes, tragic! yes, unfair, even!) and reproduced on pink paper and pasted into wooden jewelry boxes, purses, hats, etc., interiors suggesting clogged and cluttered vaginal openings. But Henley attempts nothing greater than the presentation of evidence wrapped in stagy metaphors, endeavoring no greater interrogation into the experience of abuse, other than to say, "Here it is. My wound." Psychiatrist R. D. Laing wrote that, "If our experience is destroyed, our behavior will be destructive." In Henley's, M.D.S.S., I'm afraid beauty, sensuality and art have come under attack once again.**

Carol was gone from the kitchen when Heath looked up from the paper. He combed his hand through his hair and thought about all the notes he'd scribbled on writers' manuscripts—*awkward sentence phrasing, too sentimental, this emotion doesn't ring true, too vague, too much explication, over-the-top.* That was his favorite, *over-the-top.* This little phrase covered a multitude of literary sins—*beyond believability, trying too hard, overwritten*—and a parade of trespasses that Heath wouldn't expend the energy to figure out. It had become easy finding fault in someone else's work, but he'd never felt he'd been as harsh as Kenneth Korman, at least that he could remember. And Carol, she wouldn't let this drop without a fight.

Heath went up to the bathroom off their bedroom, easing down on the edge of the toilet as Carol came out of the shower. She bent over, scrubbing her hands into the towel around her hair. She shot upright, tossing her hair back, spray hitting the mirror behind her. "That sonofabitch is going to be sorry he ever heard of me."

"What are you talking about?" Heath said, forcing a nervous chuckle over her statement.

"First I'm going to write a letter. Then...I don't know. One thing at a time."

Monday morning, Carol was already gone when Heath woke. She'd hardly spoken about the review all weekend, holing up in her studio downtown. He poured coffee, shuffled through the pile of manuscripts stacked in the corner of his spare-bedroom office, wondering which one needed his most fierce attention. Most of them were finished, waiting to be mailed back, but addressing envelopes and figuring postage took time and effort of a physical nature. He wasn't up for that, not on a Monday.

Morning was the best time for Heath to concentrate. Shortly after turning forty, Heath noticed his energy would start draining around eleven, plummeting shortly after lunch, some kind of blood-sugar thing, he figured. A nap, chased with black coffee and a Cliff Bar, usually put him back on track. Carol had gotten him hooked on Cliff Bars during their trip to Colorado. Before he'd met her, Heath had never been hiking. And he'd liked tromping around outdoors, though he wasn't very good at it, needing lots of water and food and rest along the way.

He reached across his desk and picked up the letter from the IRS. Near the bottom of the letter was an address directing him where to mail his new check: *Remittance Coordinator. Fresno, CA.* At the bottom of the letter he read, *If you decide to stop payment on your original 2005 From 1040ES third quarter payment check, you can request a reimbursement of bank charges. To file a claim you must complete Form 8546, Claim for Reimbursement of Bank Charges Incurred to Erroneous Service Levy or Misplaced Check.* Below the claim information was an 800 number for obtaining Form 8546, or he could go online.

*If we receive your replacement check within 30 days of the date of this letter, we will credit your account as having been paid timely.*

Heath didn't want to waste precious energy on righteousness, but it was hard not to get upset over the letter. After all, he had mailed the payment in plenty of time and now, it seemed, he was receiving a subtle threat to get another check in the mail ASAP or he'd be penalized.

Heath hadn't balanced his checkbook in six months, and had no idea if the check had cleared or not. He pulled a wad of bank statements from the filing cabinet. The check he'd written for his state taxes had cleared, but not the federal. He pictured beachcombers, bums and teenagers diving into the San Francisco Bay, fighting over soggy 1040ES envelopes, scrambling for the enclosed checks, taking them home, drying them in the sun with clothespins, then flattening them liked pressed flowers between the pages of thick encyclopedias, selling the restored checks to underworld types who had the connections to turn them into cash. But that seemed ludicrous. Who but the IRS could cash a check written to the IRS? And wouldn't the government initiate a full-scale effort to clean up the mess, retrieve the jettisoned 1040s? Heath wondered about the courier driving the truck. Had he died when the vehicle overturned, crashing through the guardrail, plunging into the Bay in a shower of white envelopes?

He called Lizzy, the accountant he'd found soon after his audit in '98. Lizzy hadn't heard of any such letters from her other clients, but another accountant had called wanting to know if she'd heard anything.

"Does it look authentic?" Lizzy asked.

Heath had never thought about the letter being a fraud.

How much would it take for an opportunist to have heard about the accident, set up a P.O. Box, pull a logo off the Internet, run off simple letters on an inkjet printer and send them out? But there would still be the issue of cashing the replacement checks. How would they do that? Heath's mind wasn't able to color outside the lines, having difficulty tracking the criminal mind, its resourcefulness, its potential. Scams like this seemed too complicated, over-the-top. Besides, how would crooks know the IRS hadn't already cashed his check? But that wasn't really the point either, was it? And how did Heath know if there'd even been an accident? He felt his sinuses starting to clog just thinking about it.

"Fax it over, Heath. I'll take a look at it."

After faxing the letter to Lizzy, he put it aside and tried to concentrate on the new manuscript he'd been working on, a first novel written by a retired lawyer who swore he had no desire to be the next John Grisham, just wanted something to do with his time. Heath had no sooner opened the manuscript to the Post-it note when Carol popped her head into his office.

"Brought Chinese," she said, rustling the white bags in her hands. "Hungry?"

Heath couldn't believe it was noon already. He checked his watch. "It's only ten thirty," he said.

"Yeah, I know. They weren't open yet. I practically had to threaten them before they'd whip up some goddamn egg rolls and moo goo gai pan. Let's eat out on the patio. It's gorgeous today."

Before Heath could tell Carol he wasn't hungry, he heard the clunk and clink of plates and glasses being pulled from the dishwasher, the back door swinging open and falling shut.

A stuffy lint-trap kind of warmth filled the tiny courtyard behind their apartment house. Heath slouched down in the chair, stretched his legs under the table and let the heat from the sun blanket his face, turning the interior of his skull bright red when he closed his eyes.

"Here. Eat," she said, pushing the plate across the glass table. He sat up. The food smelled good, rousing a hunger that hadn't been there a moment ago. Leaves continued to fall, one landing in the moo goo gai pan. Carol plucked it away, then slid her chopsticks into the mound of white rice on her plate.

"Productive morning at the studio?" Heath asked, uncomfortable with her pleasant demeanor.

"Trish called. She sold two of my pieces yesterday. The pumps, and the hat. Plus, she has a couple other possible sales that look promising."

"That's great."

"She also said Korman's a fraud."

"Fraud?" Heath said, unsure what Carol wasn't saying, something edgy and dangerous pacing beneath her words. Carol was never quick to let an argument drop, even after the opposing side conceded defeat. Heath learned that bit of information early on in the relationship during a fight over a comment he'd made about a piece of her art, a three-legged found object that she'd covered with Christmas wrap. He'd told her he liked the way she'd decorated it, even though he didn't know what it was. "Decorated? Heath, that isn't *decoration!* For Christ's sakes! It's about consumerism...Oh forget it. Fucking *decorated?*" Heath had kept apologizing while Carol had kept assuring him that it was okay, that he'd had no way of comprehending the message because he'd never studied art. The pardon left a barb, one that Heath hadn't been able to remove since the incident. Now he just refrained from saying anything about her work, and she no longer asked. Of course, as a constant reminder, she'd placed the gift-wrapped object next to the television in the living room so he'd have to look at it every time he watched football or golf.

"Trish said he's an asshole. Korman came from Kansas or Iowa, some kind of corn state."

"Well... Illinois is a corn state, Carol," Heath said.

"I know, Heath. But Illinois is hardly Chicago."

Heath didn't want to argue, suddenly seized by Carol's statement about Korman being a fraud, wondering if the IRS letter was a fraud. He was surprised Lizzy hadn't called back yet.

"Where are you?" she asked.

Heath looked up. "What?"

"What are you thinking so hard about?"

"Nothing."

"Did you check your e-mail today?"

"No. Why?"

"I copied you on the e-mail I sent to Korman."

Heath felt the recoil in his chest. The first shot had been fired. No wonder Carol appeared smug and satisfied. The battle had begun. Heath could practically hear Trish egging her on, greasing the gears of Carol's revenge with hyperbole and conjecture. Trish and Carol—art vigilantes.

Carol went back to her studio after lunch. Heath sat at his computer, ignoring "Take the Stand," the courtroom drama by his latest client, the retired lawyer. Heath was going to suggest a new title eventually, unsure how attached Edelman was to the existing one. Heath clicked the e-mail Carol sent to Korman.

**Mr. Korman, it is obvious from your review of my show at The Charon Gallery that you are new to art criticism. It is also obvious that you don't take your new craft seriously,**

**evidenced by your lack of insight and your puerile comments about my work. Most likely, you dashed off this review on your way home from my opening, probably scribbling in the dark on a napkin in the front seat of your Chevy Blazer, or Ford F150, or whatever it is you drive. Maybe you were listening to Merle Haggard or Johnny Cash while ravaging a Big Mac and nursing a 48 oz. Slurpee. Whatever it was you were doing, your mind was not engaged in the matters of art. Major magazines and newspapers across the US have reviewed and understood my work, applauding my vision, until now. Yes, just you, sir, are alone in your ignorance. Evidently (and unfortunately), displaced scholars need little else than a rudimentary knowledge of writing and composition to embark on a career of art criticism. I would hope in the future that you would treat the process with the dignity it deserves.**

**Thanks a lot!**

**Carol Henley**

Heath hoped she hadn't sent the e-mail yet, but knew she had. Korman's address was in the "Send to" box, with Heath's and Trish's at *The Charon Gallery* Bcc'd. Heath wished Carol had waited a week or so before sending it. That was the trouble with e-mail; it fed the impulsive appetite of rage. With regular mail, intention was involved, an envelope must be addressed, a stamp found, a flap licked. Not to mention finding a mailbox, or driving to the post office, diversions that could aid the cooling off process. Plus, there was always the outside chance your vicious letter could end up in the Frisco Bay, extending the cooling period. But e-mail was Uzi-proficient; you could keep firing long after your enemy was dead, no need to stop and reload, or assess damages.

Heath clicked out of his e-mail and was about to search the

Web for info on the San Mateo Bridge accident when a new e-mail arrived.

> **Mr. Korman. I Googled your name and found an interesting bio. It seems that you have been doing art criticism for eight years in Des Moines, graduated from Duke University in North Carolina (I wasn't aware Duke even had an art appreciation program), and have come to us here in Chicago fresh from the plains of Iowa, where I'm sure your conservative and naïve sensibilities concerning art were appreciated. It might not hurt to pick up a copy of Art in America, or ArtForum, try to acclimate yourself to the bigger picture.**
>
> **Best of luck!**
>
> **Carol Henley**

An intervention was needed, a power outage, something to stop her from sending more e-mails. Heath could feel her destroying her career.

When he couldn't reach her on her cell phone, he got dressed and drove to her studio. The front door was locked. The bass from her stereo thumped on the outside of the two-story building. Annie Lennox, he thought. He tried the back-door, jiggled the knob, then knocked several times on the wood panel. The glass had been replaced with plywood, then covered with steel bars in the shape of locked hearts. Carol's design and welding.

"Carol," he shouted, knowing she often listened to the radio on her headphones while blasting her stereo at three-quarter throttle. She loved the dissonance. She had to be there. Her Toyota was parked in the driveway, and as much as she liked to hike, she never went anywhere in the city without driving. He pounded harder on the door. When it flew back, a torrent of music rushed through the opening. Heath leaned away. Carol's eyes grew bright, obviously surprised to see him.

"What are you doing here?" she said, twisting the sound reduction headphones from her hair. "Wait!"

She hurried away from the door. A moment later the music stopped. Heath stepped in. "Wow. That was really loud."

"Yeah. I guess," she said, a magazine rolled between her hands. "Come on in."

Heath rarely came to her studio anymore. He'd never meant to be nosey, but his hands were inquisitive, opening oddly painted boxes to see what was inside, pulling back canvases to see what was behind. She didn't like him "snooping," as she called it, especially around works in progress and told him as such. Since he could never be sure what was off limits, he just stopped coming around.

"You okay?" he asked.

"Yeah. Why?"

"I keep getting e-mails."

She turned away, walked to the small fridge that did double-duty as an end table next to the couch. "Want a Coke?"

He nodded. "You don't seem okay," he said, popping open the can.

"Korman sent me an e-mail. Go over and read it."

Heath walked to her computer and sat on the wooden trunk Carol used as a chair.

**Ms. Henley, I am sorry you took such offense at my review. While I found the work temporarily moving, it lacked the depth to resonate, but that is not why I am answering your call. It is interesting that you mentioned ArtForum magazine, for it was in that very same publication I reviewed your installation piece in 1996. I am surprised you don't remember, because if you did, you would know that I not**

only read all those magazines, but am a frequent contributor. And furthermore, you might recall that I referred to your work in that particular issue as, "innovative," "refreshing," and "distinctive."

Also, I want to assure you that Duke University has a wonderful art program. And while you may believe Iowans to be lacking some gene that doesn't allow for the appreciation and understanding of serious art, nothing could be further from the truth. I hope this finds you well and I look forward to seeing more of your work.

Sincerely,

K. Korman

Heath sat up, noticing the issue of *ArtForum* Carol had placed next to the computer. A TicTac container made a lump in the book, marking the spread. Heath opened the magazine, read the review, then studied the pictures. He had never seen this work before.

"So, it's over?" Heath said.

"Over? What?"

"This feud. With Korman."

"Sure. I sent him one more e-mail. You can read it when you get home."

It was obvious there would be no end. Heath felt claustrophobic, some sort of transference to Korman, as if he, Heath, were the one being hounded by Carol, as if he had been the one to pry the lid off Pandora's found object, had committed the horrible art mistake. Heath even thought of emailing Korman himself, ask him to recant his criticism, even if just in an e-mail to Carol, put an end to the volleys. But maybe Korman enjoyed the anonymous scuffle, enjoyed the electronic distance of the Internet, the safety of modems and signals. Besides, it was none of Heath's business anyway.

"I'll see you at home." Heath folded his glasses into his pocket.

"I may stay down here tonight," Carol said, leaning over to kiss him on the lips. "You won't be too lonely, will you?"

At first he thought she was goading him, as she often did, accusing him of being too clingy, but she looked sincere this time, concerned, beautiful.

"I'll miss you," Heath said, pulling her close. "If that's okay?"

"We could make love...if you're not in a hurry." She stepped back, pulled her T-shirt over her head, then undid her jeans. She took his hand and guided him to the couch, dragging him to the cushions, adjusting him between her thighs.

Heath stopped at El Rancho's for a burrito after he left Carol's studio. He bought an extra one for Carol, along with an order of refried beans and rice—her favorite—in case she changed her mind and came home. He also bought a six-pack of Corona in case she didn't. He didn't really like sitting home alone, so he rented a movie for later, reward for the work he would do on "Take the Stand."

Tired of depositions, affidavits, and arguments, Heath put the manuscript aside and woke his computer to check his e-mail. He clicked the latest correspondence from Carol.

Mr. Korman, I must admit, I didn't remember the ArtForum review you did of my work in '96, and I'm sorry that I didn't, because you really missed the mark on that show as well. I happened to have a copy of that issue and reread your comments. It was amazing to me how someone could praise work he didn't understand, and with such panache and conviction. Reviewing your comments

**from that article explained a lot. I can see now how you shoot from the hip, make it sound good, smoke and mirrors. The work in '96 had nothing to do with "the industrial revolution" and "its effects on women." I am composing a letter to the editor of your newspaper, attaching copies of "informed" reviews more seasoned critics have written about my work. You are young and that is not your crime. Even ignorance can be excused to a point. But you can't keep relying on flamboyant language and elegant lingo to keep your bacon off the spit. You are nothing more than a well-dressed gatecrasher, an interloper. Consider yourself exposed.**

**Best wishes,**

**Carol Henley**

"Oh, Jesus." Heath screwed off the cap and tipped back a Corona, draining half the bottle. He belched, then took another gulp. "Christ." He wondered what drove Carol, what made her so inflexible. He wasn't willing to blame it all on her past, the abuse. It was more than that, something deeper, but he wasn't sure what. Over-the-top. Yes. Heath explained it to himself that way. Carol was *over-the-top.* Beyond believability. Trying too hard. Overwritten. Heath leaned back in his office chair and downed the last of the Corona, then pulled another from the carton at the side of his desk. He'd drink them all before they got warm. His dad could drink them the same way, set the carton on the coffee table, turn on the Bears and finish all the beer before the last one turned warm. It was as if some special physics existed in their living room, a molecule freezone where subatomic particles were frozen.

Heath went to the kitchen to eat the burrito he'd bought for Carol. He sat at the kitchen table in his underwear, staring at Korman's review, a syrup and egg yolk stain seeping through the print. Heath forced himself to read the review upside down, thinking that maybe a new perspective would render it as silly as it was, just words on the page. Not even words, just letters. And not even letters, just curlicues, lines and circles, shapes. Hieroglyphics.

The phone rang. Heath stretched for the receiver. "Hello?"

"It's me. Did you eat yet?"

"I stopped at El Ranchos on the way home," Heath said, finishing the last of Carol's burrito.

"What are you doing now?"

Her voice sounded distant, harmless. At times it was difficult for Heath to believe that this was the same woman who was so implacable and hell-bent on revenge. "Working on 'Take the Stand,'" Heath told her.

"Any good?"

"I'll earn my money."

Heath waited for Carol to say something, but the phone was silent. "Are you there?" he asked.

"I'm ready for bed. Just wanted to say goodnight."

"You okay?"

"Stop asking me that, Heath. I'll talk to you tomorrow." She hung up. It was a habit of hers, something left over from growing up in the south, he thought, in Macon. She never said good-bye, just hung up. She had managed to rid herself completely of her accent, but never realized that most people end a conversation with *good-bye.* Her mother had done the same thing when she was still alive. Heath was almost used to it.

He went back to his office and pulled a Corona from the carton. Still cold. He typed "San Mateo Bridge" into the Google window and hit search, then clicked on an entry referencing an accident involving a postal courier. There were many entries, and all of them seemed the same—a stock statement

116

from the Internal Revenue Service—except for one. This article acknowledged that the IRS was not attempting a rescue mission for the lost 1040ES checks, contending that the envelopes would sink in the bay and be impossible to recover. A tax preparer from Scottsdale wasn't convinced of that theory, saying that some 1040s could be carried out to the Pacific Ocean, maybe wash ashore at a later date. The tax man warned that affected parties should be on the lookout for identity theft, that anyone who found one of those 1040ES envelopes would know your social security number, your address, and have some idea of your income. Heath tipped his beer back and finished it.

Identity theft. Just what he needed. Now he'd have to scour every entry on his Visa and American Express bills, scrutinize every bank statement, balance his checkbook. He hated the thought of all the extra bookkeeping, the added attention he'd have to give to his paper life. He carried the carton of Corona to the living room, opened another beer, then placed the *Wall Street* disc in the tray of the DVD player. He loved Charlie Sheen in that movie.

Sheen was at Gekko's cocktail party when Carol called. Heath paused the movie.

"Are you near your computer?" she asked.

"I'm watching *Wall Street*."

"Get to your computer quick. You'll love this."

"What?"

Carol hung up. Heath rocked himself from the chair and went to his computer. He clicked an e-mail Carol had forwarded from Korman.

117

Ms. Henley, your harassment must stop. It is immature and uncalled for. If you don't like my review, then disregard it. I have already contacted the police and will speak with my Internet provider in the morning to report you, as well as inquiring into having your e-mails blocked. If this persists, I will be contacting my lawyer and looking into a restraining order. In the interim, I would suggest that you seek some sort of help, a counselor maybe, or a psychiatrist. It is obvious you are upset and disappointed, but you must find some other outlet for your hostility. Just so you know, I will NOT be opening further correspondence from you.

Along with the Korman e-mail, were nine new forwarded e-mails from names Heath recognized as Carol's friends. They were all addressed to Korman, and copied to Heath. Heath clicked on the first one.

Mr. Korman, I recently read your review of Carol Henley's show and was surprised by your ineptness. It was probably the dumbest review I have ever read. I would think that a newspaper like the...

Heath read e-mail after e-mail, more arriving as he read, all with a similar message. Heath scrolled down through the list of e-mails, now numbering close to thirty and still arriving. One came from Korman. He clicked it open.

Mr. Jarrell, I have not received an e-mail directly from you, but notice you are copied on each and every one of the e-mails I'm receiving. I am certain Ms. Henley is behind this new barrage of hate mail, but I have no idea what relationship you have to this matter. Maybe you are the "ringleader." If so, I urge you sir to cease and desist immediately. Ms. Henley is out of control and has now enlisted her friends and colleagues to join this ridiculous crusade of hers. I am saving all e-mails and addresses in the event that legal action is necessary. If you are a friend of Ms. Henley's, I implore you to talk some sense into her before this matter gets out of hand.

It was already "out of hand," in Heath's estimation, but there was no talking sense to Carol. Heath felt like a turncoat, harboring empathy for Korman, and yet, wasn't about to involve himself further by answering Korman's e-mail. Heath, upset he'd been implicated to the extent he already had, dialed Carol's cell.

"You have to stop this," he said when she answered.

"You're unbelievable, Heath! That fucker's the one who started this, not me. I thought you were "sorry" about the review, remember? You came to the bedroom all solemn and serious, acting like Korman had been unfair, telling me how bad you felt. What was that, an act? More bullshit, Heath? Christ, you can be such a phony at times."

"Why are you attacking me now?"

"Because you stand for nothing. You're a chameleon. You hide behind the status quo."

Heath started trembling, unable to speak.

"Go back to your movie, Heath," she said. "I've got to go."

"Why is everything always about you?" Heath said, stating his own anguish over the letter he'd received from the IRS.

"What letter?" she asked.

He reminded her that he'd told her Saturday morning, but she'd been so wrapped up in her own affairs, and Korman's review, that she hadn't bothered listening. He told her about the courier, the overturned truck, the San Mateo Bridge,

30,000 1040ES payments floating in the San Francisco Bay. He told her how the IRS wasn't doing a thing to retrieve the envelopes, letting them drift around for anyone to find, that he was worried someone would find his check, cash it, steal his money, and that he, Heath, would still be responsible for the tax payment. Then he told her his concern that the letter from the IRS might be part of a fraud, a monumental scam. He told her about the possibility of identity theft, and how he'd have to scrutinize each and every credit card transaction.

"Oh, that. You're agonizing over nothing," she said. "I read the letter. Christ, Heath, it doesn't even apply to you. It clearly states that if you mailed your 1040 payment to an IRS P.O. Box in San Francisco it may have been lost. You didn't mail your payment to San Francisco, Heath."

"But the letter came to me."

"They probably sent it to everyone who filed quarterly so they wouldn't have to figure out who's was lost and who's wasn't. Did you even bother checking your bank statements? Did you even call the fucking bank to see if they had a copy of your cancelled check?"

The picture on the television screen was frozen, Darryl Hannah in a gown that sparkled like a Cartier necklace, Charlie Sheen next to here, looking confident and smug making a fool of himself criticizing Gekko's expensive art. Carol hung up before he could tell her that he had searched for the cancelled check. But he knew he hadn't searched all that hard and probably should have called the bank. He flopped down in the chair. His eye caught on Carol's Christmas wrapped object staring out from the side of the television like a gaudy award. He had always wondered what was under the "decorative" paper.

Getting up, he knelt next to the piece and started scratching his fingernail at the wrapping until a tiny edge tore loose. He seized the small corner between his thumb and fingertip and ripped it toward the floor, then tore at more pieces, letting them fall around him. He ripped at the paper until the metal skeleton was finally exposed. What was it? A spittoon on legs? An elevated ashtray? A three-legged urinal? He had no idea. He'd never seen anything like it.

Ragged scraps of Christmas paper littered the floor, as if something festive had exploded. In its nakedness, the three-pronged object seemed liberated, finally freed after years of unnatural incarceration. But how would Carol feel about it now in its new emancipation? Heath toed scraps of wrapping paper and thought about getting the trashcan, then wondered if there was more wrapping paper in the closet, something that matched close enough that Carol wouldn't notice. But she would notice. Of course she would notice, Heath realized, and when she did….

Drawing the last Corona from the carton, he pictured himself standing on the San Mateo Bridge, leaning over the rail, staring down into the crystal blue water as thousands of white envelopes drifted like gulls toward the bay. Closing his eyes, he imagined the salty mist against his face, a chilly breeze feathering his hair. He raised the Corona to his lips and tilted it back. Still cold.

# ONE YEAR FROM NOW

(Appeared originally in *The Minnesota Review*)

The room is small and bright like the inside of a hundred-watt light bulb and smells serious and antiseptic like a doctor's office because that's what it is. Medical encounters render me helpless. Like a child. Even though I'm forty years old and run my own business, I tremble when the nurse slides the frosted glass window and calls my name. She tells me to get on the scale so she can weigh me— one hundred and ninety-five pounds (Christ, my clothes are heavy)—then guides me down a hall, opens the door and drops my file in a plastic holder screwed to the wood. There's a plain-colored plant in the corner of the room and two not-so-distinct chairs and an examination table covered with white paper that comes off a roll and covers the table for sanitary purposes and crinkles when you sit on it and is cold if you have your pants off, but I sit in one of the two chairs and look at a *Popular Mechanics* magazine and wonder *who reads this stuff?* and wait for the doctor. To prepare myself, I glance over at the table covered with white paper. It probably won't be necessary for me to remove my pants and sit on the cold white crinkle paper because I'm just peeing too much. That's what I tell the doctor when he comes in.

"How much is too much?"

"Fifteen to twenty times a day. Even after I go I still feel like I have to go again."

"Open wide."

He has me sit on the white crinkle paper after all, but with my pants on, depresses my tongue, feels my throat, looks in my ears, my eyes, up my nose, takes my pulse, my blood pressure, listens to my lungs, my heart, my cough, then has me pee in a cup and give it to the nurse who had weighed me, then feels my throat again.

"Do you know you have a lump here?"

I don't know anything about a lump. Even when he guides my fingers to the alleged lump in my throat I can't feel it.

"Here, press harder. Right here. Can you feel it?"

Of course I can't feel it. I'm not a doctor. My fingers aren't trained in the sensitive art of finding life-altering physical anomalies hiding in the darkest parts of the human anatomy.

"Is that why I'm peeing too much?"

"No."

"What's making me pee so much?"

"Stress maybe. Constricts the bladder. But the lump is what concerns me. We need to find out what it is."

Two weeks from now I will have my first operation ever.

The room is small and mostly pale green like the center of pistachio Jell-O, with two chairs made of metal near the foot of my bed and no plant, green or otherwise, and one window and a television on a shelf near the ceiling in the corner of the room. Somebody has turned on Family Feud and I wonder *who watches this stuff?* and the room smells of betadine and bedpans like a hospital room because that's what it is. The bandage at my throat feels tight making it difficult to breathe, but it isn't the bandage that's tight, it's the swelling from the surgery making me uncomfortable and my stomach throws a solid ball of heat up into my throat and I know I'm about to vomit. The nurse sees me gagging like a cat with a hairball and puts a cold washcloth on the back of my neck and I suddenly feel better. I learn three things during my two-day stay. One, a cold wet washcloth placed on the back of your neck will often suppress the urge to vomit and two, after thyroid surgery, if you do vomit because the washcloth didn't work, it hurts like hell, and finally, the lump they removed wasn't benign.

"It was cancer, but we're pretty sure we got it all. Thyroid cancer is very rare in men and usually only malignant ten percent of the time. But, as you know, there are exceptions. You'll be all right though."

The surgeon grabs my foot through the sheet on his way out and toggles it like a three-wood in his golf bag and I'm relieved, I think, and I visit his office a week or so later to have the staples removed and have the incision checked for infection and all looks well and he tells me that I'm lucky we found the cancer when we did before it spread to my lymph glands.

"I was peeing too much."

"What?"

While the surgeon reads my file and ponders surgical sorts of things, I explain to him why I had visited the doctor in the first place, because I was peeing too much, but the doctor found the lump instead of finding the cause of my perpetual peeing.

"How much was too much?"

"Fifteen, twenty times a day."

"That's a lot. How about now?"

"No. I only pee a few times a day now. But the cancer…"

"The cancer wasn't making you pee like that. Probably stress or something. Come back in six months and we'll check you again. I think you'll be fine."

Four months from now my surgeon, due to frustration with malpractice insurance and HMOs, will leave his practice and become a consultant for McKesson Surgical Supply.

The room is small and vaguely yellow like the inside of a crème brulee, with two windows, draperies, and several plants in the corner, including one passive fern near the cushy chair and couch. I sit on the couch because of movies I've seen and know that the doctor always sits in the cushy chair and the patient always sits, or sometimes lies, on the couch. I choose to sit, instead of lie. The couch is cushy, made of leather, and I look at the *Psychology Today* magazine sitting on the small table to my right and wonder *who understands this stuff?* The doctor comes in and I explain the surgery, the thyroid cancer, and the lump in my throat that I hadn't been able to feel and how the surgeon had removed it. Then I explain about my visit to the first doctor.

"I was peeing too much."

"How much was too much?"

"Fifteen to twenty times a day."

"Um. Thyroid cancer shouldn't increase your urinary output."

"The doctor said it was stress."

"That caused the thyroid cancer?"

126

"No, the peeing. Even after I went to the bathroom I still felt like I had to go."

"Go where?"

"To the bathroom."

"Do you still feel that way?"

"Which way?"

"Like you have to pee all the time? Do you need to pee right now?"

"No. I went this morning. I'm fine."

We talk for 59 minutes, mostly about the stress that must have been causing me to pee fifteen to twenty times a day, and my job, and my son, and my wife, and my family, both immediate and extended, and my debt, both real and imagined, my childhood, my dad, my older brother whom I hardly ever see, my hobbies which I lie about because I don't have any, my eating habits, my age, my dreams, my fears....

"Hour's up. That's all for today. Is this same time next week good for you?"

I tell him it is and shake his hand and thank him and he hands me a prescription for pills to help relieve the stress and I take the prescription and shove it in my pocket and thank him again. He tells me that my hobbies are a great asset and that I should make time for them even though I have a busy schedule and then he tells me how important it is to set aside time for myself. I feel guilty over lying about my hobbies especially after he made such a big deal about them. I thank him again and secretly wish for hobbies.

"Take three of those pills every day and if you have any problems with side effects please don't hesitate to call."

"Yes. I will...I mean, I won't."

Seven months from now I will stop seeing my psychiatrist and take up nine-ball and archery.

The space is narrow and confined and somewhat dark like the inside of a cereal box but I can see blue sky directly above me and white morning clouds lolling past and over there is my green Toyota Camry sitting in the parking lot a hundred yards away. Walls of brick rise on both sides of me like I'm standing between two buildings because that's where I am. On the pavement at my feet is a stained and wrinkled copy of the Enquirer with a photo of a two-headed frog-goat-boy(?) on the front page and I ponder the headline that reads "Child of Alien Parents" and wonder *who writes this stuff?* With my pool cue case in my left hand, my keys jangling in my right, I look over toward the parking lot, at my car sitting among so many others. Although I am still less than a one-minute walk from my Camry and a thirty-five minute drive from home, I picture my neighborhood perfectly, the Ginko tree in Irma Springer's backyard, Burt's audacious canary-yellow Hummer down the street, the Johnson's brand new tan and burgundy metal tool shed and I can't seem to bring myself to go home or move from between these buildings and for some reason my legs start to quaver and I figure it is because I have not slept in over twenty-four hours. My cell phone vibrates in my pocket and when I answer it my wife asks how I did in the nine-ball tournament.

"Third place."

"That's great."

"It's only third place."

"But it's the first time you won third place. What did you win?"

"Five dollars."

"You want me to come down and meet you, Marshal?"

"Why?"

"To celebrate."

"Third place?"

"I can meet you there."

"Where?"

"Wherever you are. Where are you?"

"Between two buildings."

One year from now my son will quit college and join an intentional community in Peru, my wife will leave me for a jury wrangler, claiming that I have lost my focus, I will pawn my archery equipment and keep the ticket in my wallet as a reminder that two hobbies at a time is more than I can handle, and my new girlfriend Cherry will come to the smoky pool room dressed in jeans, cowboy boots, and a fringed and sequined jacket and sit in the shadows on a hard wooden stool sipping her beer and even though she knows nothing at all about nine-ball, occasionally, while I'm lining up my next shot, she will smile over at me, wink, and shoot me two thumbs up. After a few dates Cherry will notice the one-inch scar at the base of my throat and I will tell her about the thyroid cancer, the surgery, and the peeing.

"How much did you go?"

"Fifteen to twenty times a day."

"I go that much when I drink beer. Did drinking beer give you the cancer?"

"They weren't related."

"Who?"

"What do you mean, 'Who?'"

"You said they weren't related. Did you mean the doctors? I don't understand."

"I meant the peeing and the cancer."

"Oh. What did the doctor say about drinking beer?"

"I don't remember."

For me, Cherry will not be a destination, nor has she been

the road less traveled. Even so, we will share many stimulating evenings discussing articles from the *National Enquirer* and watching Family Feud, not to mention the fun we will have building a plain wooden foyer-bench-that-doubles-as-a-storage-chest from plans Cherry will come across in *Popular Mechanics*.

# SUBSIDENCE

(Appeared originally in *Paterson Literary Review*)

*P*eople could think what they wanted, but there was no way June would take Harry's sorry ass back. Harry was an office furniture salesman, a lollygagger and smelly-freckle, and a dedicated alcoholic with a son by a previous marriage, a moody boy named Rodney. Rodney had quit high school, or graduated, and apparently decided to pass on college. Regardless, he was one of those tall, sullen, good-looking fellas with a head full of mystifying notions about life. You never knew what would come out of his mouth. One minute he'd be going on about communism, or fish falls, and the next he'd be saying what a nice day it was to have a picnic.

"A picnic?" I said. "Rodney, it's the middle of winter. There's six inches of snow on the ground."

"I don't see how that matters, Mrs. Williams," he said. "A picnic's a picnic. Plus...no ants."

I'm not one to kiss and tell, but Rodney would sit at my kitchen table for hours, drinking my coffee, smoking my

Winstons, telling me all kinds of crazy things while my husband Phil was out protecting and serving, keeping Hampton Hills safe. Rodney was a polite boy, always called me Mrs. Williams. And even though he was peculiar as a plantar wart, that boy was handsome as a Haynes underwear model.

When I broke my arm that spring, he came by every day after I got my cast, helping me around the house, lifting the wet clothes from the washing machine, dumping them in the dryer. One afternoon I grilled tuna sandwiches on the stove and poured him a glass of milk.

"I'm a little old for milk, Mrs. Williams," he said.

"You want orange juice. Or Coca-Cola?"

"Do you have any whiskey?" he said.

Shocked me, but I figured the apple didn't fall far from the tree. His father Harry was an on-again off-again drinker; either *on* the front porch drinking again, or *off* at a bar drinking again; either way, Harry was always drunk. It didn't happen on my watch, but Irma said one afternoon a year or so ago Harry came home early from work and there was seven kinds of hell over at their place, until June came running down the front porch steps in nothing but her bra and panties screaming her head off. She jumped in her Taurus and sped away. Irma said Harry came out on the porch a few minutes later, a beer in his hand, shaking his head and laughing, still wearing his tie and white dress shirt from work. Harry was one of those *"Fuck you and the horse you rode in on"* guys. Irma never found out what happened.

I set the bottle of whiskey down in front of Rodney.

"Would you like some?" he said.

"I count two glasses there in front of you," I said, even though I didn't much care for whiskey, not like my husband, Phil.

We finished a third of Phil's Kentucky Bourbon and I

hadn't even started dinner yet. Rodney was telling me about neon, and how it got started back in Paris in 1910, and how he had applied for a job at *IT'S A GAS*, some sign maker down in the city. "Different gases glow different colors," he said. "If you enhance argon gas with vaporized mercury, you get this really crazy, intense blue." He sat there sober as a Baptist minister, telling me how you could get over 150 colors just by combining different phosphors and gases. I loved watching his lips when he spoke, like a newscaster on CNN, his words spilling straight out of heaven. He talked about wanting to learn how to scuba dive, and about entering a jitterbug contest a few years ago with a girl named Holly.

"We might have won if Holly hadn't gotten sick. We were the favorites to win."

I told him how Phil and I used to jitterbug down at the Casa Loma when we were teenagers, that big, mirrored ball spinning like a brand-new planet above our heads, soft spots of light spilling across the room, everything sparkly. Rodney poured us each another shot and I said I'd better get dinner started.

While Rodney used the facilities, Phil called and said he wouldn't be home for dinner, that they'd busted a meth lab on the east side of Pagedale and he'd be tied up for hours with paperwork. Phil said he and his partner were going to Casey's afterward for pork steaks and beers, not to wait up.

I hung up the phone and told Rodney he didn't have to go, that Phil was going to be late. "I've already got these chicken breasts thawed," I said. "You might as well stay for supper if you don't have anywhere else to be."

Rodney asked where the aprons were and said he'd do the cooking. I pointed at the pantry door and told him to follow his nose. While he stood at the stove, I poured a couple more shots and carried his drink over. We decided to toast and I had to go back for mine, using my good arm to raise the shot and clink his glass. Some of his whiskey spilled down the front of his shirt and we both laughed like a couple of hobos and that surprised me. I hadn't suspected we were almost drunk.

I sat at the table and watched Rodney preparing the breasts, grease popping from the skillet while he rolled the pieces in flour. I tried cutting up a salad, but he made me sit while he took care of everything, all the while entertaining me with stories about strange deaths and oral galvanism, a small electrical current set up in the mouth between dissimilar metals. He said a woman in England who'd been blind since the age of twenty-two had her sight restored after the dentist removed three metal-filled molars. Rodney talked about opening up a costume shop, going to England to see crop circles, and how easy it was to build a sailboat once you understood boat design, things like displacement, center of buoyancy, prismatic coefficient. I didn't understand any of it.

I got up to go to the bathroom while he set the table. "Do you need help?" he asked.

The question stopped me cold. "Help with what?" I said.

"Anything. Getting your underpants down, or back up, or... anything. You know, because of the cast and all."

I scratched my head and told him I'd be fine, that I'd been managing okay. Since I broke my arm, I'd gone back to wearing dresses instead of jeans. It made everything easier.

He smiled, nodding, setting forks and knives beside our plates.

In the bathroom I pondered his peculiar offer of help. Was he so soused he'd forgotten who I was? Or was it some perverse flirtation? But he'd said it with such concerned straightforwardness, he might as well have been asking if I needed him to take out the trash or change a flat.

When I came out, he was seated at the table.

"Do you want candles?" he said.

"Candles? To eat with, you mean?"

"Yes, you know. Dinner by candlelight."

I had no idea what this boy was thinking about. I was at least ten years older than he was, maybe fifteen, probably twenty. And married. I pulled the candles down from the cabinet, but before I could hunt for matches, he told me to sit, lighting them with his Bic. When he switched off the overhead fixture, we sat looking at each other, our faces flickering gold in the dim kitchen.

"I'm not really dressed for this kind of soiree," I said.

"Do you want to be?"

I thought about my black spaghetti-strap dress, the one I wore five years ago when Phil and I went to his partner's daughter's wedding. I still had the heels too, somewhere in my closet. I was pretty sure the dress would fit.

"I'll go change," I said.

"Call me if you need help," he said, earnestly, nothing sly or smarmy.

What would Phil think if he came home and waltzed into this little jamboree? I went upstairs to the bedroom, closed the door and undressed in front of the mirror. I looked okay, a little extra "sweetness" as Phil called it around my waist, but my hips were still nice, and my breasts weren't bad, at least in low light. But there was no doubt I looked sexier dressed than naked. I slipped the gown off the hanger and wrestled it over my head with my free arm, wiggling to make it fall around me, using my good hand to tug it down on both sides. There was no way for me to zip it. I slipped my feet into my black pumps, then went to the bathroom and brushed my hair. If I was going to this much trouble, I figured I might as well put on a dab of lipstick, a little eyeliner. When I finished I stood in front of the mirror again, checked my hem, thankful the varicose veins hadn't shown up yet. Irma's legs looked like roadmaps of Iowa.

Rodney was sitting at the table when I walked into the kitchen. His head waggled from side to side. "Your beauty has no rival, Mrs. Williams," he said, then stood up, walked over, and pulled my chair out for me.

"Can you, uh...zip my dress?" I asked, remembering I'd forgotten to use deodorant, perspiration soaking my underarms. I wasn't even sure when I'd shaved last. Probably before the cast. I prayed that huge shrubs hadn't sprouted from my armpits. After Rodney slid my chair under me, I lifted my arm slightly and snuck a quick peek. It wasn't bad. Mostly stubble. Rodney scooped string beans onto my plate, then some mashed potatoes and carrots. He cut up the salad in my bowl, and skewered a breast for me. "Do you like the skin?" he asked.

"No," I told him. His knife hand slid past his fork hand, slicing through the tender white meat. He set the utensils on the table and pulled the skin free, his fingertips slick and glistening in the candlelight. I wished for wine. It seemed like the perfect moment for it, though Phil and I never kept it in the house.

"Your mother must feel lucky to have you, Rodney," I said, resting my cast arm in my lap, using my fork to move my carrots around. My appetite had left me.

"You mean my step-mother? June?"

"Yes."

"We really don't get along all that well, if you want to know the truth. I think having me around makes her feel old. She isn't old at all."

Irma had told me June was thirty-eight, or thirty-nine, just a few years younger than me, but she still looked good, jogging down the street in the morning, bottled water in hand, reflective tennis shoes. Young all over, except her eyes. Up close, on

136

the street or at the grocery store, her eyes looked shriveled and tight, like they were shrinking into her face.

"June's thirty-seven...and I'm twenty-eight. My father was young when my real mother had me. Of course, my dad's quite a bit older than June."

I was shocked. Everyone said Rodney was a few years out of high school, at least that's what Irma told me, and she don't chew her cabbage twice. And I'd had no reason to doubt her. After all, Rodney looked young, his skin pure as a baby's cheeks, none of that bluish beard shadow anywhere on his entire face or neck. And his fingernails were perfect, the hands of cellist.

I nibbled carrots while Rodney told me about a huge hole that showed up in some people's yard one night out west, Nebraska, or Montana. It started out six feet wide and twenty feet deep, but within a week had grown to over twelve feet in diameter and they couldn't see the bottom. All I could do was shake my head and churn my mashed potatoes with my fork. I loved watching him talk. He told me that authorities figured the hole was caused from tunnels cut beneath their property centuries earlier by ancient miners.

"Subsidences," Rodney said. "The ground just opens up. I read about one woman who was hanging out wash when the earth gave way beneath her. She dropped into a ten-foot hole. Wouldn't that be a terrible feeling?"

I nodded, knowing the feeling, at least something like it. Phil and I were in St. Louis during an earth tremor. Shook everything. Glass. Doors. The ground under our feet felt like quicksand, shifting, swaying. I'd never felt anything so unpredictable, so scary.

When Rodney finished his dinner, he carried his plate to the sink and asked if I was through eating. He took my plate and asked if there was anything I needed help with before he left. I was surprised he was leaving so soon, but then I looked at the clock. Almost nine. I had no idea it had gotten so late.

"Is there?" he asked.

"What?"

"Anything I can help you with? Anything that's hard for you to do right now?"

Yes, there was, but it was certain he couldn't help. I wasn't even comfortable asking Phil to help me bathe, wash my hair, my back. It was impossible to take showers until the cast came off. But it was only another week. "No, not really," I said.

"Really?" he said. "You seem to have something on your mind."

"Just my hair," I said, the comment sounding like a stupid joke, which I hadn't intended. "What I mean, is, it's hard to wash my hair...and my back." Oh there it was, I said it, and couldn't believe I had. I felt my face flush red and was even more embarrassed by being embarrassed.

"I'd be glad to help you with that," he said.

I rubbed my fingers over my neck, wondering if my skin had turned blotchy. "How would that work?" I asked.

"You would get in the tub and I would wash your hair and back."

"Would I have clothes on?" I asked, trying to establish exactly what we were talking about.

"Clothes? In the bathtub? Sure, why not, if that makes you more comfortable."

"Oh, I don't think I could," I said. "Even with clothes on. Let's don't and say we did."

"What?"

"It's just an expression, like, 'Nervous in the service,' you know...oh, never mind."

He seemed real confused, but he smiled and told me good-night. I thanked him for his offer and showed him to the front door. He bounded down the porch steps and I watched him all the way across the street, until he went in his house.

At the kitchen table, I sat in my evening gown and high heels and poured myself another shot, thinking about Rodney's hands massaging my scalp, soaping my back. Now I'd never let him give me a bath, but the fantasy alone made me feel twenty years younger.

I decided to wait up for Phil.

He came in around ten thirty and had to look twice, me sitting at the kitchen table all dolled up with the bottle of Kentucky Bourbon and two candles melting onto the tablecloth.

"Hells bells, Jess. Is everything okay?" he asked, unsnapping his gun belt, setting it on the chair. He looked perplexed, like he didn't know whether to grin or call for back up.

I went to him, took his hand and guided it up under my dress, between my legs. I couldn't remember when I'd been so wet, and by the look on his face, he couldn't either. I scooted the bottle and candles out of the way and raised my fanny onto the table and spread my legs, a foot on either chair.

"Right here?" he said.

"Why not," I said. "Then we can do it again upstairs if we're still in the mood."

Phil didn't argue, but when we finally made it to the bedroom, we were both too tired for more. The next morning, though, he didn't miss his chance before he left for work. I was still thinking about Rodney's soapy hands and beautiful fingers when Phil told me goodbye.

"Be careful," I told him. "And don't let the door hit you in the ass on the way out."

He laughed and hustled past the bed, planting a kiss on my lips before he went down the steps, his gun belt rattling and clanging.

I lounged in bed until noon. That's when Rodney came over to see if I needed anything. It was hard to believe Rodney was Harry's son; they seemed so different. Harry was a giant of a man, big in all directions, and anytime he came into a room, his head was on a swivel, his eyes radar, like he was trying to figure out who to pick a fight with, or who might shoot him, one of those *move it or lose it* types. My Phil was never intimidated by Harry, though most men were, especially ones with small hands. Harry's hands were big as chainsaws. But Rodney, he was nothing like Harry, didn't have his father's stone eyes or coarse edges.

"I'm upstairs," I yelled down to Rodney when I heard him come in. "I'll be right there." I brushed my hair, smudged on a little eye shadow, and struggled into my robe, looping the belt with one hand on my way down the steps.

"You look wonderful," he said. "You slept well?"

"Like a dead whale. Want some coffee?"

"Sure, I'll make it."

I lit a cigarette and offered one to Rodney. "Thanks," he said.

While he measured out grounds, he told me his dad came home at dawn, drunk, and slept in the bathtub. Then, as if he'd just forgotten what he'd said about his drunken father, he brought the coffee over and sat opposite me, his hair combed, his face as smooth and fresh as spring. He circled his hands on his coffee cup, his perfect fingers curled over the white porcelain.

"So," he said. "Do you want to try that bath after we finish our coffee?"

Just the mention of it made me wet and I tried not to let him see me squirming in my seat. But how could I? "Oh, Rodney, I really appreciate the offer, but I don't know how—"

"Close the shower curtain," he said.

"Huh?"

"We'll close the shower curtain, and I'll just reach my hands around both ends and wash your hair and back. Or I could wear a blindfold. That would work."

A blindfold. Well, I guessed that could work, but what if Phil happened to come home unexpected, me naked in the tub, my plaster cast propped up, my body covered in bubbles, Rodney kneeling on the bathroom rug wearing a blindfold, his arms encircling the shower curtain, and his soapy fingers in my hair? Phil had seen peculiar things during his eighteen years on the force, but nothing he'd ever told me sounded half as unsettling as the scene in my head.

"Do you have an old bandana?" Rodney asked. "Something I can cover my eyes with?"

"Rodney, I don't think it's a good idea. The cast comes off next week."

"You'd rather not? Sure, that's fine. Whatever you're comfortable with."

"Would you be comfortable? In my bathroom? Washing my back?"

"I think so."

The rush of water into the tub made my knees weak. I sat on the bed and couldn't believe I was about to do what I told myself I could never do. "Easy greasy, it's a long slide ahead," I told myself. But it did no good and Rodney was in the bathroom, testing the water, getting things ready. He told me not to come in until he had the blindfold in place. "Need help getting your robe off?" he asked from the bathroom.

"No, I can manage." Oh, I could manage, all right, manage to get myself into a real pickle. It wasn't like I couldn't wash my hair at all. I could, with one hand, but it *was* hard sinking down in the tub to rinse it without getting the cast wet. That's what I kept telling myself, even though I had done it just fine several days earlier. And, if I really wanted to, I could have gone to the salon and paid Ashley to wash my hair.

I slid the robe off my good arm first, then tugged it down over the cast.

"Anytime," Rodney said from the bathroom. There I was, naked, except for my panties. I tugged them down and wiggled them off, leaving them in the middle of the carpet. This was just foolish and crazy.

When I stepped into the bathroom, Rodney had the blindfold on, and his shirt off. "What are you doing?" I said, covering my breasts with my good arm, even though he couldn't see anything. "Why are you undressed?" His chest was beautiful, little soft hairs running down the center to his navel, his stomach firm as the hood of my Accord.

"I took my shirt off so I wouldn't get it wet," he said. "I can put it back on if it bothers you."

I glared at my hand, trying to kill the desire to touch his skin. He had arranged the soap, along with the shampoo and conditioner bottles, on the rug next to him. He even had my Loofah body scrubber sitting there. "Do you need help shaving your legs?" he asked. "I didn't find the razor and foam."

"No. No I can handle that." The hair on my legs could grow as thick as Sasquatch before I'd let any man shave me, even Rodney. "What about the shower curtain?" I asked. "Are we still employing that little feature?"

"If you think it's necessary," he said.

I didn't suppose it was, so I let it go and got into the tub. Soapsuds washed over my thighs as I eased down into the water, then over my stomach, touching the bottoms of my breasts. The water was perfect. But before I was completely acclimated, Rodney groped my shoulder and I jumped, splashing him and the floor. I apologized, explaining that I wasn't quite ready yet. When would I be? Since I'd been married, the only men to touch me other than Phil had medical diplomas on their walls. Rodney wiped the suds and water from his chest and stomach. His pants were soaked.

"Let me know when you're ready," he said, his hands resting on the edge of the tub. I enjoyed studying his body without him knowing it. The thrill of voyeurism, I supposed. But taking pleasure in it was kind of creepy.

"Are you going to do my hair first?" I asked.

"Whatever you want."

He had me rest my cast on the edge of the tub, then draped a towel over my shoulder and the cast to keep it from getting wet. Then he eased my head back, dipping water from the tub with a plastic cup, pouring it over my hair. He applied shampoo and massaged it with both hands, then did my scalp with his fingertips. Oh my God. I'd had no idea it would feel this good. Even better than Ashley. My eyes flickered closed and I felt like I was drifting through space, his touch gentle, exotic. He rinsed my hair, the water hot from his cup, running along my scalp, down the back of my neck. I shivered with pleasure, but I don't think he felt it. He used his palm to smooth the hair away from my forehead, his skin warm, soft, the other hand supporting my neck. When he worked in the conditioner, the smell of honey and vanilla filled my head. He kneaded the back of my neck, then rubbed little circles above my ears with his fingertips. I finally exhaled and felt my body slump. While my hair absorbed the conditioner, he rubbed the skin at the base of my neck. A few minutes later he dipped water from the tub, cascading it over my hair, pressing out the conditioner with his closed hands. When he spoke it startled me. I guess I had dozed off.

"Ready for your back?" he said, his voice low, almost as if he'd drifted off a little himself.

I took another deep breath and pulled myself upright. I looked over at him, his chest, his beautiful lips, and wanted to pull him in with me. But even sex would not have felt as good as what he did next. With his fingers soapy, he slid them across my skin, my shoulder blades, down my spine. His hands went to the small of my back, then under the water to the dimples above my fanny. His hands slid up over my hips, up my ribs to the edges of my breasts. My breath caught and I think I jerked a little. When his fingers when under my arms, to those soft, fleshy pits, I lost it. I couldn't remember what Rodney had called it when the ground just opened up, but I felt it, free falling down a dark hole, no bottom, no way back. I was spiraling, dizzy, and wasn't sure if Rodney actually touched my breasts, or I just imagined he had, but I jumped up from the water, screaming.

"My god, Mrs. Williams, what's wrong?" Rodney said, peeling off his blindfold. I yelped and ripped the shower curtain in front of me so he wouldn't see me naked. I only glimpsed his face, but it was white as an egg.

"Go home, Rodney!" I said. "Go home now!"

With my body hidden behind the curtain, I heard him pad down the steps. A few seconds later, the front door snapped shut. What an idiot. I felt terrible for letting him wash my hair and back, then felt worse for sending him away.

Phil and I made love like dolphins that night, me fighting off guilt with each moan and gyration. We did it twice, and were going for thirds, when we both collapsed, exhausted. When Phil started snoring, I got up for a washcloth, then stood at the window staring at Rodney's house. The lights were off and I wondered if he'd ever come back, if I even wanted him too.

The cast came off a week later. Phil drove me, and during the entire time the doctor was cutting plaster, I was remembering Rodney's hands on my back, maybe even my breasts, though that may have been a sensory fabrication. Rodney didn't come by after that magnificent fiasco in the tub, and I didn't see him again until the day after I had the cast removed. My arm was itching like crazy and Phil had taken the day off, using the time to catch up on morning television. I was in the kitchen making Jell-O when I heard all the commotion.

At first, all we could hear was shouting and yelling from Rodney's house. Sounded like Harry and June going at it. Phil had just gone back to his TV when Harry crashed through the front door carrying June in a bear hug from behind. She was kicking and screaming, scratching at Harry's arms, and naked as a Vegas stripper. Harry dropped her on the front lawn, then went back toward the house and stood on the front steps. Each time she tried to run past him, he pushed her back.

"Phil, you better come see this," I said.

About the time Phil got to the door, Harry shouted at June, "I guess if it's okay that my son sees you naked, I figure the whole neighborhood should have a peek."

June screamed back, "You're crazy as a damn shithouse rat," then stormed the porch again, trying to shove past Harry. He just put out his arms and laughed, and said, "I *am* a shithouse rat!" She kicked at his shins, trying to scratch his eyes out, yelling, *Bastard! Bastard! Bastard!* —but he just kept countering her attacks like some Kung Fu master, laughing and trying not to spill his drink.

"Damn Sam the Mustard Man," my Phil said. "Guess I better go put my pants on and break up their little lawn party."

Phil went upstairs to dress. That's when I saw him. Rodney came out of the house hugging a blanket, hurrying right past Harry. Harry just looked at him, grinning. After wrapping June in the blanket, Rodney huddled her close to him like she was some kind of refugee, guiding her up the walk. Harry just stood there shaking his head.

"What are you doing, Dad?" Rodney said, calm as a preacher. "What were you thinking?"

Harry held his post a second longer, then said, "Aw, hell, keep it in the family, I suppose."

By the time Phil came back down it was all over. June and Rodney disappeared inside the house, and Harry drove off in his Lexus. A few days later I saw Harry sling a couple suitcases in his trunk and drive away, flipping the finger to the house.

Nobody saw much of Rodney and June after that. Harry showed up several times, but never got any farther than the front porch, peeking in windows, clicking his keys on the glass, shouting for June to, "Open the damn door." She never did. I could just imagine Rodney's delicate fingers soaping June's hair at night, rinsing it with warm water, easing her backwards so the soap wouldn't run in her eyes. In the afternoons he would probably sit across the kitchen table pouring bourbon in little shot glasses, telling her stories about underground government installations and skydiving and spontaneous combustion. Oh yeah. I'd sit at the window watching their house while the television played to the empty sofa, remembering Rodney's hands on the small of my back, his thumbs exploring the dimples there, his fingers splayed over my hips, how he caressed my waist, my ribs, and yes, maybe my breasts. I'm sure June was enjoying all of that now and she'd be a fool not to. And poor Harry, out there on the porch in his wrinkled suit pants, his white dress shirt flagging out in the back, his bald spot like a landing strip for small aircraft. No, there was no way June would take his sorry ass back.

# CALLING FROM THE MOON

$\mathcal{M}$aybe it's wrong for August to sit on the screened-in back porch with a cold bottle of Budweiser, while Darlene—*God only knows where she is*—wanders aimlessly alone somewhere in the neighborhood, or some neighboring neighborhood, almost certainly lost. He assures himself he's done everything he can since her disappearance after breakfast. Everything. Phoned all the necessary authorities. Searched all the streets, the parks, her favorite stores. Called all her friends.

Now he must sit and wait, watching fireflies etch listless, drunken loops against a dying cobalt sky.

Even so, his son, Julian, fidgets next to him on the porch swing, squeaking his fingers down the wet glass of his own Budweiser, his eyes flicking accusatory jabs in August's direction. Julian's that way. Julian went to college, planned his future, his family, his finances, his investments, his retirement, his burial. It seemed that from the day he was born Julian had been planning for his eventual death. "You don't let people you love just wander off," Julian had told him over and over, over the past two hours. There was nothing for August to do but sit and take it; he would always be a disappointment to Julian.

Julian springs from the porch swing when his cell phone music plays. The theme from *2001: A Space Odyssey*, if August isn't mistaken. He never really liked that movie.

Julian checks the identity of the caller, the steady crease of his mouth a straight line between two fixed points. Without a word, Julian hurries into the house and August knows it's Julian's wife, Clarissa. Clarissa is much like Julian, having planned her life out before they met. A certified CPA with her own home and garden, her own retirement plan, her own SAAB completely paid for. Together she and Julian orchestrated their wedding, merged their holdings, assigned financial responsibilities and goals for each other, and defined their familial trajectory in advance: Two children—one boy, one girl —a dog, and two birds. But Clarissa had two girls, the dog had to be put down when it bit the neighbor's shin, and one of the canaries died from a freakish virus. Now the surviving canary refuses to sing.

August hears a scurry of intangible, squeaky whispers from the kitchen, like someone scribbling on a blackboard. Julian and Clarissa are very private, never speaking to each other in front of him, or Darlene, and always in hushed tones. August has often wondered what conversational topics were so delicate as to require these squeegee-like murmurings. Nevertheless, August is relieved to be alone again, sitting, waiting, a yellow platter of moon serving up over the holly bushes by the fence. The cicadas roister invisibly among the leaves and August takes a good long sip from his beer until he hits the dregs, then heads to the fridge for a fresh one.

When August enters the kitchen, Julian spins away on some unseen axis, burrowing his head down between his shoulders, a cupped palm covering the cell phone. From August's perspective, it looks as though Julian is imparting some profound and troubling secret to the coffeemaker in the corner of the kitchen countertop.

August strolls past, pulling open the refrigerator door—glass bottles and jars clink in the compartments—and pulls out a beer. Ignoring Julian, he guides himself back to the porch, about to sit down when the wall phone rings, a magnified, magnificent rush of promise and possibility. Leaving the bottle on the railing, August hurries back to the kitchen, even though he knows Julian will beat him to the phone. And there stands Julian, a phone on each ear, one old, one new, as if he's speaking to himself across time.

"Mother! Where are you?"

August pauses a few feet away. He wants to grab the receiver from Julian, but knows he could never wrestle it free from his grip. "It's Mom," Julian says into his cell to Clarissa, then shifts his mouth back to the older device. "Mother? Where are you? We're worried sick about you." He never once looks at August.

"What?" Julian says, his face suddenly furrowed with complex geometry. *"Where?"*

Julian swings his attention to the other phone, a slight of hand, and speaks sharply into his cell. "Just wait, Clarissa. Just wait! I can't tell what she's saying." Julian swerves his eyes back, leveraging his question toward the wall phone. "Where are you, Mother?"

After a prickly silence, Julian shakes his head, his expression both spoiled and astonished, a look that surprises even August. With eyes minted and shiny, Julian stiff-arms the plastic receiver to August and walks to the back porch with Clarissa in palm, muttering gravely, ambling like a war veteran.

"Darlene?" August says. "Where are you?"

"Oh, August, I wish you were here with me! It's so lovely!"

"Where, Darlene? Where are you?"

"The moon, August. I'm calling from the moon. And it is so spectacular."

Her voice is clear, close, and August sends his eyes toward the living room, as if she might be on the extension. "The Moon? Is that a restaurant?" August asks. "I've never heard of—"

"No, silly. The moon. The one in the sky. Can you see it from the window?"

August strains the cord tight, peeks through the kitchen blinds. "Yes, Darlene. There it is. I can see it. It's yellow."

"Golden yellow, August. Rare and absolutely golden."

August knows Darlene gets confused and is probably standing at a pay phone, gazing up in tender reverie at the same glistening planet outside his window. "Can I come get you, Darlene? It's getting late."

She informs him she's going to stay tonight, that she wouldn't miss this for the world.

Julian soldiers back into the kitchen, his tenacity restored, his gait stealthy. August gives his back to Julian to thwart the certain interruption. He knows Julian would not think twice about yanking the phone from his grip. And even though Julian never played sports, he grew up lean and powerful, all that sinew and muscle seemingly wasted on a desk chair. Julian lords over August, his arms crossed, his aftershave reaching up into August's nostrils, a stringent and citrusy scent sluicing the thoughts from August's brain.

"Darlene...are you still there?" August says softly. Julian steps closer, wearing a smile perfected through years of litigation, and places his fingers on the receiver, starts to tug it away. August jerks back, steps toward the stove, his eyes on the sky. The moon is lopsided.

"I have to go, August," Darlene says. "But I will call you tomorrow. Now don't you worry. Oh, and there's chili in the freezer if you get hungry."

"Darlene!"

Hastily, Julian pries the phone from August's fingers.

August doesn't care; he knows Darlene is gone. Julian is speaking into dead plastic when August shuffles to the back porch, to his waiting beer, the moon cutting a bright profile along the bottle's glassy edge. She sounded so near, August thinks. He eases down into his rocker, the cushions sighing softly when he gives his weight to the chair. He presses the bottle to his lips, moving his tongue to control the flow, a thoughtless maneuver he's performed for decades, like breathing. Where's the nearest pay phone? he wonders. There aren't that many anymore. How hard could it be to find her?

"What's wrong with you?" Julian says, marching toward August's rocker.

August glances up, setting his beer on the small glass snack table. Cash Points, he thinks. Near the Amoco.

"How could you let her go out by herself?" Julian shouts, not attempting to funnel his fury. "You know she gets confused. It's just stupid. How could you? We need to find her."

Julian wandered off years ago, and August never did anything about it. Julian was a teenager then, and in the waning heat of summer while Julian was waxing his car, August stood in the driveway, speaking to him about the effectiveness of using a circular motion. Julian continued buffing a hard candy shine into the fender of his Chevy Nova, not saying a word. With rag in hand, Julian suddenly spun from August and went in the house. August stood there for over forty minutes, waiting in the driveway, but Julian never returned, leaving August to replace the lid on the can of Turtle wax before it dried out.

August stands, pulls his trousers up to the shelf of his belly, but they'll not hold there for long, gravity being what it is. He tilts the bottle back, then sets it down and fishes through his pockets for car keys. The spacey tone of Julian's phone drones again. He speaks abruptly, turning on his heels, trundling to the privacy end of the porch. August slips past and heads for the garage, hoping to reach his car before Julian can follow.

August is backing down the driveway when he sees Julian leap from the front porch, waving his hands at August's Taurus, the cell phone clutched in his palm like a detonation device. August takes his eyes to the garbage cans, the rearview mirror, backs out into the street and drives away, Julian shouting after him. He knows Julian will follow in his BMW.

August cruises by the Cash Points and spies a young woman wearing a tan hunting cap and speaking on the phone, pacing and smoking, staring up at the moths circling the street lamp. August pulls in beside her, rolls the window down. "Excuse me, ma'am, have you seen an elderly woman about five-foot tall wearing a flowered dress and house slippers?" The girl looks shocked, then annoyed, but smiles and shakes her head, adjusting the cap until the bill points skyward like the opened hood of a car.

August remembers a pay phone at the entrance of the Walmart but before he can pull away, Julian's BMW angles to a halt in front of his Taurus, blocking his exit. Julian jumps out and starts speaking before he reaches the driver's side window of August's car.

"Why didn't you wait, dammit? Come get in my car. We'll search together."

August suggests they search separately, cover more territory and all that.

"No, let's stick together for once," Julian says, jerking August's door open.

"Let me at least park my car over there out of the way," August says, tugging to free the door from Julian's grasp, suddenly sorry he caved in so readily to his son's demand.

They drive in silence, the inside of Julian's car as quiet as funeral parlor carpet. August can barely stand it, the absence of normal road noise—the shrill whistle of air tricking through metal, the clatter and squeak of brackets and clamps. In the square hush of the car Julian exhales his disappointment, sighing audibly, once in August's direction. When Julian's cell music plays, he glances over at August, his face muddled with panic and August knows Julian doesn't want to hold counsel in front of him.

"You could lock me in the trunk until you're done talking on the phone," August says.

"Real funny, Dad. Real funny."

Julian will now speak in conversational shorthand. August has heard it before, the "Yes...you know...remember? Yes, that's right...what I told you last time, remember? That same thing. Yes, that's right." August considers jumping from the car. They've driven past every pay phone in a five-mile radius when August suggests the pay phone at Walmart. Julian, glancing at August while talking to Clarissa, turns at the next light. Minutes later he pulls the BMW past the entrance and August tells him to stop, that he wants to check inside.

"Why?" Julian asks. "Does mom like coming to Walmart?"

August pops the door open and tells Julian he'll only be a second.

As the years wore away, Darlene fell subject to frequent and severe spells of narcolepsy, some incidents so sudden and complete that they both had agreed she should stop driving. Darlene hadn't seemed to mind, telling August she really never liked the claustrophobic feel of crawling in traffic. That's when she started walking more, returning home in the afternoons and evenings to report places and things August was almost certain did not exist, not within walking distance of *their* neighborhood, anyway.

August pads toward the back of the store, his eyes darting down aisles and past colorful displays. He detours through the craft and fabric department, along rows of paints and little wooden letters and frames, then slips into a wide corridor of metal shelving piled high with pillows and comforters and blankets and sheets. When he arrives at the back of the store, he asks a woman employee manning the layaway counter if she can check the women's restroom. The woman's hair swoops in a grand breaker from the left side of her scalp to the right, cascading down over an ear pinned with a fat red hoop earring. The woman smiles at August as she walks past. He nods back, picturing Darlene sitting fully clothed on one of the toilets, dreaming of being awake. A year or so earlier Darlene had fallen asleep in one of the stalls and spent the night in Walmart. She woke the next morning and walked out as if nothing had happened, even forgetting that she had not returned home the night before. That was the first time she'd disappeared and August had been crazy with worry. He'd never mentioned the incident to Julian.

"I'm sorry, sir, but there's no one in there," the woman clerk says, stepping from the restroom, touching the earring as if to adjust it. "If you tell me your wife's name, I'll page her for you."

August looks at the woman's name tag, Maria, and tells her that won't be necessary. Moving toward the front of the store, August thinks surely if Darlene were at a friend's house, the friend would have called and told him where she was.

"Let's go back home," August says to Julian as he folds himself into the leather seat.

Julian pulls the cell phone from his cheek. "What?"

In the timelessness of the moment, August's mind reinvents

the woman in layaway, the great tidal wave of hair, the name tag, Maria. *Maria.* Latin for seas. "Let's go to the library!" August tells Julian. "I think I know where your mother is."

"The library's closed," Julian says.

"I know, but that's where she is."

August recalls the illuminated model of the large golden moon at the library, how Darlene loved going there, studying the surface, memorizing the names of all the craters, the terrae. She explained to him once about the maria, the dark featureless areas of the moon that the ancients had believed were filled with water. He imagines her standing among the dark books lit only by the glowing resin orb, her face splendorous and warmed by the soft yellow light.

"There's nobody here," Julian says, guiding the BMW into the parking lot.

As soon as Julian stops the car, August jumps out and rushes to the front window, pressing his face to the glass, his hands cuffed over his temples to cut the glare. He hurries from window to window, fighting his legs through the stiff evergreen bushes that line the building, the clumps of mulch compressing beneath his shoes. There it is, the moon, the glowing moon with the huge map behind it on the wall detailing the vast expanses of lunar surface. He knocks on the window, calling her name, then rushes back to the entrance, pulls on the doors, calls Darlene's name again.

"There's nobody here," Julian says, walking up behind him.

"Call the police, Julian. I know she's in there."

Over the next hour several police officers, along with the library director, search the premises, checking the restrooms, meeting rooms, offices, closets, storage rooms, the computer room, the research room, and basement. August checks around all the bookstands, calling her name past the numbered spines. One of the police officers, a short man with a neatly pressed blue shirt and a rabbit's foot hanging from his belt, informs August that no one is in the building.

"I promise, Mr. Lyner, your wife is not here. We searched everywhere. There's no one here."

August wakes the following morning, his knees achy, his back stiff. He must mow the lawn today. After toast and grapefruit, he calls the police again. They have not found her. "She's probably at a friend's house," the officer says. "You should call everyone you know." The officer assures August they have his number and will call if they find her. August doesn't bother telling the police that she called from the moon. It would only make them less interested in searching.

Aside from the Walmart incident, Darlene has never stayed out all night before. Mostly she just gets herself turned around down by the river and walks the opposite way out of town. And he always finds her. She's easy to spot, her white hair cut squarely at the crest of her shoulders, a wide red belt cinched at her waist—one of those fashionable accessories from the 70s —and her fuzzy Acorns. August bought her a pair one Christmas and she started wearing them everywhere. At first, because she forgot to change them for sneakers or pumps, but eventually, because she just preferred wearing the bed slippers. There is a gentle gliding to her step that he knows so well, her back straight, her arms swinging at her sides, slender pendulums waving her forward. August can recognize her from two blocks away.

He pushes the mower past Darlene's garden as a small constellation of raindrops poke craters into the soft dirt around her roses. He glances up at the dented aluminum sky, a lone drop sailing past his eyelid. He hustles to finish the yard, quickly stowing the mower in the garage when the clouds spread a shiny deluge along the driveway and street.

August is tugging off his dripping boots in the kitchen when the phone rings. He pushes himself from the chair and slides the receiver from the hook. He recognizes Darlene's voice immediately. "Are you all right?" he says. "Julian and I were looking for you..."

"You mustn't worry, August. I'm just fine. It's very dark here right now, so I can't talk long."

"Dark where? Because of the storm? Where are you, Darlene? I want to come get you."

"It's so quiet here, August. I think you would enjoy the solitude."

"Are you alone?" August asks, a pinch of pain just beneath his sternum. "Are you okay?"

"Oh, yes, yes. I'm just fine. I don't mind being alone. Not somewhere this beautiful. I wish you were here. I miss you."

"Can you describe where you're standing? Are there any street signs? Any stores or businesses you recognize? Is it raining there?"

"On the moon? Don't be silly, August. Anyway, I have to go. I'll see you tonight. Look for me."

"Wait! Darlene!"

The rest of the afternoon is a slurry of phone calls and fret, and long fruitless drives over wet streets. It has been years since August has missed an afternoon nap. Julian phoned several times, leaving messages, and August was glad he'd missed the calls. Julian said some awful things the night before, even for Julian, and there were no apologies on the machine.

August pulls the chili from the freezer, unwraps the

aluminum foil and sets the glass container in the sink to thaw. He calls the police station again, knowing a new shift will be on duty, maybe a more sympathetic and effective one. They offer the same response. Nothing yet. August will go back out after dinner. He'll drive to Haywood, to Oakdale, all the way to Creve Coeur if necessary. He tries to recall places she loved, special moments she's talked about over the years. It is hard to remember. He never thought he'd have to. Darlene's recollections had been just that, memories, not some road map to finding her.

He dumps the chili in the pot and twists the flame to high. He sits at the table, slowly rolling the cold beer bottle across his forehead, missing the smell of Darlene's neck, the way her little finger crooks to the side because she broke it as a kid riding her tricycle. They hadn't met until August got out of the Navy, but he felt that he'd known her all her life, as though he'd heard her cry the day she flipped her three-wheeler, cradled her small broken finger in the palm of his own hand. August smells the chili. He gets up to turn off the stove. Julian steps into the kitchen.

"What are you doing?" Julian asks, his jacket and tie still smart and wrinkle free, unspoiled by the day's work.

"Eating supper. There's enough for two. Want some?"

Julian shakes his head and snuffs. He scratches his jaw, then his neck, then loosens his tie. August has never forgiven himself for Julian's shoulders, how the right one is levered slightly lower than the left. Darlene had noticed it when Julian was twelve, but the doctor said it was just from the boy's posture. "Kid's slouch," he'd told them, but August knows they should have gotten more opinions, had it corrected.

"How can you eat?" Julian says. "You should be out there looking."

August is about to explain that he's been out all day, has

burned a tank of gas driving through every rainy, gray neighborhood between Pine Lawn and Webster. He scoops chili into a bowl and covers it with shredded cheese and lettuce, then seats himself at the table.

"Bring it with you. I'll drive," Julian says. "Did she call today?"

August shakes his head, doesn't want to answer for her, and can't begin to explain her strange demeanor, her odd statements. It's easier to say nothing. The chili tastes good. It's Darlene's specialty. It was the first meal she ever made him. Chili and crab cakes.

"We can't just sit here doing nothing," Julian says. "I called the police again. They're no help. We should have told them she robbed a bank, then they'd find her." Julian leans against the table and sighs. "Maybe not. Where do you think she is?"

August doesn't have a clue. "She'll show up," he tells Julian.

"She told me she was on the moon," Julian says. "She should be hospitalized. For her own safety. You can't take care of her by yourself anymore."

August and his son have had this conversation before. "Don't think you know what's best for your mother, Julian. Or me. I don't tell you how to live your life. Don't tell us how to live ours."

"Christ! That's great. Just great! She's calling from the moon and you're sitting here eating chili, giving me advice about life. That's rich!"

August gulps the last of his chili down and slips the bowl into the sink. "Go on home, Julian. I'm tired."

"You're not going with me?"

August shakes his head. "Go on home."

～

The breeze tugs and pushes at the curtains of the bedroom window. August has been lying here for hours, gazing out, his thoughts orbiting some distant nucleus of despair. There is slightly less moon tonight, a slice clearly missing, and he wonders if she will call, if she's okay. He lies motionless on his side until the moon seems to wedge in the upper corner of the window, edging its way out of August's line of sight. If he sits up or moves, it will be gone and August can almost feel the imperceptible sway of the earth's rotation. He listens as a moth knocks at the ceiling of the bedroom, clicking an erratic path across the plasterboard, mistaking it for sky.

Unable to sleep, August puts his robe and slippers on and goes to the backyard. He stands in the grass, the dew soaking through the soft sides of his Acorns.

Where could she be?

The phone rings in the house and August scurries toward the kitchen. In his haste to get to the phone before it stops ringing, he trips on the back steps, slicing open his knee.

"Hello?" he says, pulling his pajama leg up to inspect the damage. A thin ribbon of blood has reached his ankle.

"Hi, August. It's me. I really miss you."

"Christ, Darlene. Where are you? Let me come get you. Please!"

"Can you see me? Are you standing in the backyard?"

August tries to stretch the phone cord to the porch. It won't reach. He pushes the blinds aside and fixes his eyes on the lopsided egg in the sky. Clouds slide past, slowly erasing it from the night. "Yes, I can see you. I see you, Darlene!" he says, as if pretending could make it so.

"Oh, I'm glad, August. You're getting fuzzy. Lots of haze tonight. But I'm glad I got to speak with you. I have to go."

"But wait, Darlene. Wait! Don't go. Let me get in the car and…" He thinks he can follow her voice with the Taurus, certain he could find her that way. He needs Julian's cell phone. "Wait, Darlene. Do you remember Julian's cell phone number? I want you to call his cell phone, Darlene. Call it right now, okay? Darlene? Darlene?" If she calls Julian, at least they'll have the number she's calling from.

The phone goes dead. He calls Julian. "Did your mother call? Did she call you yet?"

"No," Julian says. "Why? What's going on?"

After August explains his plan, Julian dresses and drives over. They sit and drink coffee. They don't speak. They take turns looking at the clock, though it is not part of the plan, or some coordinated complicity on their part. Eventually Julian falls asleep, snoring into the well of his crossed arms, the cell phone lying on the kitchen table only inches from his thinning hair. August glances at his boy, a man now, showing signs of age. August takes his eyes to the clock above the refrigerator. The hands are bleary. Just past four in the morning. August pushes up from the table, the pain in his knee jolting to life from the sudden move. He limps to the backyard, searching the dark clouds for a smudge of light. The wind carries a fragrance of rain so strong he can taste it on his tongue. The leaves rattle and flap and August stands a long time until the first drops splash along his cheeks and forehead.

When he goes back to the kitchen, Julian is stretching his arms, his eyes squeezed shut, his face grimaced from waking. "I've got to go home, Dad," Julian says. "I'm shot."

"You okay to drive?"

Julian nods. "I'll take off tomorrow. We'll drive over to...I don't know. We'll find her."

August listens from the kitchen table, the sound of his son walking down the hallway, across the living room rug, the front door clicking closed. A sound almost insignificant if not for the silence that follows. The rain puddles along the back

161

steps and August refuses to think about all the wonderful times he and Darlene have spent together, the kind of memories that haunt when all hope is exhausted, the ones that shuffle through lonely rooms, empty closets, and weary hearts. August arches his back and feels the vertebrae realigning themselves, crackling like brittle branches. He thinks they all may crumble one day, a tide of bones tumbling down into his legs. He sees himself that way: hollow, a sack filled with sculpted armatures of cartilage.

For the next few days, August and Julian search surrounding towns, visit hospitals, bus stations, malls. They crawl under bridges, sneak into alleys, force their way into abandon buildings, even a few dumpsters, exploring areas so awful August can barely stand to look for fear of finding her there, praying he won't.

She still calls, but less frequently now, her voice growing listless with each conversation. He asks if she is hungry, cold, scared, alone. She assures him she's fine.

"I may not be calling for a while," she says. "But you mustn't worry."

"But, Darlene, if you could just tell me where you are, describe your surroundings, I could come get you, bring you home."

She laughs a little. "Oh, August. You're so funny sometimes. I have to go. I love you."

"Wait…"

August places the phone in the cradle, feels a perplexing gravity at his knees. He ambles to the back porch, down the steps into the backyard, his bare feet slicing through the grass, cool moisture collecting in the spaces between his toes. Over the past week, August and his son shared the common goal of finding Darlene, the bond as sound as the tragedy. But the tie faded quickly when the situation turned seemingly hopeless. Without Darlene, August and his son were like negatively charged magnets, repelling each other. Julian hasn't bothered calling the past three days.

August stands motionless in the grass, a comforting numbness spreading through his limbs. His eyes are tired and start to eclipse when he hears the doorbell in the house. Julian, maybe. August won't go in. He does not want to speak to his son.

A man's voice calls from the gate at the side of the house. "Mr. Lyner?"

August turns toward the sound. Darlene stands on the back walk, her dress rumpled with ridges and craters. Her face glows between the two officers. A mirage. A reflection of the past.

"August?" she says again, drifting toward him across the lawn.

She doesn't become real until she touches his face. Something in his chest spins when the warmth from her fingers penetrates his cheek. "Hi, August," she says. "I've missed you." August pulls her to him and feels a sudden weightlessness.

The officers follow across the yard, explain to August about the homeless shelter in Pine Lawn. August knows the shelter is over twenty-five miles away, too far for Darlene to have walked.

August thanks the officers and leads Darlene into the house. He makes tomato soup, arranges a dozen Saltines on a clean plate for her. While she eats, he watches her, studies the shadowy blue half-moons beneath her eyes, the smudges on her cheeks and chin. He asks why she went to a homeless shelter.

"Oh, that's just where I ended up when I got back. I was going to call you and ask you to come get me," she says, raising the spoon to her chapped lips.

Upstairs he runs a hot bath for her, helps her undress. She is still beautiful and he can't pull his eyes from her naked body. Bubbles erupt into the air when she eases down into the sudsy water. August balls up the dirty dress to put in the hamper. Gray dust and something like sand falls from the pockets.

August closes the lid of the toilet and sits. Darlene has her eyes shut, smiling up at the ceiling like a child. He worries the day might come when Darlene will become unreachable, just as Julian had become all those years ago. Maybe that time's already here. He's not ready for it.

August will not tell Julian she's home. He's already decided. Saint Sebastian Sanitarium is filled with lunatics. That's where Julian wants to send Darlene, and August has neither the vigor nor the doggedness to fight, only the declining rotation of his own potency. He's not sure how long he can keep her return a secret.

That's when he hears the front door open and shut. Julian calls from downstairs, his footfalls hard, echoing through the house. "Mother!" He starts up the steps—"Mother!"—and August hurries from the bathroom, pulling the door closed behind him.

He meets Julian on the steps, palms out, shushing him.

"Where is she? Is she okay?" Julian asks.

August nods, taking Julian by the shoulder, turning him back down the steps. He guides Julian into the kitchen, explaining that she's already in bed, asleep.

"Where was she? Is she okay? Does she need to go to the

hospital? The fucking police left a message on my cell phone over two hours ago! Why didn't you call me?"

"I was getting ready to when—"

"Bullshit! You should have fucking called as soon as she got home. Jesus, you're unbelievable. When were you going to call? Or had you decided to let me find out by myself? Fuck, you are such a bastard!"

"Don't speak to me that way, Julian."

Julian throws himself in the chair. His cell phone plays its haunting tune. August goes to the sink to wash the dishes, while Julian speaks with Clarissa.

Julian nods to Clarissa on the other end of the line, as if she can see his agreement, his eyes red, angry, then says into the phone, "No, she's been home for over two hours! Yeah, he didn't even fucking call me. Can you believe that?" Julian is quiet for a beat, then says, "Yes, I know. There's going to be some changes, Yes, yes, of course I will," and palms his phone without saying goodbye.

"I'll be bringing paperwork by tomorrow for you to sign," Julian says, standing, straightening his tie.

August walks over with the dishrag. "Paperwork?"

"To have Mom admitted to Saint Sebastian."

"No, you're not."

"Yes I am. You know I don't need you to sign. I can prove you're unfit to take care of her. You can barely take care of yourself!"

"You have no right to come into this house and start telling me I'm unfit. Telling me what I am going to do! Now get the hell out of here!"

"You're a joke. You don't even know what's best for her. I'll sign the fucking papers myself, you know! Clarissa and I will make sure that Mother is taken care—"

"Goddamn you, Julian! Get the hell out of this house! Now! Our life is none of your fucking business!"

"She's my mother! She's my fucking business!"

Before he knows it, August has slapped Julian across the face. He heard the sound, feels the sting in his palm, but it still doesn't seem possible. He fully expects a return blow from Julian.

Julian's eyes are frozen in a half-squint. He shakes his head and begins rubbing softly at the new red blotch gracing his cheek. August cannot tell his son's emotion, if he is about to cry or rage. Without a word, Julian snatches his cell phone off the table and sweeps from the house. August hears Julian's car start, the tires squealing as he pulls away.

August walks to the back porch, wipes his eyes. He is not sure what to do, wondering if Julian truly has the power to have Darlene committed without his permission. He is scared, trembling, and wishes Julian were dead; a thought he is ashamed of, but can't rescind; a notion that would horrify Darlene if she knew.

He will call a lawyer in the morning. He will make sure Darlene is never out of his sight. He will take her away if need be, pack suitcases and drive somewhere in the car, leave everything else behind. They'll disappear together.

He tilts his head back and traces his gaze along faint constellations he has no names for, planets he learned about in school that hold no meaning. The emptiness of the night frightens him, tightens beneath his ribcage until he can hardly breathe, everything adrift in an endless black arc of sky. He cannot fathom Darlene being taken from him and placed under a stranger's care without his permission, as if all their years together did not even give him a say in the matter. He slips his hands down into the empty space of his pockets and stares at the last thin slip of moon just beyond the trees.

# SPOKEN WITH AUTHORITY

*F*uck!

That one word spoken with authority, not in anger, but with masculine passion to put the point on a point! Jesus, it was like being thrust into the world of men, where men discussed things that required words with more amperage than the watered-down versions of profanity I heard at home. No, this place was real, a place my father wouldn't even fit in, a place that shot me skyward past my dad's stilted station as husband, breadwinner, and swearing flunky, a place crusted over with stubble-faced old men leaning forward on rock-hard knees, a place where arms swung wide like the blades of arthritic windmills and gnarled fingers poked sternly into imaginary chests if a tale was to be told correctly, a place where no one was ever surprised, or shocked, or dismayed, a place where the story of one man's tragic tale was met—with no attempt to top—by another's in the spirit of solidarity, conspiring against the cosmos with the same tenacity the gods had conspired against them, a place where men's spittle and fire fueled the gravity of every yarn and landed on your forehead if you were unfortunate enough to be sitting too close.

The barbershop. That's where I first heard it. I was almost eleven when my parents let me go by myself.

I can still picture that old man sitting there, blue shirt and matching pants, some sort of mechanic's jumpsuit, an oval sewn onto the left chest of the shirt and the name *Earl* stitched elegantly in satiny scarlet thread. His hands were maroon and bent, the fingers amber near the tips where his cigarette rested. His face was a craggy leather bag, his skull narrow with thick slate hair rolling back in a natural wave on top, trimmed thin as sprinkled pepper down his neck and around his ears. His knees poked at the material of his trousers like the fat ends of Louisville Sluggers, while the bottom cuffs crept up his bony ankles exposing droopy thin white socks and black shoes sturdy as cinder blocks.

"A maple tree! That bastard was this fucking big around!"

*Earl's* voice was a rusty razor on a grainy strop, his spittle glittering through the shaft of sunlight, red eyes narrowed like a killer's, arms bear-hugging some invisible trunk for *us* to see. Us. He didn't exclude me because I was a kid. A couple of times he even looked right at me, those big mitts of his clamped to his knees. Veins thick as lamp-cords crisscrossing the backs of his hands, winding around his wrists. Scared the hell out of me and the only words I heard for the duration of my time in the chair were *cocksucker, son of a bitch* spoken as one word, and all derivations and compound varieties of *fuck*. I was astonished, terrified and relieved when the barber swung the apron from my chest with a matador's flourish and held up the mirror for me to admire the back of my head. I nodded, smiled nervously and dug in my pocket for the crumpled bills, still picturing *Earl* clutching that bastard of a tree, praying I'd never see him again.

# PUSH ME

(Appeared originally in *Flint Hills Review*)

*J*ackie always says the same words. Push me. I always say no.

From the moment I proposed to Clair six months ago, Jackie, my ex-wife, has been sitting in my head like a guest on *Oprah*. Two nights before my wedding and I can't stop picturing her with the clingy blue sweater she had on the night I met her at Concert in the Park in Clayton. The same sweater she donated to Goodwill three years after we were married. "It's only a sweater," she had said, kissing me, pulling me into the mound of clothes on the bed. God, how I loved that sweater.

At the center of all the cheering, chortling, elbowing men, a girl takes off her blouse and skirt and starts dancing on the coffee table and I wonder if it's sturdy enough to support her. Not that she's fat or anything, she's actually quite trim, attractive. But the table is chintzy. Harris bought it at Big Buys after his divorce.

Harris, my best man and long-time friend, organized this ritual and now holds a beer in one hand, his arms extended out to the sides of the young girl's legs to catch her if she stumbles. It's a cautionary gesture, like spotting someone on the bench press—only he's grinning like a crocodile in a petting zoo, his tie hula-hooped around his neck. Bachelor parties are a bad idea, especially for second marriages, but Harris insisted.

I'm trying to ignore my ex, concentrate on the stripper sling-shotting her bra over the heads of whooping portfolio managers and corporate tax attorneys. I have to look away when the stripper kneads her breasts. It looks painful.

"She's kind of cute," my ex says referring to the stripper. Jackie is back in my head, stunning in the white evening gown she wore the night I passed the Bar Exam. An ivory limo had pulled up in front of my apartment and honked. Our chauffeur for the evening, Buddy, drove us around St. Louis, then dinner at *Harry's*, finally parking on the levy of the Mississippi River. Buddy leaned against the front fender, smoking cigarettes. Jackie and I drank rum and Coke and made love in the back.

"Why don't we go up on the roof and talk," Jackie says.

I get up to leave, grabbing my overcoat from the hall closet.

"Hey, wait!" Harris shouts over the clapping and whistling, his shirttail blown out of his chinos like a spinnaker. "You look glum, man. Where're you going?" His loafers are gone, and his jaw is thrust out like he's ready to pummel me with questions.

"Up on the roof," I tell him.

"By yourself? Why do you want to be by yourself?" The ash from his raspberry-flavored White Owl breaks loose, melts another hole in his rug. "The party's down here, Bro! Don't do the morose-loser-loner thing tonight, okay?"

"I'll be back in a few minutes. Just need some fresh air." Harris lives in a twenty-story apartment building overlooking the Mississippi River, an incredible three-sixty view of St. Louis and Illinois.

"What is it with you and that roof?"

I shrug. He'd never understand.

"Here, wait a sec," Harris says, dashing to the Coleman cooler, returning with a cold Budweiser. "Take this with you. And don't jump off the roof!" When he laughs, his face flushes white for a second as if he's about to puke, but he recovers so quickly I think I imagined it. Jackie—dazzling in the red sequined dress she wore to the hospital on our eighth anniversary (I dislocated my shoulder in Rigazzi's parking lot trying to prove I could still do a handstand)—assures me I didn't.

After climbing the three flights of stairs, I push open the metal door. Jackie is leaning against the brick wall that borders the roof of Harris's apartment building. She's gazing across the labyrinth of lights and skyscrapers, her skintight pink running suit more astounding than ever. "You know, you could just call me in Atlanta and we could talk," she says. "Anytime you like."

I nod and set my Budweiser on the wall, wondering why there's only one star in the sky. I'd thought about it, knowing I didn't want to risk her new husband answering the phone.

"Matt won't care," Jackie says.

"What?"

"Matt won't care if you call the house. We talk about you all the time."

"You do?"

"Sure. It's cathartic, you know. We don't dwell, though. It's not like an obsession."

I still can't understand why she moved to Atlanta so soon after we divorced.

"I met Matt," she says. "That's where he's from."

Leaving made it easier somehow, she'd told me, that we would have been hanging onto each other out of some desperate attempt to piece *us* back together, that staying would have ruined everything over time.

She spins around, places her hands on my shoulders, teeth sparking through the tiny space of her smile. "Let's go to your first apartment, Taylor! Remember that cute little place you had on Maywood Avenue with the claw-foot cast iron tub?"

Before I can agree, Jackie is easing her lovely bare leg into a deep sea of bubbles. "This is such a great tub!" Squatting down, she's as luscious as the first time we made love on the balcony of her apartment in Clayton. When she sees me staring, her expression darkens. "You know I don't look like this anymore," she says.

"What?"

"This body you're gawking at is when I was twenty-three, when we first met, Taylor. I've put on a few pounds. You haven't seen me since the divorce. I even found a few gray hairs."

Still wearing my overcoat, I climb into the tub and sit facing her, reaching out to cup her breasts. She shakes her head. "My breasts have changed too, Taylor. Remember? The cancer? The surgery? They're not the same anymore."

Dropping her eyes, Jackie scoops a handful of suds from the water, sticking them to my chin. She reminds me it was a tough time for both of us, that it changed us and there's nothing to be sorry for. Nothing to regret.

"I didn't stop loving you because your breasts…changed."

"I never thought you did. You know, Taylor, we were young. Who expects things to change?"

She told me once that she could never have guessed how the cancer would shape her life, how the fear would never quite leave her, even when she thought it had. It rearranged her, our relationship. She never expected that either. The cancer focused her life, made the important things sharp and clear, everything else a blur.

"I ended up in the blurry part?" I ask.

"Look, Taylor, it's not like that." Jackie touches my ankles under the water. She needed different things, needed to know she was with someone who wouldn't struggle against memories, or hold on to how things were without even knowing it. With me, she could never be sure, and that was no fault of mine. She said it was about her, what *she* needed.

"I don't *struggle against memories,*" I say.

"You're doing it right now, Taylor. That's what you're doing here. Don't you see?"

I wasn't sure if I saw or not. After all, how do you stop a memory? "Can I take your picture?" I ask.

"Why?"

"I don't know."

She nods a reluctant approval, wiping the soapsuds from my chin. I pull my phone out of my coat pocket, sudsy water dripping from the lens. I dry it with the cuff of my shirtsleeve and place her in the frame. About to click the picture, Jackie places her hand in front of the camera. The phone takes it anyway and I'm certain I have a wonderful shot of her palm.

"Wait," she says. "Take it this way."

Suddenly her breasts are scarred and disfigured, the coloring no longer matching the skin of her stomach and shoulders. I had forgotten how she looked after surgery— swollen, bruised, the incisions bright and ruddy. Then more operations. More healing. And many months later, how she looked the evening she sat up in bed and said we needed to talk. All that night, and most of the next day, she'd tried to explain why she had to leave, that she had already rented an apartment across town. I took off work and helped her box her things, rented a truck, spent the night in her new bed, made love in the dark. We both cried, then fell asleep. She was gone in the morning, running. The note said she would call me in a few weeks, and asked that I not contact her. I dressed and went home.

"Don't look so gloomy." She stood up in the bath, her skin glistening gold in the candlelight. "Let's go back to the roof."

The evening is cool, breezy on top of Harris's apartment building. Wearing the white terry cloth robe I stole from the Hyatt in Maui on our honeymoon, Jackie faces the city, the Arch, the lights of the riverfront, her ebony hair waving out from behind her ear.

"It just seems like there was something I could've done differently, Jackie. You know…if I just would have had more time…"

"No, Taylor, that's just it. You couldn't have prevented what happened to us anymore than I could've prevented the cancer. It just happened."

A suffocating dread washes over me, some terrifying helplessness folding in on my gut and I can't breathe. I inhale roughly, pushing at the wall with both palms, and for the first time all evening I'm picturing Clair, my fiancée, her white shoulders, her slender neck, the shape of her face, but I can't see her features. The first time I saw Clair she was standing next to one of her marble sculptures, the stone figure in repose, smooth and simple, a shape fixed and elegant and impervious to change. Clair invited me to her studio after the opening, showed me her chisels, let me run my fingers along the burnished skin of her work. That was over two years ago, when everything was new and made me forget. Now I'm afraid of diseases that grow without warning, the impermanence of desire.

When I look up, Jackie is barefoot, standing on top of the wall, her back to the city. She's wearing the black negligee she wore the night our condo was broken into. We'd just returned home from a *Radiohead* concert and found the place a wreck. After the police left, I started cleaning up. That's when Jackie strolled out of the bedroom wearing nothing but the silk nightgown. "They didn't get this, Taylor!" She leaned against the doorjamb, eyeing me back to the bedroom.

"Will you come down off the wall?" I reach my hand out to her. She smiles.

"Push me," she says.

"What!"

"Push me, Taylor."

"I don't want to."

"Push me."

"No."

"Please. For us."

I take a step closer and place my palm on her tummy. She touches my cheek and I shove her, gently. She's gone. Stepping to the wall, I lean over and watch her rush away from me, the gown tangling and flapping like a flag around her body. "Call me sometime, Taylor," she says, her voice shrinking.

I can't watch. I go back to the party.

"Where have you been, man?" Harris asks as I walk through the door dragging my overcoat. The young stripper is performing some kind of nude tiptoe ballet across Harris's sofa, the cushions slumping beneath her pointed toes. Men crumple dollar bills and toss them at her feet. "I thought I was gonna have to send out a posse, Hoss," Harris says, aiming his cigar at the girl. "Leanne over there has a friend coming in about twenty minutes and they're gonna treat us to a little lesbo show."

"Gosh, that really sounds fascinating, Harris. But I'm not feeling so great. I'm just gonna shove off." After much wheedling, haranguing and beseeching, Harris finally gives up on all the verbal head-butting machismo crap and lets me leave with my dignity.

The street is dark and drizzly as I walk to my car. Looking up, I see Jackie still falling from where I pushed her from the roof. She has on the faded peach sweatshirt she was wearing the last time I saw her, the night I spotted her and Matt eating wings and nachos at Brannigan's. She looked happy that night. She never saw me.

# SLOW CURVATURE OF DESTINY

(Appeared originally in *The Baltimore Review*)

*W*e built the sky, gave it a fresh coat of midnight blue, hot-wired the stars, found wind under boulders, caught clouds escaping to the sunset and told them to empty their pockets. Rain rain rain rain. Raining ever since Ketti left. Can't shut it off. Water's reached the second floor window. Straddling the shingles on the roof, I smoke skinny cigars and flip butts and watch boards drift by, clothing and corn-fed cows, soggy dogs and oil drums, lampshades and ragged sheds, mobile homes with people inside, brewing dinner, clinking spoons on China plates, scratching their heads, plugged to the radio, ears to the flood. That's the big news around here. Brown water so thick you could run a marathon, race Jesus to the far bank if you could find it. I give them mobile folks a friendly wave, hope they see me, toss me some food, but they don't, moving off swift, tide swinging their yard barge out of range.

Ketti possessed a powerful love—Mother Teresa, Florence

Nightingale, and Sara Lee balled into one—set on salvaging what she could of the world. We married young, Ketti and me, happy as bunions on a big toe, and up until three days ago, she was right here, doing cartwheels, shaving her legs, bleaching her hair purple to match her fingernails, sitting cross-legged on the porch swing, concocting gourmet meals from corn flakes and string beans, consulting the I Ching, kicking back, popping Pabst and all the while our television suffered the fritz. Did we care? *Oh I did!* but Ketti said, Don't be silly! and she grabbed me by the wrists, swung me round the room. My boots shot from my feet and slammed the wall. She swore she'd swing me till I came to my senses, till I gleamed and whinnied and surrendered all fret over the frazzled tube, till I gave up all worry over getting old, or growing bald, or falling down cracking a hip, not having work or insurance or a pension or a pot to catch pity in. I promised and pleaded over and over and she flung me out the window, tackled me halfway cross the lawn, pounced on top, tickled my sides till I giggled like a fool in front of our neighbors, Cyril and Elsie Buick. Jolly-eyed, I shrieked and howled and felt myself flush pink, nearly wet my pants. Ketti's big brown eyes ate me up. Her crazy laughter floated me off the ground like an alien abduction and I tingled all over from the stroke of her fingers along my ribs. We made love right there on the front lawn with Elsie Buick shrieking, scaring the hogs, and Cyril Buick banging his walker, yelling, threatening to ring the sheriff, the mayor, and the FB of I. Did we care? *NoSir!* That's when we built the sky, hot-wired the stars, unleashed the wind, and bullied the clouds and the waters rose rose rose rose and Ketti rowed away from the porch waving and sunny, slanting the wooden skiff across the glassy current searching for critters and creatures and a way of life to save, rescuing the sons and daughters of absolute strangers, cleaving the sonic rush of river to her breast, shining away, tracing the slow curvature of destiny; tiny, then gone.

# RECIPES FOR HAPPINESS

*I*n Willamine's room all the shadows are the color of gunpowder. They have attached themselves to all of her possessions: the oatmeal-colored woven wicker chair near the front door, the oyster blue vase from her Grandma Ida's estate, the photo of her young parents in bathing suits smiling from a beach in Nice, her extra pair of tortoise shell bifocals that never venture from the kitchen table. Some of the shadows attach themselves to Willamine in unflattering ways if she sits too far from the square window in her kitchen.

Flab hangs from her arms and her ankles are the same diameter as her calves. Consequently, her slippers are smashed flat from the enormous pressure they are under. She wears a dress of uncertain hue that seems to work for all seasons. She rarely moves from the window except to cook meals on her new Hotpoint range, which the deliverymen carried up to her apartment on the third floor and placed in the exact location where the old range sat for over twenty years.

Willamine has in her possession the Recipes for Happiness, given to her by her grandmother, Ida. And if she can take the proper action, she is sure the Recipes will be the trick to rid her apartment of these bothersome shadows. In order for it to work, though, she knows she must share the Recipes of Happiness with the world. She's not sure how she knows that, just something that speaks to her when she lies awake in bed at night. At present she has not been able to force herself into sharing them with anyone, and her lack of courage fills her with anguish and remorse.

Every day she sits like a sniper at the square window, her chubby fingers interlaced, her hands folded in her lap like a small brain. Shadows fill the room behind her, changing incrementally in size and direction but only when she is not paying attention to them. Even though she rarely regards those shadows, she is thankful that they change. It gives her a peculiar sense of hope. She especially avoids the rather large shadow that has attached itself to her and her chair.

A young couple walks past on the street below. Willamine can see very clearly the tops of their heads, the man's bald spot, the woman's gold butterfly hair clip. They're holding hands. Wind stirs leaves and paper cups around the feet of the lovers. Willamine had a lover once, Geoffrey, when she was 35. She was still rather trim then, 140 pounds or so, and they were in love. At least she was, and that was enough for her. It didn't have to be perfect.

Yellow Post-it notes cover her refrigerator door. They have curled upward like damaged shingles on a wind-ravaged roof. Under each note is a sharply distinct shadow and she doesn't understand why the manufacturer couldn't have put a thin strip of glue at the bottom of each note to avoid the unnecessary, troublesome curling and the resulting shadows. But she knows she has no right to criticize anyone about anything. After all, she herself is ineffectual.

Each note is a reminder; what medications she must take

and when, reminders to check the calendar, the day, month and year, make sure the stove is turned off after cooking, wrap the garbage and place it in the hall for Mr. Kilbride, her one-eyed neighbor—'gouged out in a brawl,' he'd once told her—who takes her garbage down to the dumpster in back of the building. There is also a note to remind her to prepare her laundry for Mrs. Filo who picks it up on the first Tuesday of each month, another to remind her to tip the grocery boy, and turn off the television before she goes to bed, and other notes to guide her through her life.

There is also a note reminding her that on the third Wednesday of each month at precisely 9:30 in the morning she will get a call. It is now 9:26 on the third Wednesday of the month and in four minutes the phone will ring. It will be a nurse, but more correctly, a technician. Ms. Welch. In anticipation of the call, Willamine wets her wrists at the sink, watching the sheet of water swell and ripple, running from her pale skin like winter snow melt, then sits at the kitchen table with the plastic case opened, the case the hospital had given her after her surgery. The phone rings. She picks up the receiver and places it down in the cradle provided inside the box. She removes the two bracelets from the case, each with a wire attached. One wire is white, the other black. Each bracelet looks exactly like a man's expandable chrome watchband, except without the timepiece—timeless watches, she thinks, amused by her novel and useless idea.

For her size, Willamine has relatively small hands but her wrists have a hefty padding of flesh. The wired watchbands will be uncomfortably tight when the test begins and will leave red marks on her skin, like scars, making her hands look like they've been sewn back on after a horrible accident. Ms. Welch will be checking her pacemaker. There is also a white plastic-covered magnet the shape and size of a donut inside the case.

When prompted by Ms. Welch, Willamine grasps the white magnet, which always brings to mind one of those small white sugary donuts—maybe because she's hungry, never eating before the test (she's not sure why)—then runs the magnet over the scar where the pacemaker is buried inside her chest while Ms. Welch tests it from her office ten miles away. Over the phone, Ms. Welch makes any adjustments to the pacemaker that might be required. She feels nothing as Ms. Welch slows or quickens the device that regulates her heart. She and Ms. Welch have done this so many times over the past five years that they perform this ritual without words.

When the pacemaker was installed, Willamine was 49 years old and weighed 175 pounds. She knows she's gained over 150 pounds since then and that she will not live much longer. She must act soon if she is to do that which she believes she was born to do.

When the test ends, Willamine puts the phone receiver back in its cradle on the kitchen wall, removes the bracelets and is about to place the white magnet donut in the plastic box when the phone rings. She answers and hears the warm liquid voice of Ms. Welch asking her if she feels all right, if she's experiencing any shortness of breath, dizziness or discomfort. Willamine does not like the questions and doesn't trust the pleasant new tone of Ms. Welch's voice. Ms. Welch has not spoken with her in over two years and this worries her. She answers no to Ms. Welch's inquiry and doesn't dare mention the breathing difficulties.

"I want you to call if you start feeling any of those things, okay?" She nods, knowing not to ask if anything is wrong because she doesn't want to know, and hangs up the phone. She knows today is the day she must take action, knows it with excruciating clarity, but can't figure out why today feels any different than any other. It just is.

She takes her station by the window. New thoughts do not come easy. Most of the activity in her mind is recycled from the day before, or from television. New thoughts, when they occur, sometimes frighten her.

The couple with the bald spot and gold butterfly have moved on, but the wind continues to stir the trash and debris below Willamine's window giving her a new idea. After thumbing through the Yellow Pages, she calls the Have-it-Now Rental Center and orders a copier to be delivered to her apartment. They will bring it this afternoon. She thinks about closing the shade over the window to make the shadows disappear, but then she'd be forced to sit in darkness. She turns the television on instead. *The Price is Right* is playing so she twists the volume up until she can hear the show from her chair at the window. A boy shushes by on a skateboard below. His hair is orange. Wind pushes paper and leaves up behind him and the shadows under the leaves move swiftly, cunningly, almost without notice.

Two sweaty men curse and grunt as they bustle through the doorway of Willamine's apartment. They carry a copier that is roughly the size of a small car engine. On top is the package of pink copier paper she requested.

"Three flights of steps! Christ, they need an elevator in this damn building!" The man with hairy arms speaks to no one in particular, removes his cap and brushes his bristly forearm across his forehead to remove sweat. The other man is young and slender, like a girl, Willamine thinks, and he smells like wet puppy fur. His head is on a swivel, his eyes devouring everything in Willamine's apartment. His lips are one thin line, unmoving, and she is certain that the young man is bewildered by her size, wondering how such a giant can live in such a small place.

The men have placed the copier in the middle of the kitchen table. "Do you want us to leave it here," asks Hairy Arm Man, his eyes now roving the interior of her dwelling for a more suitable spot. There is none to be found and the man gives up the search with a shrug of his lips. He holds the yellow copy of a service contract in his meaty hand, the knuckle of each finger hosting a sparse patch of black hair.

Willamine says nothing, signs the paper. Hairy Arm Man plugs in the copier, runs off a duplicate of the agreement and places it on the table before they leave. She knows that her tortoise shell bifocals have been smashed under the copier. She heard the crunching sound as the men set the copier down. She could tell they heard it too but acted as if nothing were wrong.

Listening to the gunshot-echoes of the deliverymen's shoes clomping down the wooden steps, Willamine is about to close the door when she notices a young man lingering in the shadows along the hallway. At first she thinks it's the peculiar young deliveryman from the Have-It-Now Rental Center, the one who looked like a girl, and maybe he has stayed behind to kill her, or rob her, but then she notices that the man is not young at all. He is gaunt with a blue cast to his skin, looking like a faded tattoo, or a ghost. She starts to ease the door back into the jamb when the man looks up at her. For one brief, impulsive moment he seems familiar and she thinks, Geoffrey! Her heart quickens, or maybe it's the pacemaker. Could it be Geoffrey? No, Geoffrey would be sixty by now. Wouldn't he? She wasn't sure. The man didn't look sixty. But how would Geoffrey find her. She closes the door quickly.

A knock at the door briefly dismantles her. She ambles over to check the Post-it notes on her refrigerator. Nothing is scheduled for today. Another knock. Willamine does not like unplanned visits. "Just a second," she says, instantly wishing she had remained quiet. The television is playing too loud. She turns it down and stands at the door.

"Willamine?" a voice calls to her from the other side.

Unable to contain her enthusiasm, she shuffles closer, whispering Geoffrey's name like a prayer... geoffrey geoffrey geoffrey. There is silence filled with fret. If it is Geoffrey, what will he think? She runs her hands over her wide hips.

"Are you still there?" she asks.

The voice assures her that he is and asks if he can come in. Not for many years has she felt such electricity. Oh, if it were only possible to take a pill and lose two hundred and thirty pounds in a second! she thinks, wringing her hands beneath her breasts.

"Geoffrey, is that you...?" she asks, melodious as a lyric.

After a moment, the voice outside the door returns a sad message indeed. "No, I'm sorry, Willamine. It's Todd. Your brother."

Willamine looks over at the picture of her parents, Roger and Mitzi—their faces frozen in paranormal happiness, their swimming suits still wet after 45 years—and imagines the man on the other side of the door with Roger's electric-blue eyes and Mitzi's perfect skin and sculpted cheekbones. She keeps the photo of her parents on the kitchen counter next to the pink toaster. It is the only picture of Mitzi and Roger she has. She admires her parents' courage, their ability to take action. Mitzi and Roger knew from the moment she was born that they couldn't take care of a child. They, like Willamine, had things they were born to do and a child would only slow them down, so Roger's mother, Ida, raised her. Mitzi and Roger always visited on weekends, every weekend, unless they were in Vegas or Seattle starting a new business or running down a big deal. She loved the stories Roger told her and how his eyes sparkled like blue popsicles. He would pick her up and swing her around, tell her the whole world was hers for a smile, and so she would smile, and giggle, and laugh. Her mother, Mitzi, was gorgeous, actress-caliber beauty, and Willamine always hoped to grow up half as beautiful. Mitzi would fix Willamine's hair when she visited on weekends and paint her nails red, brighter than the reddest rose. The visits became fewer after Todd was born. She never knew Todd very well because he traveled with Mitzi and Roger. Boys were easier to take on the road, easier to travel with. No one had to explain that to her. It was pretty well known. She admired them for taking Todd on their journeys, showing him how to be a man of the world. Boys had to learn that or they'd be eaten alive.

The last time Willamine saw Mitzi and Roger was 36 years ago. Her parents had found a place in London and were going there to live. Todd was already in London, staying with a nanny. She had seen her parents off at the airport. Ida drove Willamine home after the plane left the runway. Willamine received postcards for about a year.

"Willamine, I need to talk to you," the voice of Todd says.

But how would Todd know where to find me? she wonders, then thinks. Grandma Ida must have told him before she died. She never mentioned that she was ever in touch with Roger, Mitzi, and Todd.

"What do you want?" she says.

"You asked me to come. So here I am."

Willamine had never talked with Todd, had never asked him anything.

"How do I know you're Todd?"

"When Grandma Ida died, Uncle Marvin gave you a stack of my letters from Grandma Ida's safe deposit box."

"I still have those," Willamine says, opening the door slowly.

Todd enters the apartment and stands like a post in the center of the kitchen. He looks so much like Grandma Ida that Willamine figures he could pass for her ghost in heaven, if that's where she is. His eyes are brown, not blue, and his cheekbones are jagged, not smooth or beautiful like Mitzi's. Acne scars cover his cheeks and his hands are spindly and grayish looking. She knows that he couldn't be much more than forty-seven, but he looks unhealthy. She's only seen him twice in her life. He was just a baby. She drags the oatmeal-colored wicker chair to the center of the kitchen and directs him to sit down. She sits by the window, looks down at the street. An old man is falling into a restless sleep on the park bench, his head jerking upward in surprise each time he jolts awake.

"I see you have the copier again," Todd says.

"What do you want?" she asks, wondering what Todd meant; she's never rented a copier before as far as she can remember.

"I came to remind you, like you asked." Todd's eyes no longer roam the apartment and now rest gently on some unknown spot on the wall. He fumbles his thumbs in his lap. "Mitzi is dead."

Willamine nods her head and pictures Mitzi, her lavish smile, her precious skin, and knows that Mitzi would never have agreed to death. No, Mitzi would never die like regular people; she'd be carried away on a cloud at the exact moment of her finest and most radiant beauty. She glances over at the photo of Mitzi and Roger. No, Mitzi would never just die.

"May I call you Willow?" Todd asks.

Willow. No one has ever called her Willow. It's kind of pretty. "No. Just call me Willamine."

"Okay," Todd says.

"You came all the way from England to tell me that Mitzi

died?" she says, taking her eyes back out the window. The old man is gone and the slats of the bench throw perfect even shadows on the sidewalk.

"Yes. That's why I'm here. Don't you remember?"

Willamine shakes her head.

Todd lets his eyes fall into his own shadow. "Roger is dead, too."

"How did he die?" she asks.

"Car accident. And I'm sorry to say they had nothing to leave you. Roger and Mitzi died broke."

That's not Roger, she thinks. Roger will die trying to stop a train or falling out of a hot air balloon. And broke? Not Roger, not her father. The world is yours for a smile! A smile! No, he wasn't broke. She looks at the photo of Mitzi and Roger and it hasn't changed. Roger is still tan, his eyes wired to the sky, his smile a million dollars of potential. He would never be broke.

"Is that why you're here? To borrow money?" she asks, picturing Grandma Ida, her narrow face and tight eyes warning her about Geoffrey. Geoffrey had wanted to marry Willamine, but Ida said he was only out for her money. Willamine would inherit all of Ida's property and stocks when Ida died. She hadn't cared why the young man wanted her and knew in time that she could imprison him with her amorous attention, her easy-going manner, and her delicious food. But Ida insisted on testing Geoffrey, explaining to him that Willamine's parents were poor good-for-nothing vagabonds and that Willamine would no doubt die penniless and that all of the wealth he was looking at around him would go to her only son, Roger. This was a lie, of course, and Ida had never planned on giving Roger "one dull dime," as she put it. As planned, Willamine had listened from the kitchen. Geoffrey said nothing for a minute, then stated, somewhat indignantly, that he loved Willamine very much and wanted to, "...marry *her,* not her *wealth!"* Even though Willamine knew this would make a fool of Grandma Ida and anger her, she didn't care. She loved Geoffrey. But he stopped coming around soon after.

Willamine crumples her hands into her lap and looks out the window, the trees throwing tiger-stripe shadows across the park grass. After a moment, she pushes herself up from the chair and shuffles to the bedroom, careful to keep her slippers beneath her feet. In a few moments she returns carrying a check—filled out and dated, very legible, her signature neatly penned in the lower right-hand corner—and reaches it out to Todd. Todd looks at her and doesn't take the check. She feels that he has learned a good deal of etiquette through his travels.

"I don't need your money," Todd says, his fingers bony, looking broken and useless in his lap. "On this day five years ago Grandma Ida died. At the funeral Uncle Marvin gave you my letters and you told Uncle Marvin you were surprised that Mitzi, Roger, and Todd were not attending Grandma Ida's funeral. That's when he told you we had been killed in a car accident four years earlier in London. You were quite shocked, as anyone would be, and Uncle Marvin was equally shocked Grandma Ida had not told you. You came home and sat right where you're sitting now and said you never even had the chance to meet me. That's when I came the first time, Willamine."

Picking up the photo of Mitzi and Roger, Willamine tries to picture her parents nestled in satin-lined coffins, but their smiles are too convincing, too captivating to succumb to death.

"I've been coming every year since."

"Why?" she asks.

"To remind you that Roger and Mitzi and I are dead, just as you asked."

She looks over at Todd, at the sad smile carved into his face. A moment later he's gone.

Willamine walks across the empty room to her caterpillar-decorated recipe box next to the stove. The lid of the box is hand-painted with pink letters that read, Recipes for Happiness. She extracts an index card, one of many Ida has given her over the years. She opens the lid to the copier and places one of the index cards face down on the glass realizing she can probably fit four or five per sheet if she turns two perpendicular to the other three. After arranging the cards on the glass, she runs one copy to see how it looks. Very legible. She wishes now that Todd had stayed longer; he could have helped, but she feels fortified by his visit.

Willamine puts all her weight behind the kitchen table, pushing it and the copier closer to the window. "Don't give these recipes to anyone, Willamine," Grandma Ida had warned her. "They've been in our family for over three generations."

The first copy lands in the tray and is still warm when she drops it out the window. She slips the next copy over the sill as well, watching the sheet cut the air like a scythe, at first, then shift back and forth like a porch swing.

Willamine pictures Ida sitting up in her grave, thin as clothesline, her jaw and arms moving in sync like a clunky mechanical toy, yelling for her to stop. "Don't you dare!" Willamine ignores Grandma Ida and pushes the button again and another copy floats into the tray, which she promptly drops out the window.

After fifteen minutes of releasing copies out onto the street below Willamine loads more paper into the machine, and arranges five new recipes on the glass, discarding the previous five out the window. She decides to make paper airplanes of the next five Recipes so they will sail farther from the building, over to the park across the street. Roger had shown her how to make paper airplanes, showed her each fold, made it look simple. She gets it almost right, folding the wings one extra time, but it doesn't seem to affect them aerodynamically and they shoot across the street, drifting through the branches of the lindens lining the sidewalk before falling to the lawn. An hour later she is down to her last twenty sheets of copy paper. In her caterpillar-decorated recipe box, there are maybe fifteen recipes left, but the Have-It-Now men only brought one ream and she wishes she had ordered more. She knows she must make due.

Beneath her apartment, the street is littered with recipes and paper airplanes, like fallout from a wartime propaganda effort. Willamine is pleased. She takes great effort with the last twenty airplanes, taking time to aim each one, though they fly haphazardly when they catch in the breeze. As the last airplane leaves her hand, passing over the windowsill, she notices, for the first time, the shadow just beneath it, disappearing over the sill like a gray, translucent serpent.

The recipes were Grandma Ida's most prized possessions, the only nurturing feature of Ida's otherwise bitter and miserly life. Willamine knows she owes Ida a debt of gratitude for raising her, staying with her all those years when Mitzi and Roger and Todd were exploring the world, but her time with Ida has left behind this residue of shadows, these vague smudges of life that are colorless, fleeting, empty.

Willamine removes the last five index cards from the copier and turns them over in her hands like a magician preparing a magic trick, then rips each one into pieces and opens her palms. The scraps float down from the window like parade confetti. On the sidewalk below, three boys are laughing, having a paper plane fight with the Recipes for Happiness. A bent, haggard old man in a dirt-brown coat picks up one of the pink sheets, gives it a rudimentary nod, then crinkles it over his face and blows his nose. After a couple more tugboat-blasts, he balls up the sheet, tosses it toward the gutter and shambles away. Standing in the shadow of a tree is a man and she thinks it might be Todd, tries to recall the color of his eyes, not really sure if she would recognize him by the top of his head, and not completely convinced that he really exists; his visit already seems as though it happened thirty years ago, if at all. The man steps out of the shadow and picks up one of the paper airplanes with the Recipe for Happiness, looks at it for a moment, then looks up at her and cocks his arm back, sailing the airplane toward the sky, toward her. For one long, capacious moment the plane hangs in the air, floating back and forth beyond her window, just out of reach.

# THE FRED ARBOGASTER

(Appeared originally in *The Southwest Review*)

*D*idn't happen with a bang or a zing, my first step toward independence. Just showed up in the mail one day. Years later it would all make sense. But not that summer, not at twelve. I took the package to my room, tore open the envelope and dumped out a rectangular clear plastic box no bigger than a Three Musketeers. Inside the plastic box: the Fred Arbogaster, just like in the magazine—shape and size of a robin egg but bright yellow, two shiny treble hooks hanging from its belly, a tiny chrome shovel for a lip. Off its tail was a thing called a hula skirt—white and yellow rubber bands it looked like to me. But anyone could tell; that skirt was life itself to a bigmouth bass. I left the Arbogaster in the box, held it up to the window, slid it back and forth picturing hungry green shadows darting out from weedy banks to snatch it.

Mom made us a great lunch. Pork roast sandwiches for my dad. Peanut butter and jelly for me. "You can help your father pack the car after you tend those teeth." Even at five in the morning she wouldn't let me leave without brushing.

The sky was a black sheet of stars. Pop was busy at the back of the Pontiac. In the dark, the trunk space glowed like a portal to another world. "Grab the rods, Drew. Put them in the back seat."

At the bait shop he bought three dozen fathead minnows and a box of night crawlers thick as licorice, then asked if I wanted a Snickers for later. While he paid, I searched the plugs on the far wall. Not one Arbogaster. I smiled, patted the box in my shirt pocket.

Perfectly flat. First ones on the lake at dawn. Before sunlight burned above the trees, the wooden skiff was gliding toward Smeltzer's Cove, the electric motor quiet as grass. At his favorite hole he slowed the boat, said there was a tree or something below the water. Braided rope slid slowly through his coarse hands until the anchor hit bottom.

"Hand me your rod, Drew. I'll tie you on a hook and fix your bobber." I stared at the red and white bobber in his hand. How many bobbers had he fixed on my line? —how many fathead minnows and fidgety worms on my hook? I didn't think it would be this hard. "I'm gonna fish with this, OK?" I said, slipping the clear plastic box from my pocket.

Steam rose from the Thermos cup on his seat. Peeking out from his hip pocket was the leathery edge of a billfold. A small tear in the back of his coat showed a puff of white stuffing, while blue cigar smoke circled over his shoulder, drifting behind him across the water. He never talked much while we fished, not ever, but this was a new kind of silence, that much I could tell.

# LAMINATING THE PAST

(Appeared originally in *Pisgah Review*)

Something black flew across the night sky. Ted watched. Standing between the curtains and the bedroom window, he believed that on this particular night the object was as black as something could be, blacker than the bowl of mountains surrounding the valley, blacker than the scraggly bare branches of the dogwood outside his window. Absolute blackness, some sort of purity, he figured. And even though the object was gone, the impact of it lingered on his retinas while he studied the dingy evening sky, the city lights of Asheville flickering below like the last struggling embers in the dark crater of a dying volcano. Here was Ted, standing at the window staring into the breach of the new millennium, wondering why he felt so crappy about everything.

"Teddy. Are you voting there?"

"What?"

"I said, 'Are you voting there?' With your legs sticking down below the window curtains it looks like you're in one of those voting booths."

"Have you ever voted, Shelley?"

"No. Why?"

"Then how would you know what they look like?"

"I don't know, movies maybe? Conditioning?

Ted, wearing only a short robe and boxers, spun from the window, splashing the curtains apart to face Shelley. His hairy belly protruded through his opened robe. Shelley was lying under the covers propped up on one elbow, sopping up the last of the baba ganoush with a wedge of pita bread.

"Jeez! How is it that you're twenty-nine years old and have never voted? It makes no sense! That's exactly why you don't date out of your decade, Shelley, exactly why!"

"What are you talking about? — 'date out of your decade.' What the hell does that mean?"

"It means, that if you were born in the fifties, you date someone born in the fifties. If you were born in the sixties... you get the idea. Then you have something in common, you know, you can relate to the same things. You're never more than nine years apart in your thinking!"

"You gotta be shitting me, Teddy. You don't really believe that?" Shelley scooted her back up against the headboard letting the comforter slip to her waist, exposing the bluebird tattoo above her right nipple.

"Yeah! Yeah! I do. The world is changing so fast that if you date out of your decade you're dating an alien, like from a different universe. Hell, at the rate things are changing, pretty soon, if you're not dating someone born on the exact same day as you, you'll have nothing in common!"

"Oh, brother!"

"Oh brother, my ass! The William Tell Overture?—a perfect example! Tell me about the William Tell Overture."

"You think I don't know what the William Tell Overture is? Briskly paced with a capering quality...lively...composer, Rossini — but not my taste. I prefer Philip Glass, Gorecki, The Sex Pistols."

"Exactly! My fucking point exactly!"

"Now what?"

"If you were born in the fifties like me, the William Tell Overture would not be briskly capering of a lively quality blah blah blah!—it would be the fucking Lone Ranger! Yeah, Hi Ho fucking Silver, away! That's what it would be. If you were born in the fifties you couldn't listen to the William Tell Overture without thinking of a masked man on a white horse and his goddamn zombie sidekick, Tonto! They stole that music from me! If you were born in the fifties you would understand!"

"Have you taken a Prozac today? You're creeping me out."

"I'm going out on the back deck and smoke a cigar."

"Teddy, it's dark, and like thirty below zero or something!"

"Yeah, right, Shel. Why do you always have to exaggerate?" Ted rummaged through the pockets of his robe looking for his lighter.

"Oh boy, What's up, Teddy? I know that tone."

"Why does something have to be up? I just need a smoke."

"Look, I know you just turned forty-nine and you're supposed to be morose and unreasonable, but is that any reason to deprive me and General Blinkingham from having a good time on your birthday?"

"Jeez, Shel. Do you have to refer to my dick as General Blinkingham? Is it because you were born in the seventies? There's something psychotic about anthropomorphizing my penis!"

Shelley slid her finger along the edge of the bowl and brought out the last dollop of baba ganoush and promptly popped it in her mouth, sucking her finger clean.

"Forget this! I'm gonna go smoke." Ted bent over to look for his slippers. The space under the bed was thick with dust anomalies.

"Oh, come on," Shelley said. "I'm just kidding. Come to bed, birthday boy. Don't make me beg." She patted his side of the bed. "At least tell me what's wrong before you go."

"Okay, Shel. How about…1969?"

"Shit, here we go again. Let's see, I was doing the backstroke in my mother's uterus trying to avoid being gang-raped by a billion frenetic sperm cells, while you were receiving a tonsure so you could go fight in Vietnam for Nixon. Is that about right?"

"See, this is exactly why you don't date out of your decade!"

"Oh, come over here and tell Shelley what's bothering her big Teddy Bear.

Ted jerked his robe closed and turned to leave the bedroom.

"Don't leave. I'm just trying to cheer you up. Is that a capital offense?"

"I don't want to be cheered up. I want to smoke my cigar."

"Not until you tell me what's wrong."

"You wouldn't understand."

"Try me."

"It's just…everything."

"There, see. And you thought I wouldn't understand."

"Christ, Shelley, sometimes I just want to pop you one!"

"Do you want to pop me one? Then pop me one. Here!" Shelley kicked off the blankets and knelt upright in the middle of the bed, tapping her finger on her chin.

Ted tried to ignore Shelley's other tattoos: the small bluebird near her ribs that almost matched the one on her opposite breast, and the bluebird just above her pubic hair. He'd seen the flock a million times, but somehow they bothered him, as if they'd been rendered out of perspective or something. He couldn't figure it out.

"No...I don't...but it's tempting!" he finally said.

"Stay. Talk." Shelley sat back on her heels, her legs folded under, arms laced beneath her breasts.

"Look, I had a revelation and I just need to sit with it awhile...*alone!*" Ted pulled a cigar from his pocket.

"Oh, I see. You had a depressing thought and now you need to nurture it with self-pity and mutant paranoid delusions until it becomes a full-blown depression requiring additional medication. I bet you weren't breast fed as a baby, were you?"

The next morning Shelley strolled into the kitchen, rubbing her eyes, and spied Ted sitting at the table in his boxers, blue ones with tiny yellow toasters. She eased up behind him, wrapped her arms around his shoulders and kissed the small patch of hair at the base of his neck. "Happy Birthday!"

Ted didn't bother turning around. "That was yesterday."

"You only turn Forty-nine once!" she said, a little too cheerfully for eight in the morning.

"Yeah, right. We'll see how perky you are when your odometer hits thirty in a couple of months."

Shelley leaned forward, resting her chest against his back to peek over his shoulder. The kitchen table was covered with cards and papers. Ted's worn brown wallet was spread like a rancid sandwich on the table, stripped of all contents. He was holding the U-Haul tape dispenser.

"What's going on here?"

"Laminating some things." Ted stripped off a five-inch length of clear 2-inch wide tape and placed it on the table, glue-side up. He lifted a card from the pile and laid it on the sticky side of the tape.

"What's that you're laminating?"

"My draft card." He pressed it down, then stripped more tape from the U-Haul dispenser, placing the new piece over the card, encasing it.

"Your draft card? You're forty-nine! I doubt you need a draft card."

"No, I don't need my draft card, at least I don't think so. But I keep it as a reminder."

"Of what?"

"The war, Shel, the goddamn war! Remember?"

"Vietnam?"

"No, the Revolutionary War!—of course, Vietnam! What do you think?"

"You didn't even go to Vietnam. You were stationed in Okinawa, driving trucks or something, and screwing the locals!"

"You just don't get it, Shel." Ted trimmed the excess tape around his draft card, then pulled another card from the stack.

"Your social security card!" Shelley leaned over and pulled the small card from his hand. "Wow, this thing is really in good shape. Is it the original?"

"Yeah, of course," he said, snatching it back and laying it on the table.

"You're going to laminate your social security card? Do you think that's really necessary?" Shelley said.

"Necessary? Christ, I don't know. I don't really care. I don't want to find out a few years from now, when I really need it, that it's so worn out you can't read the fucking number anymore. So, yeah, I'm gonna laminate it."

Shelley hovered behind him a moment before heading over to the counter to make coffee. Yawning and stretching at the sink, she held the carafe under the faucet while reaching down with her left hand to pull her bunched panties from the cleft of her behind. After switching the coffee maker on she went back over to the table and sat across from Ted.

"What's this one?" she asked, picking up a satiny-white piece of paper and studying it.

"It's my fishing license," he said without looking over.

She made a slight snuffing noise. "I didn't know you fished."

Ted briefly raised his eyes toward Shelley.

"Gosh, it's from like over five years ago," said Shelley, her attention fixed on the small scrap of paper, "and it still looks this good! I've got hair appointment cards from a *week* ago that don't look this good."

"I think it's printed on some kind of space-age shit that never wears out," Ted said. "They should make boxer shorts out of that stuff. My boxers are all wearing out."

"I hadn't noticed."

"Yeah, look here." Ted pushed away from the table and spread his legs to reveal a smiling gap just below the seam of the crotch.

"That's where your balls rub, Teddy. You've got huge balls."

"Huh?" he said, scooting his chair back to the table. "My balls are huge, huh?" He laid out more strips of tape.

"So why are you going to laminate your fishing license if it's space-age material? Besides, I don't think it's good any more, Teddy. It's expired."

"I don't know if it's space-age, Shel. I just think it is, you know, some kind of special formula shit. And I don't care if it's expired. Do you see me wearing a fishing vest and carrying a pole?"

Shelley got up to pour coffee. "Ready for a cup?"

He nodded. The dispenser made a squealing noise as he stripped more tape.

"Why save an expired fishing license?" she asked as she set the coffee cup down next to him.

Ted scratched his chest, combed his hand through his hair. He closed his eyes, lifted the cup under his nose and sniffed the coffee, slow and long. "Have you ever had coffee cooked over a campfire?" he asked, looking over the rim of his cup.

Shelley shook her head. He figured she didn't know what he was talking about, so he was about to explain. He could feel his expression go slack when he was headed back in time, as if his mind had to disengage from his body in order to find the tag end of his thoughts.

"My son cooked coffee over our campfire when we went to the Boundary Waters."

"David?"

"Yeah, David. He was a real outdoorsman," Ted said, smiling at the picture he saw in his head of a lean, bearded young man, shoulders flared like a sail, organically tanned. "It was his idea to go to the Boundary Waters. I'd never been fishing and he was probably sorry he ever asked me. All I did was complain—the rugged campsites, the long, grueling portages, the mosquitoes. Christ, the whole time I'm complaining, he's doing all the work—setting up the tent, cooking the meals, cleaning up the dishes, taking down the tent, stuffing our back packs, purifying our drinking water, carrying the canoe over his head like some kind of bushman, never saying a word."

Ted shook his head and slurped his coffee. "Do you know you have to hang your food from a tree before you hit the sack at night? That's right, Shel. Bears! They get into your food packs if you leave them on the ground, or worse, in the tent. The first night, while David was down cleaning the dishes and pumping water into our bottles, I brought the food pack into the tent. Jesus, David must have thought I was an imbecile but he didn't say a word. He just grabbed it and showed me how to tie it up in a tree. He told me to make sure I didn't have toothpaste in the tent, or chewing gum or anything that had a sweet smell. Hell, the first night I couldn't sleep, thinking about a bear ripping through the tent because I'd dropped a Tic Tac in my sleeping bag."

Shelley chuckled and sipped her coffee. Huddled in the chair, she pulled her legs up and wrapped her arms around her knees, supporting her coffee cup with both hands. Steam rolled up under her chin.

"You know, Shel, that was the best time I ever had in my life. I told David that on the drive home. He shook his head and smirked. He didn't believe me. God, Shel, I would give anything to have that time back. I hardly remember the bad stuff, the wet clothes, the cold, the bugs and all that. I just remember the last morning we sat by the fire drinking fresh brewed coffee." Ted gazed past the sliding glass doors and could almost hear the fire crackling, almost see it spitting sparks, the sky a seamless gray fog. Tops of pine trees looked like pencil points sticking up through the mist. It had been completely quiet except for the occasional cry of a loon and the low rush of a waterfall near their campsite. They'd hardly spoken the last morning, just paddled and fished and shared the silence.

Ted cradled his coffee in both hands, his elbows on the table.

"Why don't you call him?" Shelley said.

Ted couldn't bring his eyes from the backdoor. "David? No. I haven't talked to him in over five years, not since I divorced his mother. I don't think he'll ever forgive me for that." Ted put down the coffee and picked up the fishing license, measuring it with his eyes to figure out how much tape it would take. "Look. I don't want to spend the day laminating the past," he said, ripping a length of tape from the dispenser, careful not to smudge the sticky side with his fingers.

"You mean *lamenting,* don't you?" Shelley said.

After thinking a moment, Ted finally said, "Yeah, whatever."

Ted set the fishing license on the tape, positioning it just so before sandwiching it with another piece over the top. "You know, Shel," Ted said, "David is almost the same age as you…"

Shelley and Ted looked at each other for a long second before she shrugged. Then, with lips together, she gave him a half-smile. "Care if I laminate some stuff?" she asked.

"Be my guest."

They spent the remainder of the morning laminating every non-plastic card in their wallets. Shelley remembered some business cards she had, plus her haircut appointment card, and her tanning membership card, so they laminated them as well. They laminated pictures, bookmarks, leaves, coins, M&M's, in case of a sugar emergency, an unpaid electric bill, the remote controls for the TV and VCR—so they'd be easier to keep clean —and some of Shelley's rust-colored hair for Ted's wallet.

"Let's go to a movie!" Shelley said, admiring the stacks of neatly preserved items. "I love matinees. Plus, we can pick up more tape while we're out."

# YIPS

(Appeared originally in *Talking River Review*)

When my mother phoned this morning she told me she was dying of syphilis. No one dies of syphilis anymore, I told her, but she was inconsolable on the phone. Being the concerned and loving daughter, I went over. Krystal, my mother, refused treatment, set on using her "illness" to retaliate against my stepfather. Her plan, as she described it in maliciously twisted detail over tea cookies and brandy, was to re-infect him continually with the hideous disease, which she believed he had given her. My mother wasn't certifiable, but she was given to frequent mental misfirings. However, she wasn't delusional about my philandering stepfather. Edward was the worst sort of horn-dog. Still, I couldn't believe he'd given her syphilis; they slept in different bedrooms, opposite wings, separate realities.

Convinced that Edward was a scoundrel and not to be trusted, my mother thrust a plain manila envelope into my hands, said it was filled with incriminating documents about his taxes and investments. "Don't be afraid to use it, Charlene," she said. "It will ensure your inheritance and monthly stipend." Certain she was dying, again, Krystal wanted to make sure I'd be taken care of properly. With my degree in astronomy and never having worked a day in my life, I had given my mother plenty reason for concern. And coupled with the fact that Edward had never officially adopted me, she was more convinced than ever I needed an edge.

Patting the envelope with her frail hand, she told me to keep it for the right moment.

I took it from her, kissed her on the forehead and left. Within thirty-five minutes I was in the parking lot of Castlebrook Hills Country Club. It's what I do when I'm stressed, or bored, or anxious; it's just what I do. I play golf.

Castlebrook Hills is one of the more prestigious and progressive country clubs, and one of the few attempting to restore the tradition of caddies. There're only a handful of boys today, mostly high school age, a few college. It doesn't bother me that they snicker and elbow each other when I come into the clubhouse. It's easier for me that they've traded stories; less explaining on my part.

At thirty-eight, I am relatively unattractive, single, and flat-chested, but blessed with the long, shapely legs of my mother. I must admit, from the hips down I'm pure goddess, just like my mother, even though the rest of my body seems like the product of failed concentration on God's part. I don't have facial hair, grotesque physical anomalies, or bad skin, but the equation of my features doesn't add up to beauty. I am plain, and I dress accordingly and wear my hair short. My posture is straight and erect, and my shoulder blades protrude like boat keels, giving me more topography going than coming. And so far, my butt is holding up well, egg-shaped, while not ostentatious. My mother was beautiful in every sense, except that maybe she loved too deeply, too unrestrictedly, and her hate plumbed the same depths as her love when her love capsized, if you can say that love capsizes. She is large-breasted, just like her two sisters, and for a long time it was hard to understand why the phenomenon had skipped me. I am convinced now that it is a matter of arrested development, that my breasts are just waiting for the right moment to *bang* into existence. It can happen. It's how the entire universe came into being.

I was drawn to a new caddy, one of the older boys, college-age, with cheeks sunk in like wet sand. The smooth terrain of his tan skin pulled taut over the shiny edge of his cheekbones. The caddies are always tan, contrasting my bleached-out sunblock-60 skin.

His name was Tyler. He looked down at the floor, grinning, trying to conceal it. Whistles and whoops came from the locker room. Tyler picked up my bag and followed me out to the cart, but not before sending a few smug glances over his shoulder back at his peers. I guess he figured I wouldn't notice.

Whenever I step onto a golf course I picture my stepfather. Maybe it's the dewy fragrance of mowed grass, or the refreshing sting of morning air, but I doubt it. Edward taught me how to play when I was fifteen, providing me the one pastime that could help fill the insurmountable void of my life. Without golf I would die. Unfortunately, my addiction to the game has not made a proficient golfer of me. Edward says I lack concentration and passion. But even he will admit that when I swing a driver my form is impeccable. He thinks it's his influence, attempting to lay claim to the only aspect of me that he approves. I attribute my exquisite form to theft, studying the greatest women golfers ever, Joanne Carner, Betsy Rawls, Nancy Lopez, and of course, Mickey Wright, whose form I most tried to emulate. But not the mechanics of it, just the illusion. Like my poise, stolen from old movies—Loretta Young,

Audrey Hepburn, Charlotte Rampling—everything about me is stolen, right down to my breeding of wealth, which was stolen from Edward. It's not really breeding, though, as Edward is so quick to point out. "Don't confuse arrogance with breeding. They're not the same." Of course he's right. I have only arrogance. He has both.

Preparing my putt on the first green, I hoped today would be different, but with Tyler holding the flag, I could already tell it wouldn't. I lined up over the ball for a sixteen-footer when my hands jumped. The putter kicked the ball to the left, landing it farther from the hole than when I started. Tyler told me to take it over.

I said no. Tyler laughed and shook his head. He has gorgeous legs and I have the yips. It's a stupid, uncivilized ailment supposedly brought on by performance anxiety, a type of dystonia—a neurological disorder that causes involuntary muscle contractions. No one can seem to find a cure. I've tried hypnosis, acupuncture, visualization, and a vegan diet, but nothing works. When the yips hit me, I get nauseous, like motion sickness, and my body tightens.

My mother never played golf and couldn't understand why anyone would, except maybe for the fresh air. She was pragmatic about most things, finances, cooking, and politics (except for her conspiracy theories), but like her two sisters, my mother had lashed her faith to tea leaves, astrology charts, and tarot cards and if she'd been born a few hundred years earlier, she would surely have burned at the stake. Of course, if you ask her, she'll tell you she was. My mother was a regal oddity, a lavish piece of dime store jewelry, and it was that which had so attracted my stepfather. He'd collected such treasures, lost and shiny objects buried in the sand, cast off by society as cracked and worthless and took them home to place in front of his indulgent parents. And being the charismatic youth, Edward had no trouble getting them to accept my mother.

Today would be hell. The second hole had proved as disastrous as the first. I closed my eyes and practiced a technique I learned from my Yoga instructor and was soon drifting above a white island surrounded by emerald sea. A warm breeze carried me aloft, over the island. Swooping down closer I could see the sand, perfect and white, every grain calm and pristine, unhurried. Exotic birds skittered along the edge of the surf, escaping the foam. When I opened my eyes, I felt better. Tyler was holding the flag but he was a blur to me. The dimples on my ball looked like craters on the moon. The hole, several yards away, looked as wide as a freshly dug grave. I lined up over the ball and slowly released a breath, but just as I started my swing forward, my wrists jerked, sending the ball bouncing across the green into the sand trap.

I attacked the manicured grass with the blunt nose of my putter. Tyler rushed over and grabbed me in a bear hug, lifting me from the ground before I could execute further damage to the green. When I stopped struggling, he put me down, then went over and picked up my club. Squatting down, he gently tamped the earth with his fingertips, like the Dali Lama of the putting green, offering solace to the fucking dirt.

On the fourth tee, I sliced my shot into the trees. The only thing I've found to relieve my yips is sex. I guess I could take a pill, but I'm not into drugs. Besides, most of the caddies are willing to accommodate me, even if for no other reason than how easy it is and when I turn to walk into the woods, I hear the cart squeak. Tyler follows. The path is well worn.

From under the dark canopy of tanoaks, palms and Pacific madrones, the fairway beyond the cover appeared sharply green. Dried leaves and twigs crunched under Tyler's feet as he walked behind me and I thought of Harris. Harris was the most beautiful boy I had ever known.

When I was young, my stepfather and mother threw elaborate parties. They were actually my stepfather's idea, but my mother was congenial and supportive, even though quietly, or not so quietly sometimes, she detested them. The party that stands out most in my mind was one he threw at the end of every August for the caddies before they went back to school. All of my stepfather's friends and business associates were invited, giving the boys a chance to make important connections with people they might otherwise not meet. But for Edward, it was mostly a chance to drink and flirt with the wives, and my stepfather never missed an opportunity for either.

I had just turned fifteen a month earlier and had a crush on one of the caddies, a senior in high school named Harris. He was always around the house for one reason or another, making extra money doing odd jobs for my stepfather—painting the guest cottage, repairing the stone wall that ran along our property, refurbishing my stepfather's duck decoys. Harris was a bit of an artist. Anyway, at the party, I had coaxed him to my room under the guise of showing him my album collection. It was an impressive collection and I could tell he was a bit jealous and awed. Before long, we were necking on the bed, sitting at the edge with our feet on the floor, twisted toward each other in the most painful way. Harris was kissing me when he started to put his hand up under my blouse. I stopped him because I was embarrassed. I pressed his hand against my stomach, holding it there, not wanting him to go further, but not wanting him to remove it. I loved the humid touch of his palm on my skin. When my stepfather appeared in the doorway, I thought I would throw-up. Everything happened so fast.

Harris jumped up from the bed. I remember the shouting, the white-terror on Harris' face, the rush of his footfalls as he fled down the stairs to the living room, the slam of the front door, the vacuous silence he left in his wake.

Edward glared at me, then pushed the door to my bedroom closed. What happened next was more illusion than solid, more like a movie than reality. Edward came over by the bed smelling of alcohol and without a word, put his lips to mine. Before I could catch my breath, I felt his tongue fill my mouth. Seconds later, he jerked away with the puzzled expression of someone who'd just awakened from a deep sleep. He took his eyes to the floor, then back at me, his mouth a square empty hole. He rushed from my bedroom.

The next day Edward took me to the club, started teaching me how to play golf. I had never seen him so patient, so loving, so nervously distant. He treated me with the compassion of a caring stranger, regarding me with the astonishment of a different species, smiling as if that alone could eventually undo his three seconds of bad judgment. He bought me lunch, introduced me to his friends, and the bartender, Albert, and the owner of the Castlebrook Country Club, Mr. Mason. We drove to the amusement park with the top down and he bought me funnel cakes and cotton candy. From the top of the Ferris wheel, I saw the speck of Edward in the crowd below, hands in pockets. Then later, caught the blur of him as I spun past in the hooded carriage of the Tilt-A-Whirl. And watched him slump on a bench, worrying the ink off the red paper tickets as I waited in line for the roller coaster. Watching Edward go through these pathetic gyrations was both tragic and contemptible, as if junk food and carnival rides could restore the boundary he'd erased the night before. Even so, I hoped from some hidden corner of my brain that it would work. The episode in my bedroom was never spoken of, nor did it ever happen again. And after that night, he never hugged me, or touched my hair, or let himself be alone with me in private.

Tyler said nothing when we got back to the golf cart, but I knew my yips were gone. I finished the last fourteen holes eight over par, which is really good for me. After throwing my clubs in the trunk of my Benz, I handed Tyler a fifty and headed for the bar. He tagged along.

"Can I call you sometime," he asked.

I stopped and turned toward him and wanted to be kind but I knew I wouldn't. "There's no reason. You did a fine job today. It was fun."

I strutted into the clubhouse, the arms of my sweater lashed over my shoulders like a needy drunken lover, and plopped down on the barstool. "Albert. I need a martini." Albert went right to work, but not before sending a glance toward the table by the window, my stepfather's table. Edward was there, legs crossed, smoking a cigar and wearing a yellow polo shirt, neon green slacks and white shoes.

"Poppie," I said and made the kissing noise he hates. "My game was inspired today. You should have seen me."

"Everyone saw you, Charlene," he said, letting his fingers smoke the cigar, pointing its fiery poker end at me. He shook his head and looked down at his green slacks as if they could advise him on what to say next.

"Why do you do it, Charlene? To embarrass me? It doesn't embarrass me. You're the fool, not me. Do you think people don't know what you're doing in the woods?" His head continued shaking long after he'd run out of words. I sipped my martini, then plucked the olive out with my fingers and crushed it between my teeth. The pimento shot across the table and landed a few inches from his drink. I hadn't meant to do that.

Edward straightened in his chair, then stood and dropped his napkin on the table after wiping his mouth. "Come take a ride with me. We need to talk."

"But I have my Benz here. I can't just leave—"

"Have Nestor bring it to your house like he always does," Edward said.

Edward must have seen the shock register on my face. Nestor often drove me home in my Benz if I drank too much at the club. One of the many perks of Castlebrook Hills. And Nestor didn't mind. He often helped me into bed, undressed me, undressed himself. It was equitable and I enjoyed it when I wasn't too drunk to remember, but it bothered me that Edward knew. He seemed to know everything about me.

Edward's taupe limo waited out front. We sat in the back and the driver pulled slowly from the club, palms swaying outside the tinted glass. I settled in across from Edward, my back to the driver, my eyes on the rectangle of back window interrupted only by the silhouette of Edward's rather large head.

Edward puffed his fat cigar and stared at me, his head screwing side to side. "Why don't you find a man and get married. You're an attractive woman. You could have your breasts done, and—"

"What's wrong with my breasts? You don't like my breasts?" I said.

Maybe I shouldn't have done what I did next. I tore open my blouse. Edward shut his eyes and turned away in disgust, his lips knotted as if he'd just bitten into something sour.

"They're not that offensive," I told him. "You really should take a peek."

"Button your shirt, Charlene. For Christ's sake!"

I fastened two buttons, but they didn't match the right holes, throwing off the alignment of my collar, making it cockeyed, as if my blouse had been in a car accident. Edward ran his thick cigar hand through his hair and I watched for the ash to fall on his head.

"You're as nutty as your mother. I swear to God!"

Edward poured himself a scotch, drained the glass, then poured another. He took a deep breath, then pushed his lower lip out over his upper until it met the bottom edge of his mustache. Edward did all his thinking with his lips. "It's your mother. We must do something about her. She's crazy."

"It's probably the syphilis," I said. "It deteriorates the brain, you know."

"Can you be serious for one minute, Charlene? Krystal is *your* mother and she's very sick. I would think you could muster some civility for her sake."

"Hey, I'm as serious as syphilis here. What do you think is wrong with her? She seems the same to me."

"Stop talking about syphilis!" Edward shouted, his face a sack of red corpuscles. He closed his eyes and started some kind of Zen breathing exercise. After a moment his calm was restored. He measured his words carefully as if he had to pay for each one. He told me my mother had a brain tumor, believing that's why she was acting so crazy. He said she was convinced she has syphilis and would sneak into his room every night...naked...and try to have sex with him while he slept, then start calling him a bastard when he woke up.

Edward was riled up again. He looked at the carpet, flicked the powdered end of his cigar in the ashtray, forgot about the breathing and downed the scotch in one stroke. Refilling his glass, he nudged it toward me, making an offering of alcohol. I declined, wondering if my mother knew she had a brain tumor.

"She was diagnosed over a month ago, but the doctors aren't sure how long it's been there," Edward said. "They say it's growing slowly, but it's going to start causing real problems soon."

I fiddled with the buttons on my blouse, regarding the awkwardness of my clothes, feeling like a teenager who'd lost a wrestling match with her date at a drive-in movie. Did the tumor cause my mother to act so crazy? But she was always a little crazy. If she dies, it will be just Edward and me. That is a disturbing thought. Edward is the sum of my family. One of my mother's sisters is dead; the other is in an institution, insane. I had forgotten that. My mind is a flip chart of intangibles. Is it hereditary? Could a brain tumor cause the yips? Maybe Edward's lying. He certainly isn't above lying! But not about this. Not even Edward would lie about this. Krystal looked fine this morning, angry and full of spirit and spite. How many times had she been dying? How many years had she convinced herself and others that she had six months to live? What was different this time? Edward. That's what was different. He'd never taken her death predictions seriously before. Was Edward acting? But why? The envelope. The manila envelope. The incriminating documents. Was that his angle? Sympathy? Solidarity? No? Yes? I couldn't understand why she hadn't told me herself.

"She's crazy. Don't you get it? She's a fucking stamp without glue."

The limo stopped in front of my condo. "It's about the envelope, isn't it? That's what this is all about," I said.

"Envelope? I don't know what—"

"Mother gave me the envelope this morning, Poppie. Is that what's got you in a lather? Don't worry, I have no intention of using anything she gave me."

Edward grimaced, shaking his head. "Christ, Charlene. Have you looked in *the envelope?* It's nothing but garbage.

There's nothing in that envelope except your mother's delusions."

That wasn't exactly right. I had looked when I got to the country club. There was a coupon for fifty cents off a box of Kotex, along with some other coupons for Heinz ketchup, Silk Soy, Listerine, and Bumblebee Tuna. There was also an ad for Freedom cell phones, some newspaper clippings, mostly obituaries and personals, a handbill for Moss Electrical Supplies, a Lowe's hardware circular, several pages of a Land's End catalog, sweepstakes entry forms, an astrology chart, and a wad of grocery and ATM receipts that dated back to 1997.

I scooted across the seat, pulled the handle on the door, then tugged at my skirt when my feet hit the sidewalk. Edward seemed like a small colorless pearl sitting in the back seat of his limo.

About to close the door, I felt myself hating him for the truth that I kept tripping over. Except for his drinking, his relentless cheating on my mother, and those three seconds in my room when I was fifteen, Edward had been decent to my mother and me and I hated him for that. I hated the elasticity of those three seconds, how they'd stretched themselves effortlessly over the last twenty-five years of my life. I hated the incongruity of Edward's actions, his tongue polishing the backs of my teeth, his shame and remorse, his elitism, his caring eyes, his patience teaching me golf, his wandering starved gaze, his gentle touch, his maleness, his awkwardness, his arrogance, his endurance.

"Please come by later, Charlene," he said, leaning across the seat, sunlight plucking the silver strands in his hair. "Talk to your mother. There may still be time. She'll listen to you."

"I'll come after Nestor drops off my car," I said, holding the edge of the door, the breeze cool on my cheek.

Edward drifted back across the car, retreating into the

shadow of the backseat, the roofline of the limo decapitating his head from my view. I flung the door shut. In seconds, the limo was a block away, the size of a pea, and I was thinking about Edward inside, how his fingers once virile and wiry were now translucent and brittle with arthritis. I thought about the lushness of my mother's thick eyebrows, the beauty of her full red lips mouthing strange proclamations. I thought of the manila envelope sitting on the back seat of my Benz where I had thrown it after laughing myself silly. I thought about a hot shower, about Nestor bringing my car to the condo, about Nestor knocking on the door to the bathroom, telling me he brought my car back, his dark, tentacle fingers unbuttoning his shirt.

# A STONEMASON ON OCRACOKE

The engine overheated. He was a long way from Carrolton Oaks, with its maples trimming the nearly silver sidewalks, the fine stone and frame homes rising from a blanket of shimmering grass. Standing at the front of the Cadillac, Marshal looked east, then west, trying to figure out where they were, then glanced at Lizzie in the front seat. An informal survey of the area found the First Original Free Will Baptist Church at one end of the block, the Hope Free Will Baptist Church at the other. Smoke from the engine swept past him with the burnt-varnish smell of anti-freeze and he knew they were still a long way from Ocracoke.

The engine overheated. She was a long way from Carrolton Oaks, the easy, shaded streets, the lovely magic of a neighborhood block party. She looked out the window. Hardee's sat on one corner, McDonald's the other. Smoke from the engine swept past Marshal in a way that almost erased him and suddenly she felt hungry. They'd driven all night and she had no idea how far they were from Ocracoke.

Squinting through the smoke, Marshal wondered how long

Lizzie would sit in the car with the windows rolled up and no air conditioning. The outside air was in the upper eighties, the humidity even higher. North Carolina should not be this hot in November. He'd noticed a severe change in temperature when they drove through Raleigh around noon. He doubted Lizzie had noticed, wrapped in the cool Cadillac air, her profile mashed against the headrest, a tentacle of drool linking her lower lip to the upholstery.

She had to pee. Leaning forward in the seat, she searched the area for some kind of public restrooms. Not seeing any, she decided on Hardee's across the street. Maybe she'd get a shake. Some fries. "Do you want anything, Marshall? I'm going over to use the restroom." She pointed at Hardee's. He swiveled his head toward McDonald's, then back to her.

"I don't like Hardee's."

"I know."

He watched her cross the street, then searched for a gas station. Seeing one that looked to be over a quarter-mile away, he took out his cell phone. No signal. He looked back toward the gas station, the word *Rocket* leaning as if the word itself moved at great speed. He knew he'd get no help there unless he needed a slushy drink and a beef jerky. Maybe they'd know someone who could help, though. He looked back toward Hardee's, then started walking, sun splashing off chrome bumpers, soda cans, and metal signs along the street.

Where's he going? she thought, sitting at a table by the window, sipping a strawberry shake. Dipping a fry in ketchup, she wondered what his old girlfriend looked like, why he was so set on seeing her before she died. He'd never said a thing about her till the phone call from Ocracoke two nights ago. Had he been in touch with her all these years and failed to mention it, maybe via e-mail, thinking it was some Internet *pal* connection not worthy of discussion?

No one had been more surprised by the phone call from Ocracoke than he had. They hadn't spoken in over twenty-five years and he'd had no idea Marsha moved to an island. He wasn't even sure how she found his number—he only wished she'd phoned him under different circumstances. Sweat ran into his eyes. She had been so gorgeous, so buoyant. He wiped his brow with his fingertips, the *Rocket* station seemingly edging away at the same speed he approached it. The idea that Marsha was dying would not quite register. She was fifty-five, or maybe fifty-three, he couldn't remember for sure. An artist, but he didn't know if she still painted. He wondered what she looked like now, if her illness, whatever it was, had stolen her splendor.

If this chick isn't dying when we get there, she'll wish she was, Lizzie thought, momentarily shocked by her own hostility. She had never been jealous of other women before, had never had reason to. Marshal was, if anything, devoted. She dipped another fry and looked out the window, no longer able to find Marshal on the street, her view blocked by a Verizon truck parked outside. Marsha. And Marshal. How odd that seemed, these old flames, their names like matching luggage.

Road Service answered on the third ring. He tried to explain to the woman where the car had broken down, between the First Original Free Will Baptist Church and the Hope Free Will Baptist Church. "Yepper, I know the spot," the woman said. "I'll dispatch someone. Should be there in about twenty minutes." He went inside for a Coke and a bag of Doritos. After he paid, he stood a while soaking up the air conditioning, popping chips into his mouth and munching them unconsciously. Hardee's seemed a long way off, the sign dwarfed and toy-like from a distance. Would Lizzie wonder where he'd gone? He was surprised when she'd agreed to accompany him to Ocracoke, but if the situation were reversed, he knew he'd never let her go see Roger by herself.

I wonder how Marshal would feel if Roger called and said he was dying and asked me to come see him one last time? Her milkshake made a horrible snot-rattling noise as she sucked the last of it up the straw. She hadn't wanted to go with Marshal, knowing she would miss her bridge club. Her partner, Betty, had pleaded with her. "Let him go," she'd said, then reasoned, "what's he going to do with a dying woman?" "I have to go," Lizzie told her. "It's not right for him to have to go alone." Betty, the most competitive woman Lizzie had ever met —and one hell of a bridge player—rolled her eyes and sucked impatiently on her cigarette. Of course, Lizzie couldn't help but wonder if Marshal had wanted to visit his old girlfriend by himself. She had asked him straight out the night of the phone call, and, without as much as a blink of hesitation, his answer came as soft as a kiss, "No."

Maybe he should have come by himself. He had wanted to, at first, when he heard Marsha's voice on the phone, but that was also why he practically begged Lizzie to come—he didn't feel he could trust himself around her. After all these years, he still suffered a peculiar intoxication for her, and the sound of her voice made him a bit loopy. He hoped Lizzie hadn't detected the crazy sizzle deep in his gut. And even though Marsha was dying, he had imagined sitting next to her bed, feeding her soup, combing her hair when she was too tired to keep her eyes open. And, of course, he'd bathe her, running the warm washcloth across her bare shoulders, a rivulet of sudsy water sliding down between her breasts. It would be hard not to stare, as he was doing now in his mind, the small heart tattoo just below her navel, the robust arc of her hips. Oh, it would be very hard not to stare.

Is he thinking about her...sexually? How sick would that

be, a dying woman and all? Of course he was, she thought. Men's minds were wired for opportunity. Oh, and what an *opportunity* this was, the helpless, needy lover reminding him of those old golden times. And who could be upset by one last deathbed fling? Was he thinking about her now, kicking himself for having practically begged me to come? She looked out the window, angry at the stupid truck blocking her view. All kinds of empty parking spaces out there and he had to park in that one? Maybe she would stay in this town, whatever it was called, not even go to Ocracoke. Marshal could pick her up on the way back. Wouldn't he love that, all alone out there with Georgia O'Keefe, the ocean fanning its lovely spray across their faces? Maybe he could stretch a few canvases for her, swish her brushes, adjust her easel until the light was just right! Brother! Lizzie dumped her tray in the trash on the way out the door. When the too-bright reflection off the white Verizon truck snatched her eyesight temporarily, she spun from the glare, swimming a hand in her purse for her sunglasses.

Marshal dropped his Coke can and Dorito bag in the trash on the way out. He paused a moment to check if he had brought his sunglasses, then remembered removing them when the car had started churning out blue smoke. When he walked from beneath the mothering shade of the gas station's huge canopy, he was once again under the scorching scrutiny of the sun, his feet kicking his deep plum shadow back toward the car. The afternoon had become a wall of obstinate air, each footstep a deliberate and strenuous act. How long would it take to fix the car? Would they still make the four o'clock Swan Quarter Ferry, or would they have to take a later one? He saw a flatbed tow truck pull up a few blocks away. A man jumped out and walked to the Cadillac.

Lizzie didn't know what to tell the man, other than the car had overheated. "Lots of smoke," Lizzie said, her arms crossed, wondering why Marshal hadn't returned. She didn't know anything about cars. "Let's have a look-see," the bony man said, his jaw and cheekbones nearly skeletal. He had black grime beneath his fingernails, but a pleasant manner, and a smile well-worth looking at. He leaned into the gaping maw of the Cadillac and it seemed for a moment he might disappear into the wires and hoses. Lizzie looked toward the *Rocket* gas station, wondering if Marshal was still there, if he'd noticed the repairman. "Blown head gasket," the man said, wiping his hands on a greasy rag. "Can you fix it?" Lizzie asked. He laughed, not mean, but empathetically, and Lizzie knew it wasn't good. "No, ma'am. Have to haul her to Kenny's up there on the interstate. He'll fix it. Heads are his specialty." Heads are his specialty, Lizzie thought, not having a clue what that meant. "You have the keys?" the man asked. Lizzie pointed toward the ignition.

"Head gasket," Marshal said, repeating Lizzie's words. "That should still be under warranty." He watched the man hook the Cadillac to a cable and winch the car onto the flatbed. "Have a place to stay tonight?" the man asked. "No, we have to catch the four o'clock Swan Quarter Ferry to Ocracoke," Marshal told the man, then added, "A friend of mine is dying." Marshal included the last part as if that one grave detail might ward off the inevitable disappointment coming his way. The man shook his head. "I'm real sorry, folks, but you wouldn't make the four o'clock now if I drove you there myself." "How about a later ferry?" Marshal asked. "No later ones," the man said, "not this time of year." Marshal looked at Lizzie. She looked back and shrugged, quietly gloating over her astonishing good fortune, it seemed to Marshal. "Can this Kenny fellow fix it by tomorrow?" Marshal asked. The man nodded confidently and scratched behind his ear. "How 'bout I drop you folks at the Comfort Inn up on the interstate? You can get a shower, a nice dinner in the restaurant, and a good night's sleep. Kenny'll have you on your way by eleven tomorrow morning, most likely. Make the four o'clock to Ocracoke."

～

*A friend of mine is dying* was more than a little dramatic, Lizzie thought, sliding the electronic key over the motel room lock. It was embarrassing. What was the tow truck driver going to do, pull a head gasket out of his jeans and fix the motor right there on the street? "'A *friend* of mine is dying,' Marshal?" Lizzie said. "Really! According to you, you haven't spoken to her in over twenty-five years. How could she even know you anymore?" Marshal shambled past her, dropping his suitcase near the TV, then went to the bathroom and shut the door.

I'll have to call her, he thought, checking for toilet paper before he sat down. Marsha will wonder what happened. What if she dies before I get there? He couldn't stop wondering how she looked, if she still had auburn hair, if her eyes were still green. That's stupid, he thought. Of course her eyes are still green! He pictured her calves, the creases at the sides of her mouth, the two distinct dimples at the apex of her bottom. Whenever she would roll onto her stomach, he would trace his fingers along those perfect indentations, letting his fingertips rest there as if those gentle dips represented the origin and general structure of the universe.

It was a mean thing to say, Lizzie thought. Why wouldn't Marsha still know him? Twenty-three years of marriage hadn't changed him that much. She felt rotten for her bitchiness and yet it was hard not to be bitchy with Marshal sitting on the motel bed talking with his old girlfriend on the phone, explaining how the car broke down, then something about head gaskets, the First Original Free Will Baptist Church and the Hope Free Will Baptist Church, and suddenly Lizzie found herself engaged in a childhood game she and her sister had played while her mom sat on the phone for hours, a game that had once been played for new cars and millions of dollars and permission to start dating. "Do you want to go down to dinner with me?" Lizzie said, sitting on the edge of the bed listening to Marshal talk with Marsha. "No, No," Marshal said into the phone, obviously unaware what she was saying. "Do you want to sleep with your old girlfriend, Marshal?" said Lizzie. "Oh, we'll have to see," Marshal said, staring at the television, "it could take all day. The man said there were no later ferries." "Do you want a divorce, Marshal?" "No, no, I promise. I'll call you if I do." Oh the hell with this! Lizzie thought, storming from the motel room.

Marsha sounded so bright, it was hard to believe she was dying. Was it really possible to postpone death? Marshal wondered. "I'll postpone it for one night," Marsha had told him on the phone, and he hadn't known how to respond. He'd heard how people lingering near the precipice of the great beyond had an innate sense of their impending finality, but could they control it? Could they really decide when? And how accurately? To the hour? The minute? It seemed preposterous, but Marsha had never set her course by the compass of others.

This had become a strange and sparkling day, as most strange days are, troubling, yet fascinating in its break with routine, each and every moment like a rare and glittery object plucked from the earth. However, strange days could quickly become wearisome, the aimless undercurrent stretching and constricting, and Lizzie was almost woozy from its sway. She ordered absently from the menu, drinking from her water glass until the young waitress brought her tea. She sipped the tea and thought about all the years she had enjoyed sitting at the regal post of Marshal's unwavering affection, the way he touched her skin as if he'd never felt flesh before, the way he studied her body as though it were the first time he'd seen a woman naked. And if his attentiveness had waned even a smidge over the past few years, she was not aware of it, and always felt supremely loved. With the napkin from her lap, she gently dabbed her eyes and cheeks, trying to keep from smearing her makeup.

~

Marshal woke early and jogged toward the pink wash of dawn rising against the highway overpass. Kenny had said he would have the car done by ten, and would have one of his men pick Marshal up at the motel and bring him back to the shop to pay. When Marshal got back to the room, he heard the shower running and wondered if Lizzie had eaten breakfast yet.

Lizzie stood beneath the hot spray too sick to eat. She'd hardly slept at all, unable to remember the last time she'd eaten supper alone, much less in the impersonal and aesthetically challenged surroundings of a motel restaurant. When she'd returned to the room the previous night, Marshal had spent the rest of the evening staring at the television like a captured spy, as though he were afraid that speaking might compromise some secret in his heart.

"I'm going to the breakfast room," Marshal said to the bathroom door. "Do you want a muffin?"

"No." She was about to add, "thank you," then heard the loud snap of the door going shut.

~

Marshal thought the repairs were reasonable and even though Kenny had assured him the car would be just fine, he was leery of switching on the air. He opened his window and followed the signs to the Swan Quarter Ferry. Lizzie slept with her back to him, her face propped against the passenger side door.

She heard gulls even before she opened her eyes. Their Cadillac sat in a long line of cars, and a hundred yards beyond the vehicle at the front of the line floated a huge ferryboat moored between massive algae-stained wooden poles. Cars had not yet started boarding and Marshal was gone from the Cadillac. He'd left the windows down and the breeze was surprisingly pleasant. Just then she felt the bite of a mosquito and slapped her arm, leaving behind a dime-sized spot of blood. Wasn't it too late in the year for mosquitoes?

His stomach knotted, anticipating the reunion with Marsha. From his station on the picnic table he could see Lizzie sitting up now, looking around, probably wondering where he was. The idea of Marsha postponing her death was still troubling him, had troubled him all the past evening, and he had been relieved Lizzie had not been in a talkative mood when she returned from the dining room, seemingly content to read one of her magazines and go to bed early. When he came back from his own dinner, she was already buried in covers. He had no idea how she could fall asleep so easily. He hadn't slept at all, tossing and turning all night, while she lay there still as a wrinkle.

She wanted something and got out to find a vending machine. Maybe she'd see Marshal. That must be him sitting over there on that picnic table, she figured. Adjacent to the white ticket building, stood a line of vending machines under a small overhang. She opened her purse to find her wallet.

230

Even though he wasn't hungry, he was surprised, and a bit disappointed Lizzie hadn't thought to buy him something. She sipped her diet Sprite and offered him pretzels from her bag, but he declined, getting out of the car as soon as the ferry was underway. "I'm going up on the top deck," he said. She nodded.

What was she supposed to do? They had never been on a boat together and this could have been very romantic, under different circumstances. She got out and grabbed both rails as she climbed the narrow metal steps leading to the upper deck. She didn't see Marshal. People leaned against the railings and tossed chips to the gulls, the birds following the boat so closely it seemed they were tethered to the craft with invisible strings, darting and diving and squawking, fighting for scraps in the churning water. It was beautiful.

It was beautiful. Marshal wished Lizzie had come up to enjoy the view with him, his eyes stretching across the sound, the blue bowl of sky resting on the blue table of water. For every mountain and hill surrounding their home back in Carrolton Oaks, Pamlico Sound countered it with a smooth and sprawling vastness that was breathtaking. He stepped into the passenger lounge and sat at one of the tables. Two young boys were watching the television in the corner of the room. Vending machines lined the back wall, Coke, Pepsi, Snacks. Outside the windows on the opposite side of the boat, stood Lizzie, her back to him, tossing the last of her pretzels to the gulls. She seemed content being alone and he didn't want to disturb her.

She figured he wanted to be alone, that's why he made himself scarce. Maybe he had gone back down to the car. He seemed aloof. How would she feel if she were going to see Roger on his deathbed? The truth was, her old flame burned out long ago and she wouldn't go see Roger if he were dangling from a cliff by his fingertips. Roger was scum, a bastard, but she'd never told Marshal that, enjoying the trace of boyish jealousy that colored Marshal's eyes when she spoke of her college lover. She had never lied to Marshal—she and Roger had enjoyed good times—but Roger was deceitful and a cheat and she felt dismally flawed she had ever loved such a man. Loving Marshal had given her new hope.

Hope was the name of the town they'd spent the night in. That's why the church had been called the Hope Free Will Baptist Church, Marshal finally realized. He'd been playing it over in his head—hope free, hope free, hope free—and the name seemed dreadfully wrong for a church. When he got to the car, Lizzie was asleep in the front seat. He stood at the rail, knowing he'd wake her if he opened the door. The afternoon had cooled. Chilled by the ocean air, he pulled a jacket from the trunk, then quietly latched the lid closed again. He watched the ocean without expectation, the flat purity of water and sky. A short while later, a faint stubble of land appeared near the horizon.

"Is that Ocracoke?" Lizzie asked, getting out of the car, rubbing her eyes.

"I think so," Marshal answered, a pink-tinged sky closing around the tiny lighthouse.

When they departed the ferry, Lizzie read the directions and told Marshal where to turn. Left at The Shipwreck Motel, then right at Surf Coffee, and follow the road for three-tenths of a mile. Coffee sounded good to Lizzie and she wondered if the shop was closed for the season. The entire island seemed closed for the season, no one about, all the windows dark. The motel had a light on in the lobby, but it seemed low wattage and not very inviting.

When Marsha had insisted over the phone that he and his wife stay with her, that they could have her studio, explaining that she no longer used it and that it had a futon and bathroom, Marshal had told her they'd think about it. He hadn't bothered to ask why she no longer painted, and hadn't bothered mentioning to Lizzie about staying at Marsha's. They'd broach that later, or maybe he and Lizzie would stay at The Shipwreck, although it hadn't looked very inviting. He spotted a mailbox with the name, Creston, and pulled in.

The headlights burned bright along the white driveway. Something crunched beneath the tires, as if they were driving over bones and skulls. Upon further examination, Lizzie saw that the surface was covered with shells!—clam shells, mollusk shells, sea shells of every kind. She wondered if they might pop the tires. The porch light snapped on and a woman with the vibrant build of a long-distance runner came bounding down the steps. Lizzie looked over at Marshal. Marshal shrugged and threw open his door.

"Oh, Marshal!" the woman cried. "You look just fabulous!"

She hadn't changed one bit in twenty-five years, Marshal thought, her breasts breaking like waves beneath her tank top, her hips as smooth and full as an autumn moon. Caught on an errant breeze, her perfume reached him a second before her body. She wrapped him in her arms. "I am so glad you could come. I'm sorry you had so much trouble." She spun toward Lizzie and embraced her. "It's so nice to meet you."

She smells so good, Lizzie thought, and why wouldn't she? —she hasn't been cooped up in a car all day. And she certainly isn't dying. Marsha led the way to the house, her hips working the spandex material, with Marshal following. Marsha made coffee and pulled a pound cake from the fridge, then proceeded to catch up on old times with Marshal, what they'd both been doing since they'd seen each other last. What's this chick's angle? Lizzie wondered, sipping her coffee, trying to keep a bite of crumbling pound cake balanced on her fork.

"You're both probably wondering what this is all about," Marsha said.

To Marshal's great surprise and mortification, Marsha proceeded to tell her story, how she'd inherited a bundle of money when her mother died, then bought this place on Ocracoke and stopped painting, stopped everything in her life to pursue her spiritual path.

"Let's sit by the fire pit," Marsha said, interrupting her own story.

Fire pit? Lizzie thought, putting on the sweater Marsha had brought from the back bedroom. Lizzie looked over at Marshal, who had declined the jacket Marsha had brought for him, assuring her he'd be fine.

Fire pit? He knew what a fire pit was—he'd just never sat around one. He'd heard of sweat lodges too, something else Marsha talked about with great enthusiasm as she led them down the back steps to the glowing portal of fire in the backyard. Marshal sat in the lawn chair with the breeze at his back so the smoke wouldn't burn his eyes. Lizzie evidently hadn't figured it out and was rubbing madly, trying to swat away smoke as if it were a swarm of gnats.

"Here, Lizzie, sit here," Marsha said.

Lizzie's eyes burned and she hated that she had been stupid enough to sit in the path of the smoke. And what was all this talk about sweat lodges, and spirit guides, and walking on hot coals? Certainly Marsha didn't expect her to walk over burning coals, or huddle over blistering hot rocks. If Marshal wants to do those things, then let him, she thought. But I'm not. I'll walk back to the Shipwreck.

"Look, Marsha, I'm sorry," Lizzie finally said, "but I thought you were dying. You don't even look sick."

Marshal looked at Lizzie, then at Marsha. Lizzie was right, of course, but he wished she hadn't been so direct. Maybe Marsha was getting to the part about her illness, or whatever it was that was killing her. Even to him, though, it seemed a lengthy preface, the walking on coals and all that other business.

"Yes," Marsha said, "I know it's confusing. I am choosing my death tonight. I was going to do it last night, but when Marshal called and said your car had broken down, I figured it could wait one more night."

"You brought us here so you could commit suicide?" Marshal said.

Marsha smiled and touched Marshal's knee. "No, nothing like that. My spiritual guide calls it energetic death. He says we all choose our death, we just don't realize it. I'm just choosing mine consciously. Native Americans and Tao Masters have done it for thousands of years."

Lizzie could not understand why this woman with her entire life ahead of her was smiling at the thought of choosing her death. And Marshal, he looked stunned, like someone had smacked him in the face with a shovel. Lizzie wasn't buying it for a second. She wasn't sure what Marsha was up to, but it wasn't any *energetic* death.

*Energetic* death? Marshal had never heard of such a thing. Why would anyone want to die intentionally, or *energetically?* He looked over at Lizzie and when her eyes reflected back the fire, he turned away. He glanced at Marsha and even though she was still holding her smile, it had turned terribly sad.

Marsha explained that she would like them to stay the night, that they should sleep in her bedroom instead of the studio. It would be more intimate. She had already made arrangements to sleep on the screened-in porch, showing them the pillows and blankets stacked on the floor, the incense, the candles. It was eerie, Lizzie thought.

"What are we supposed to do?" Marshal asked.

"Just be witnesses to my passing," Marsha answered, lighting the candle with a long match.

Lizzie wasn't sure she could do this.

Marshal wasn't sure he could do this.

Marsha showed them to her bedroom.

"Shouldn't we watch you or something?" Marshal said.

Marsha shook her head and touched his wrist. "No. I've left a number for you to call on the kitchen counter in the morning. Thank you both so much." Marsha kissed Lizzie and hugged her tight, then kissed Marshal, holding him for a long time. "You're the most special man in my life," she said, a tear rolling down her cheek, "my soulmate."

Soulmate? Lizzie thought. Wasn't that the eighties or something?

Soulmate. He'd forgotten about that. Marsha had always said they were soulmates, that that was why their names were so similar. He hated seeing her cry, hated that she was going through with this silly plan. She was such a striking and creative woman, and talented, and young, throwing it all away over what?

No way was this woman going to die tonight, Lizzie thought, and suddenly wanted to stay because the whole scenario was so ridiculous. She could hardly wait to tell her bridge club, especially Betty. She wondered if Marshal would say anything when he came out of the bathroom after brushing his teeth. Did he believe this crapola? He hadn't said a word since they'd retired to Marsha's bedroom. When they'd left

Marsha, she was lying on the floor surrounded by glowing candles, the pong of incense fouling the air.

He hated incense and hoped Lizzie wouldn't say anything about it. When he and Marsha shared an apartment, she always burned it and he could never get use to the smell, or the way it plugged his sinuses. He figured he was allergic to it.

"Do you think it's silly?" Marshal asked Lizzie, pulling the comforter up around his neck. They had been lying in the dark for over ten minutes.

"Marshal, it is probably the most insane thing I've ever heard. I just hope she doesn't burn the house down with all those damn candles and kill us, too."

Marshal woke the next morning to the sound of sobbing. He checked to see if it was Lizzie, but she was gone from the bed. He got up and slipped his robe on, walking quietly toward the living room. Lizzie was seated on the couch, nestling Marsha in her arms. Marsha was crying. Lizzie shook her head at Marshal and shrugged.

"You're still here, Marsha! That's good news, right?" Marshal said, lashing his robe tighter.

No, it is not good news, Lizzie thought. This woman is in serious need of counseling.

"Oh, Marshal, I feel as useless as a stonemason on Ocracoke," Marsha said. "I can't even die properly. I have failed at everything, and now..." Marsha couldn't finish her sentence, suddenly overwrought with another crying jag.

"But, I'm a stonemason," Marshal said, bewildered, wearing that same stunned, shovel-smacked look.

"It's just a figure of speech," Marsha said, sitting up, wiping her eyes. "Don't you see? There's no need of a stonemason on

Ocracoke because everything is built on wooden piers. When I thought of you coming here...oh, this is so embarrassing...I fantasized about you living here with me. Oh, I am so sorry, Lizzie. I hadn't even met you. Now I can see how perfect you are for Marshal. Anyway, last night when I decided to go through with my plan, I realized that you didn't belong here, Marshal. You would never fit in here, a stonemason. There'd be nothing for you to do and that's just how I feel about my life, like a stonemason on Ocracoke." At this, Marsha sank into Lizzie's lap and continued, as though she'd never stopped, with her sobbing.

Marshal looked at Lizzie. Lizzie looked back at Marshal.

They had breakfast at the Tackle Box diner, then dropped Marsha at her house before catching the noon ferry back to Swan Quarter.

Leaning against the rail on the upper deck, Marshal pulled Lizzie close, his arm around her shoulder and was thankful she hadn't brought up Marsha. He was more than a little mortified by Marsha's histrionics, but at least she'd calmed down before they left. He was even kind of proud of Lizzie for inviting Marsha to their home in Carrolton Oaks for Thanksgiving. And Marsha seemed genuinely moved by the gesture, even though Marshal was fairly certain he'd never see her again.

"Roger was a total asshole," Lizzie said.

"What?"

"Roger, my old boyfriend from college. He was a total asshole. He screwed every woman with a pulse, not that that was a prerequisite."

Marshal fell quiet, stunned by Lizzie's disclosure, always harboring a smoldering resentment over her old college flame.

"Really? You never said anything like that before about him. You always said how—"

"I know..." She snuggled in closer to Marshal, digging a handful of his goldfish crackers from the bag and tossing them to the gulls. He held her tighter, digging his free hand into the bag when she spun toward him and pressed her lips to his.

# ABOUT THE AUTHOR

 Lonnie Busch is an award-winning author whose short fiction has appeared in *Southwest Review, The Minnesota Review, The Baltimore Review* and other magazines. Among his awards for fiction are the Clay Reynolds Novella Prize for his novella, *TURNBACK CREEK*, finalist in the Tobias Wolff Award for Fiction, the *Glimmer Train* Very Short Fiction Award, and others. Busch is the author of several novels, *CARGO HOLD 4, PROJECT ÜBERMENSCH, ALL HOPE OF BECOMING HUMAN, THE CABIN ON SOUDER HILL and THE BALDWIN HOTEL,*

Busch is also a painter, animator and illustrator, and has created artwork for numerous corporations, ad agencies and institutions, including the "Greetings from America" and "Wonders of America" Commemorative Stamps for the USPS.

See Busch's other collection, *TURNBACK CREEK: A NOVELLA & SIX STORIES.*
https://lonniebusch.com

www.ingramcontent.com/pod-product-compliance
Lightning Source LLC
Chambersburg PA
CBHW031945240626
47153CB00003B/870